M000189992

A LITTLE VICE IN PARADISE

VERY VERO * BOOK TWO

GRETCHEN ROSE

A LITTLE VICE IN PARADISE
Copyright © 2022 by Gretchen Rose

ISBN: 978-1-955784-59-7

Melange Books, LLC
White Bear Lake, MN 55110
www.melange-books.com

This novel's story and characters are fictitious. Except when they're not. Certain actual events, long-standing institutions, agencies, and public offices are mentioned, but the characters involved are wholly imaginary. As regards real events: Space and time may have been rearranged to suit the convenience of the book, and with the exception of public figures, any resemblance to persons living or dead is coincidental.

No part of this book may be reproduced or transmitted in any form or by any means, electronic or mechanical, including photocopying, recording, or by any information storage and retrieval system, without permission in writing from the publisher except for the use of brief quotations in a book review or scholarly journal.

Published in the United States of America.

Cover Design by Caroline Andrus

I dedicate this book to my Vero Beach family, friends, and neighbors. You are my inspiration. And to the love of my life, Mel Laracey, thank you for always encouraging me to write and for providing a wickedly funny male perspective when my imagination flags.

Many thanks to Marc Esposito, Special Tactics Officer, USAF for providing me with the Special Forces jargon and terminology and to language consultant, Carlos Villarreal for correcting my deplorable Spanish.

"There is no remedy for love but to love more."

—HENRY DAVID THOREAU

CHAPTER ONE

NO WONDER

It was after six, Friday, the end of another grim workweek, and Vero Beach was sweltering at a sultry ninety degrees. But that's not why Andrea Nelson was hot under the collar. She was a Florida girl. Cool and dry behind the wheel of her gorgeous, new automobile, she was ruing the fact that she'd ever leased the damn thing. How was she to keep up the payments on the ridiculously expensive Benz with no source of income in the foreseeable future?

As she turned onto A1A, Andrea thought about the torturous phone calls she'd fielded—since the Dow took its historic plunge—from realty clients who were desperate to sell their properties or who'd gotten cold feet and walked away from good-faith deposits. It had been another tough slog in a long succession of brutal days. She had but one prospect, and that was a long shot. Andrea had never been more terrified.

She willed herself not to obsess. Some things were simply beyond her control. The weekend stretched before her, and Andrea was ready to kick back with a glass of wine and lose herself in Debbie Macomber's newest release, to forget all about her troubles and the housing bust. When she pulled up onto her driveway and spotted the battered Jeep Safari parked there, she knew that wasn't going to happen anytime soon. A glance back at the curb confirmed her fears; the trashcan she'd put out in the morning was conspicuously absent.

Damn it! Would that man never let her go?

Before closing the garage door, Andrea loped to the mailbox to retrieve her mail. When she found it empty, her anger notched up a level.

She burst through the door only to find her mail strewn on the kitchen counter and Derrick sprawled on the sofa. To make matters worse, Beau—the little traitor—was curled up next to him. Andrea slammed the door, and Beau vaulted off the sofa and trotted to her. His little pink tongue was curled over his muzzle, and it was clear to see he was eager for a cuddle, but Andrea was having none of it.

Derrick pretended not to notice her irritation. His eyes remained glued to the ballgame airing on ESPN as he grabbed the half-empty bottle of beer from off the coffee table and took a swig. "Hey babe, your mother called." Slyly, he ventured a glance in Andrea's direction. "How come so late?"

Andrea's patience was worn to a thread, and her frustrations came pouring out. "What are you doing? How did you get in? You can't come sneaking around here." At the sound of Andrea's raised voice, the cairn terrier hunkered down and slunk out of the room.

Derrick straightened in his seat and swiveled to face her, a bemused expression on his face.

Andrea knew him so well; she could read his mind. This man-child thought she was being overly dramatic—some hormonal thing. Which only infuriated her more.

"Baby, come on," Derrick soothed, but his words were drowned in Andrea's tongue-lashing.

"Don't baby me," Andrea snapped. "This is *my* house! You are not allowed to waltz right in and make yourself at home whenever you please. Haven't I made that clear?"

"Please, don't be that way," Derrick wheedled. "I wanted to see Maddy… and you."

"You know the custody terms. Madison's all yours tomorrow." Andrea swooped in, snagged the beer bottle from Derrick's grasp, and crossed to the kitchen sink. As she poured out the contents, her eyes flicked to the counter where her mail was scattered.

"And you have no right to go through my mail. I could take out a restraining order, have you arrested. Is that what you want?" Andrea pivoted and glared at her ex.

Derrick unfolded his lean frame and came to his feet. "I thought we agreed to be nice to one another. For Maddy's sake."

"Nice is one thing." Andrea thrust a palm before her to keep him at bay. "Breaking in is another. Now go."

Before Derrick could react, the front door flew open, and in walked the child of their union. At the sight of her mother and father—together at home—the teen's face lit up. In an instant, Andrea's ire was replaced with regret. How could she be angry in Madison's presence? The kid wanted nothing more than for her mom and dad to reconcile. Poor thing.

"Daddy!" Madison crossed to Derrick, her arms outstretched.

"Look at you, Maddy." Derrick held the girl to his chest. "You get prettier every day, honey."

He was right, Andrea thought as she watched Maddy dissolve in her ex-husband's embrace. That fact brought her no joy. With her mass of sun-tinted hair and gold-flecked eyes, Madison looked like a young ingénue—wholesome and heartbreakingly beautiful. And that would have been fine had the girl not been developmentally challenged. How was she ever to protect this innocent creature?

"Hi, Maddy," she said, tamping down her fears. "I didn't hear the bus pull up. How was kickboxing?"

Madison disentangled herself from her father's arms, and Derrick flopped back down on the sofa. "Hi, Mom. It was good. Watch this." She struck a pose, balled fists before her face. "Ha!" she exclaimed, executing a swift kick.

"Wow! Impressive," Andrea said as the girl fell into her father's lap.

"What's up, Daddy?" Madison gazed into Derrick's eyes, twisting a lock of his long, thinning hair around her finger.

Damn. The child is a natural vixen.

"Nothing. Just wanted to see my girls, is all." Derrick eyed Andrea warily.

"I'm starving." Madison turned to Andrea. "What's for dinner?"

"Dinner?" Andrea shrugged. "Gee, I don't know. I just walked in the door myself. What are you hungry for?"

"Pizza," Madison and Derrick chorused.

Andrea rolled her eyes. Her ex-husband wasn't a bad man, and he adored his daughter. But Derrick had never grown up and wasn't about to. He was nothing but a great big kid, someone else for her to help support and care for. Andrea sighed. "Okay, pizza it is." She'd been spared the ordeal of preparing a meal, and for that she was grateful. "South Beach or Davila's?"

Later the same day, Andrea sat at the kitchen table with her phone to her ear. "Derrick said you called, Mom."

"Hey, Andy. Yeah, that man of yours and I spoke at length."

"Humph," Andrea snorted. "He's not *mine* anymore." Margaret Sheridan's throaty voice, with its barely perceptible southern drawl, had its usual soothing effect on her. What would she ever do without Mom, Andrea wondered, at the same time dreading the day when she would have to do that very thing? "He's a piece of work all right."

"Has he gone?"

"He and Maddy are walking Beau. The poor dog is conflicted. He's crazy about Derrick, but every time he comes around, I go off on him—Derrick that is—and Beau skedaddles under the bed to wait it out. He's not good with confrontation."

"Who is, darling?"

"Aw, Mom, I don't know. What the heck am I going to do about Derrick? How am I ever supposed to get a new life, if I'm forever stuck in the old one?"

"We're always stuck in the old one. There are no clean breaks, my dear."

"Some people seem to make them."

"They're not evolved. Caring beings…care. They don't just dispose of people when their warranties expire. Divorce is like Velcro."

"Velcro. What?"

"You try to rip it apart, but there's never a clean break. Each little cog gets stuck in a depression and holds on for dear life. It's a messy business."

"That's encouraging."

"How are *you*, sweet?"

"This recession is killing me. Our sales have stagnated. I'm getting beat up daily at the office. On top of that, my boss's new assistant has taken an instant disliking to me, and she's making my life a living hell." Andrea put a palm to her temple and exhaled, but her pity party lasted only an instant. "I'm okay," she said, straightening her spine and putting a smile in her voice. "I got a call today, a potential buyer."

"Wonderful! Tell me about it.

. . .

The next morning, Andrea was more nervous about a showing than she'd been in a long time. It was 2008, and the housing bubble had burst. She had nothing going but this one, enigmatic client, and she needed to put her best foot forward and sell him.

The traffic light at the intersection of A1A and Beachland Boulevard changed to red, and she flipped down the visor and gazed at her reflection in the mirror. It was high time she broke down and had some fillers, she thought, maybe a little Botox—get rid of those worry lines.

And no more crying in your pillow, girlfriend, her inner voice admonished, *or you'll have to lift those sagging eyelids, as well."*

Andrea was fully aware of the sobering fact that she was selling good taste to mega-millionaires—little Ms. Vero Beach, with plenty of class and no means. She had to look the part, and it was all so expensive—clothes, car, hair, nails, on top of Maddy's school, the mortgage, food, and lawn maintenance. The list was endless. And now her mother's place, the familial estate, factored into the mix.

She couldn't fault her dad. Dr. John Sheridan—a general practitioner beloved by patients and family alike—had been an astute businessman. He'd provided for her mom and the kids, setting up trust funds and insurance policies. But who would have thought he'd pass away at the ripe old age of forty-nine, and that the biotech meltdown in the year 2000 would ravage his well-laid plans?

The rambling, two-story house on Greenway Drive in Old Riomar was paid for in full, but Margaret was years behind on the property taxes, a sum now higher than the cost of the original structure. After years of neglect, the roof needed to be replaced, the stucco redone, the kitchen and baths completely renovated, and the overgrown landscaping tamed. The entire two-and-a-half-acre parcel demanded a thorough makeover. Andrea figured it'd cost about nearly two million to bring it up to speed. Or they could sell it for a song and install Margaret in one of those high-priced retirement communities. One way or another, she knew she had to make a decision about Casa Rio.

The light turned green, and Andrea drove past the offices of Heller, Ivan, and Cain, the most highly respected law practice in Vero. The esteemed firm occupied a stately, three-story edifice set upon a prime corner location. She cast an admiring glance at the attractive structure, and a sense of pride washed over her. This was where Prestige Realty entrusted its escrow accounts, such a solid and trustworthy institution.

~

Andrea had gotten it all wrong. Behind that grand exterior—one which spoke of strength and permanence—a maelstrom was brewing. Never mind that the reception area and inner halls, with their elaborate moldings and elegantly wainscoted walls, exuded grace and refined elegance. Forget the fact that the interior atmosphere was typically hushed and solemn so that, upon crossing the threshold, one almost felt as though they'd entered a place of worship. Because, in a way, they had. Here, billable hours were venerated. Lawyers and their clerks went about their daily activities placidly. Perhaps Valium was dispensed through the water fountains. Who knew? But today was different. Today, all hell had broken loose in the corner office of senior partner, Floyd Heller, Esquire.

The charmed life Floyd had led was kaput. But Floyd wasn't Carla's only worry. It was her predicament that weighed heavily on her mind, her culpability in his madness.

"Jeez, what did I tell you?" Floyd bellowed, pounding a meaty fist on his walnut desktop. "Move the Griswold money over into the O'Keefe account."

"I did that, Floyd," Carla swiped the back of a hand across her damp upper lip. "But we're still short." The middle-aged brunette finger-combed a lock of hair away from her flushed face. "And there's not enough in the checking account to make payroll."

"How much are we short?" Heller bounded from his chair and began pacing.

"Twenty… thirty thousand. I don't know. Maybe more."

The stocky attorney stopped beating a path on his Wilton carpet, pinched his nose, and appeared to calculate in his head.

Carla's heart was pounding in her chest. No job was worth this amount of stress. Early retirement was looking damned good about now.

"Is that all?" Heller planted himself before his assistant, and she cowered before him. "That's doable," he said.

"It is?"

Suddenly, the attorney seemed to take notice of Carla's agitated state, her trembling lower lip and wild eyes. "Hey, hey," he said, waving his hands before him. "Calm down."

Floyd let his paws gently come to rest on the troubled woman's shoulders. "There now," he soothed. "Come here and take a load off." Floyd led Carla to a guest chair in front of his desk, indicating that she should sit, and the flustered woman fell into it.

"I'm sorry. I was merely venting," Heller soothed. "It's going to be okay. We'll be fine."

"Really?" Carla croaked. "We will?" She desperately wanted to believe Floyd's lies but was no longer capable of maintaining that fantasy. She knew this pyramid scheme she'd helped construct was on the verge of collapse.

"Sure, sure." Floyd plastered an insincere smile on his face. "Just transfer what you need from my personal checking to cover the difference in the O'Keefe account. Tell bookkeeping to print the employee checks as they always do. Let me know what that comes to, and we'll transfer that amount into the firm's checking account. I'm expecting escrows from two of Sally Bray's clients this week, and then we'll be flush again. No worries. This is just a little tight spot. It's not like we haven't had them before, you know."

"You're right, but—"

"No buts about it, Carla. Make the calls. Then take the rest of the afternoon off, why don't you? Treat yourself to a mini-pedi at Tootsies. Put it on my account."

"Okay, Floyd," Carla said. But she knew Floyd had finally gotten them in too deep.

It had all started innocuously enough, the little discrepancies, the deceptions and the cover-ups. "Just have to tide things over," Floyd had said the first time they'd come up short. And she'd agreed. Surely, every company deals with such things from time to time, she'd told herself when she'd first learned that Floyd was robbing Peter to pay Paul, borrowing from escrow funds to pay his household expenses.

Floyd was a good man, a family man, and a solid citizen. He contributed generously to a host of charitable organizations, attended

Sunday services at the Community Church, and had no vices that she knew of except, perhaps, for a fondness for a tumbler of Maker's Mark at the end of a long hard day. And who would begrudge him that? Carla had stood by her man, Floyd being the only one she had. She'd been loyal, true blue—in good times and in bad. But now she was ready to cut and run. There was only so much standing by a girl could muster. At some point, when the earth was sliding out from under one's feet, they had to jump off in hopes of landing smack dab into a new reality. Carla was praying for that second chance.

CHAPTER TWO

WHO IS THIS GUY

Supremely conscious of her undulating fanny, Andrea prayed that her client's attention was riveted on the gorgeous interior, the splendid light fixture, anything other than her ass. "The floors are travertine, the carpets, Stark. Note the fabulous chandelier, one of Waterford's last custom orders. Sad that they closed the factory, don't you think?"

Andrea was climbing the sweeping staircase two steps ahead of Mr. Daniel Armstrong and babbling.

"I've had enough," Daniel said, pausing mid-landing.

Shit!

"But you haven't seen the guest bedrooms or the carriage house." Andrea struggled to keep her voice from wavering as her heart plummeted. She was losing him, and she needed to make this sale. There was so much at stake.

In desperation, Andrea did her magic trick. She held her breath and blessed Daniel, wishing him great good fortune. Then she recalled her first big sale to her first multimillion-dollar client, Sid Reso, CEO of Exxon Oil International. She'd been so nervous making her presentation, speaking much too quickly and stumbling over her words.

"Slow down, Andrea," Sid had interrupted. "I'm going to buy, and I'm going to buy from you. Just relax. Take your time and sell me." Sid had been the quintessential manager on a mega scale. He'd spent a career surrounding himself with experts, and he knew how to get the very best out of every one of them. His influence on her had been nothing short of life altering. Sid was gone now, but his memory lived on, and once again, Andrea was thanking him and heeding his advice.

"Oh?" Andrea smiled, affecting an I've-not-a-care-in-the-world attitude. But then her eyes met Daniel's, and she nearly faltered.

Whoa!

Her heart quickened. With his sparkly blue eyes and well-defined jaw, the man before her was drop-dead gorgeous. How could she possibly be so involved in her own drama not to have noticed such a thing?

Must be losing it.

And then her eyes fastened on Daniel's large hands, the smattering of golden hairs creeping up his wrists into his perfectly pressed Brooks Brothers shirt cuffs, his blunt, neatly clipped fingernails.

Dang!

Andrea imagined those hands caressing her body, and her mouth went dry.

What is the matter with me?

"Alright. Tell me what's missing here," she said, struggling to keep her voice from tripping into its upper register.

Daniel gazed back at her, and then he, too, appeared momentarily flummoxed. Pivoting, he sat down on the landing, extending his long legs before him.

Andrea regarded those legs, the bulging quads faintly outlined beneath his khakis, and she felt a stirring in her groin.

How long has it been since I've touched a man?

"I don't know," Daniel said. "It's just too—"

"Perfect?" Andrea sat down beside Daniel, and when the tender flesh of her thigh brushed against his, she had all she could do to keep from crying out. "Too antiseptic? Is that it?"

"Maybe." Daniel threw his hands in the air, indicating the general environs. "I just can't see me... I mean *him* here."

"Tell me about this client you're representing."

Daniel's brow furrowed. "He likes... I don't know... atmosphere."

"Umm. Atmosphere." Andrea grinned wickedly and patted his arm. "Well, we can't purchase the Ocean Grill. At least I don't think so."

"That's a boatload of atmosphere." Daniel's penetrating eyes searched Andrea's, and she felt her cheeks warm.

"I'm sorry," he said, suddenly all business. "I'm wasting your time."

Dear Lord, don't let me lose him.

"Not at all. We simply must find the ideal place for you... for him. Tell me what's wrong with this picture, and I'll have a new itinerary for you tomorrow."

Daniel shook his head. "I can't think," he said. "I'm hungry. How about we grab a bite to eat and discuss it over dinner?"

Andrea breathed a sigh of relief. "Fine by me," she said brightly. "I'll just call my mom, have her meet my daughter when she gets home from school. Where shall we go?"

"The Ocean Grill, of course."

~

Andrea arrived at the famous landmark before her client. Although she deplored tardiness, she was beginning to think she was taking punctuality to the extreme; she always arrived early! Sid had been whispering in her ear to slow down, but she'd ignored him. Instead, she'd charged across town doing five miles over the speed limit—all the while talking on her cell, relaying instructions to her mother. She was going to hang on to this guy for all she was worth. And if she were honest with herself, it wasn't just about finding the ideal house, closing the deal, and moving on.

As usual, the Ocean Grill parking lot was full. Andrea had to circle around and back onto Ocean Drive a couple of times before she scored a space. While scurrying toward the entrance, she devised a plan. She would cajole the hostess into reserving a table for her, despite the fact the Grill's policy was no reservations for parties of less than five.

Once inside, she wended her way through the gift shop to the podium in the entryway.

"Hey, Mary!" A genuine smile split her face. She hadn't expected the owner to be manning the station.

"Hey, yourself," Mary said. "What can I do for you?"

"A huge favor. I've got an important client and—"

"Say no more," Mary interrupted. "We've got you covered."

"You're the best."

"We take care of our friends." Mary winked at her.

～

Perched on the observation deck atop the dune line on the north side of the restaurant, Andrea's mind was full of Daniel and the sale she needed to make. But the beauty of the setting seeped into her consciousness, imbuing her with a sense of contentment, and her heartbeat slowed. It was twilight, and the heat had bled out of the day. The sky and sea were a uniform silvery gray, the tide lapping at pilings supporting the weathered facade. A few stragglers remained onshore— sunburned kids digging in the sand for ghost crabs, a pair of ancient, stooped and leather-skinned beach-walkers—while across the way, Mulligan's was doing a brisk trade, honky-tonk music spilling from its open doors.

Then Daniel was pulling up in his Jaguar, and Andrea waved her arms over her head, directing him to the side lot.

"Daniel," Andrea nodded toward the proprietress, "Mary and her husband are the owners of this fine establishment."

Daniel stepped up to the reservation desk and thrust a hand toward the attractive restaurateur. "Very pleased to meet you."

"Mary, my client, Daniel Armstrong."

Mary widened her eyes and shot Andrea a conspiratorial grin. It was a fleeting, subtle reaction, but Andrea knew what Mary was thinking: the gent was hot.

Mary took Daniel's hand in hers. "It's a pleasure to meet you, Daniel. Are you looking at property?"

"Yes, ma'am."

"Well, you won't be disappointed. Vero's great, and you're in good hands with our Andy. She's one of the best."

"I'm well aware of that fact."

Just then, a petite blonde darted from the dining room into the entry, coming to stand beside the proprietress. "This is your server," Mary said, nodding toward the vivacious twenty-something. "She'll escort you to your table and take very good care of you." The pert young waitress pivoted on her heel and made for the crowded dining room beyond.

"Thanks, Mary." Andrea followed the waitress, and Daniel put two fingers to his forehead in an abbreviated salute. "Nice to meet you, Mary," he said, before hastening away to catch up with the two women.

"Oh, and Andy," Mary called after them. Andrea turned to her. "Charlie is in the kitchen tonight. So, whatever you want—"

Andrea gave Mary a thumbs-up before circumnavigating the colossal round table at the front of the restaurant where a large, boisterous party was seated. Then she zigzagged through the maze of smaller tables in pursuit of the waitress.

"Here we are," the young woman nodded toward the only unoccupied window side table.

Daniel rushed in and pulled out a chair, and Andrea allowed herself to be seated.

"Menus," the waitress said, placing bills of fare before them. "May I get you something to drink?"

Daniel cocked his head, looking pointedly at Andrea.

"I'll have a glass of the house white wine."

"And make mine a Dewar's and water."

"Okay. I'll be back to tell you about the specials. In the meantime, I'll have waters and a loaf of freshly baked sourdough bread out to you in a minute."

"Love this place," Daniel said, once the waitress had dashed off. His eyes roved about the cavernous room lavishly embellished with a cache of salvaged treasures collected from around the world—hand-painted tiles from Portugal, metalwork aged to a dusty patina, rusted bells and lanterns. "It's so—"

"Atmospheric." Andrea finished Daniel's sentence and grinned at him.

"Lovely," Daniel muttered, gazing into her eyes.

Andrea peered at him. "Excuse me?"

Daniel scowled, digging two fingers into his temple.

"What's the matter? Do you have a headache?"

"No. I'm just a little stressed." Daniel squinted, tracing his fingers across his five o'clock shadow. "I'm under the gun to find a property and close on it. The person that I represent is..." He glanced around as if to ascertain there were no paparazzi, recording devices in hand, within earshot, "rather well known, to put it mildly. As I explained earlier, he doesn't want to invite prying eyes or media hoopla. That's why he chose Vero. It's a classy, little seaside town where celebs' rights to peace and privacy are respected."

Andrea nodded, thinking that was certainly true. She was acquainted with a good number of movie stars, film directors, and pop singers, to say nothing of many bestselling authors, high-powered media moguls, and Fortune 500 CEOs, all of whom owned properties. "You're absolutely correct, but I'm not naming names."

"There you go."

The waitress arrived with their drinks. "Shall I tell you about tonight's specials?" she asked, setting their beverages before them.

"I know what I want," Andrea said.

"Me too." Daniel waved a hand in Andrea's direction, indicating that she should order first.

"Would you ask Charlie if he can scrounge me up some stone crab claws?"

"Sure thing." The waitress scribbled on her pad.

"For my sides: a baked potato, and the creamed spinach, and a Caesar salad to start."

"You got it."

"I'll have the prime rib, extra thick-cut, medium rare, and the same sides as my partner, here." Daniel looked to Andrea and raised his eyebrows, affecting a rakish pose.

Momentarily taken aback, Andrea covered by sipping her wine. "Umm," she murmured. But the warm glow that suffused her was not from the wine, but rather at the word *partner*.

"Coming right up," the perky blonde chirruped. Then she pivoted and sprinted toward the kitchen with the speed of a gazelle.

"Cute kid." Daniel nodded toward the girl's retreating figure. "If only they could bottle up her energy, they'd make a fortune hawking it in the gift shop."

"I know her family. Good people."

"Why doesn't that surprise me?" Daniel teased. "Seems as though you're on a first-name basis with the entire town's populace. I bet you know every available property, as well."

Andrea studied Daniel's face, and her smile sagged. "I'm afraid I've let you down," she said. "I really thought you'd like the house in Orchid Island."

"I *did* like it. It was just…" Daniel peered out the window, "a little cold." He turned back to Andrea.

"Generally, when there's no furniture in a place, it comes off as rather cold. I'll grant you that."

"Point taken. But my client's a bit of an eccentric. He can afford palatial, but he prefers something grand yet intimate at the same time."

"I see," Andrea said, although she didn't see at all.

"I'm sorry to be so difficult."

"Nothing of the sort." Andrea's mind was racing.
What can I show him? What would fit that bill?

~

After they'd finished their dinners, they strolled out past the reception desk. Mary had long since departed to be replaced by the usual hostess. "Goodnight," she called to them as they bypassed the gift shop and stepped outside into the night's warm cocoon. The two paused on the deck, turning back for another glimpse of the ocean, now sheened in silver, only to be bedazzled by a luminous moon— nearly full—poised over the darkening horizon. The same magnetic, inexorable force that drew the tides now seemed at work on the two of them, pulling them irresistibly toward the side observation deck.

Andrea leaned out over the rail, breathing in the briny tang of the sea. "What a moon," she exclaimed.

"Maybe it's an omen," Daniel said, his eyes fixed on the oversized orb.

"It surely is," Andrea agreed. "By this time tomorrow, it'll be full, and we'll have fulfilled your mission; we'll have found you the perfect home-away-from-home for your client."

Daniel's eyes detached from the softly gleaming orb in the sky to gaze at Andrea. He sucked in his breath and then slowly exhaled.

Andrea turned toward Daniel, a small smile playing about her lips. "What are you thinking?"

In a weak moment, perhaps because the moon was beaming strange cosmic particles down upon him, Daniel positioned an index finger under Andrea's chin, tilting her face toward his. His fingers splayed across the back of her head, sifting through her silky, ash brown hair as he covered her lips with his.

It was a delicious kiss, and Andrea melted into it. But then she realized the folly of the situation and drew away. "Oh, dear," she said. "This might complicate things."

"A man, a woman… How complicated can it be?" Daniel reached for her, but Andrea backed off, and the spell was broken.

"Are you kidding me?" she said. "PDC!"

Daniel looked mystified.

"Pretty damn complicated. Besides, you don't know anything about me. I have lots of baggage."

"You're right. I'm sorry." Daniel put his hands in his pockets and turned to face the parking lot. "I don't know what came over me," he mumbled, as he ambled off in the direction of Ocean Drive.

Now I've gone and hurt his feelings. Can I do nothing right, today?

Andrea trotted after him. "Wait up," she called, and Daniel obliged. As she neared, he turned and smiled at her, but Andrea could plainly see the smile did not reach his eyes.

Yep. You've done some pretty serious damage.

Andrea only hoped Daniel wasn't so put off that he'd find another realtor. How she wished she wasn't so needy. She was always walking this tightrope—juggling—performing a balancing act while keeping all the balls in the air. It was exhausting. She reached out and linked arms with Daniel.

If Daniel was surprised by this sudden intimacy, he didn't show it. Initially, he offered mild resistance, but then, ever the gentleman, he allowed himself to be manipulated.

"Look, Daniel," Andrea said, as they strolled arm in arm toward her Benz. "I like you. I really do. And I want to help you find the ideal house for your client. But you need to understand something…"

"Oh?"

"I'm not a free agent."

Daniel made as if to pull away. "You don't have to explain—"

Holding firmly to Daniel's arm, Andrea cut him off. "Yes, I do. But please, I don't want to go just yet. Would you mind if we took a walk? Let our dinners digest?"

She gazed up at him, and Daniel's stony countenance softened. He looked into her gold-flecked eyes and then shook his head as if to clear it. "Okay."

Andrea steered Daniel south toward the Driftwood Inn while the moon inched higher in the sky. The moon, she thought, looked like a golden egg. She only hoped it would prove as rewarding. "Please, tell me. Just who *is* this client of yours?"

"Madame, I am pledged to secrecy."

"Come on. I thought we were going to bare our souls." Andrea pretended to pout.

"Whatever gave you that idea?"

"I guess because I was about to bare mine."

"That certainly isn't necessary. In fact—"

"You know nothing about me," Andrea said, thinking she should have let him kiss her. "And I know nothing about you. You are, perhaps, the most mysterious client I've ever worked for. And that's saying a lot."

"Oh, spare me."

"Hey, I worked with Sting in Miami."

"You're joking."

"Nope. I'll tell you about it sometime. But about this fellow you represent… He could be a gangster… or a terrorist, for all I know."

"True. However, I assure you he's neither."

"I believe you. But what's your connection to this character?"

Daniel stopped walking and stared into space for a moment before answering.

Why is he so cagey?

"I'm just your average Joe, trying to make a living," he finally said. "I'm in the employ of a very important man, and he affords me an extremely comfortable lifestyle. So—"

"So, you're not going to tell me a thing." Andrea struggled to keep the disappointment from her voice. "I guess I'll have to live with that." They stood before a squat stone column topped by an ancient, rusting lantern. "Here we are."

"And what place is this?" Daniel eyed the oceanfront compound. "It reminds me of the Grill."

"It's the Driftwood Inn, silly, another of Waldo Sexton's architectural creations. Surely, you've been here?"

"Can't say as I have."

17

"Well, then you're in for a treat." Andrea steered Daniel toward the saloon. But rather than enter, they veered to the right, following the meandering walkway.

Andrea bent down to point out a detail underfoot. "See. Here's Florida." She indicated the bits of tile, which had been set in mortar in a fair representation of the Sunshine State.

"Very clever," Daniel said with little conviction to his voice while eyeing the crude mosaic.

"And here are the Florida Keys." Andrea pointed to the southernmost tip of the peninsula where several vintage latchkeys had been mortared in.

"Ah."

They continued on to the portico, past a crude wooden dining table with a mammoth single-plank top, and out to the boardwalk. Once again, that strangely engorged moon captivated them, and their eyes latched on to the shimmering sphere.

"La Luna," Daniel muttered.

"Didn't you just love *Moonstruck*?" Andrea gushed. "What a movie! Cher was amazing… and Nicholas Cage… with that enormous chip on his shoulder and no arm attached to it."

"Yeah." Daniel sighed, and Andrea reached for his hand. Suddenly, she felt the need for a tether, something to keep her from spinning off into space.

Standing there—at the edge of a continent—gazing out over a black sea and a firmament lit by a single, glowing pendant, both seemed lost in thought. Then they spoke at the same time. "I'm not a —" Daniel said.

"This is one—" Andrea laughed, self-consciously, and turned to Daniel. "Sorry, you first."

"I just wanted to tell you that I'm not a free agent, either."

"Really?" A cold stab of fear sliced through Andrea's heart. She'd been a fool, gotten her hopes up.

"You might as well know. If you google me, you're bound to find out anyway."

"Find out what?"

"That I'm married."

"Oh. Well…" Andrea's smile froze. She pivoted away from Daniel and turned her gaze back to the obsidian ocean.

"I'm in the middle of a nasty divorce. It's been brutal."

"Hey, you don't owe me any explanations." Andrea turned back to Daniel. "I really should be going. Shall we start back?"

"Sure. But just one thing…"

"Yes?"

"What's *your* marital status, if you don't mind my asking?"

"Divorced. Although my ex doesn't seem to think so. He's having a difficult time moving on."

"I can understand why," Daniel muttered.

"Anyway…" Andrea retraced her steps, through the portico, the Florida Keys inset in mortar, past the gargantuan, plank-top table, and Daniel followed. Once outside the compound, the two strolled abreast. This time, however, there was no physical contact between them. Rather, it seemed as though they were separated by a great divide. And at that moment, neither appeared inclined to have it otherwise.

Andrea finally broke the silence. "Do you have children?"

"Unfortunately, no. My soon-to-be ex-wife didn't want children."

"You did?"

"Oh, yeah. Still do. I'm not *that* old, you know." Daniel turned to her, a wry half-smile on his face.

Andrea chuckled, and the chasm between them narrowed a bit. "Believe me. They can be more than you bargained for."

"Tell me about your kids."

"Only one. A girl." Andrea stopped and pointed. "There's my car."

"I'm sure she's beautiful, just like her mother."

A troubled expression crossed Andrea's face. "What time shall we go back at it tomorrow?" She pressed the unlock button on her car key, all the while praying that Daniel would be up for another round of showings.

"I'm not sure."

Andrea felt her heart leap to her throat. She was losing him. "You know," she said, an idea suddenly forming. "I think I have an unusual property you might take a shine to, Daniel. What I have in mind isn't located in a gated community, but it's an architectural gem situated on a very large, private parcel."

Andrea shot a sidelong glance at Daniel, noted his eyebrows rise. "I warn you. It'd take some fixing up, though. Are you interested?"

"Intrigued," Daniel said. "Meet you at the office at nine-thirty?"

"Great." Andrea slid behind the wheel. "See you then. And thanks for dinner."

"My pleasure." Daniel closed the Mercedes driver's door, and, as the car pulled out of the parking lot, raised an arm and waved.

Andrea tapped the horn while thanking her lucky stars. All was not lost; tomorrow was another day.

CHAPTER THREE

SELLING THE FARM

Daniel followed Andrea's progress as she cut across to Beachland Boulevard. She was a beautiful woman—smart—and she knew her stuff. But what was that nonsense about deal-brokering for Sting? He didn't question Andrea's veracity. She'd probably sold the rock star some property in Miami, thereby becoming a bona fide groupie with privileges. That sort of thing didn't impress him. Still, there was something fragile about her, and he couldn't pretend he didn't feel an attraction. More than that, he sensed a well of sadness in her, and all he wanted to do was take her in his arms and make things right...

Stop!

Daniel put the kibosh on that daydream. His personal life was a mess, and he didn't need one more complication, especially one involving a woman!

As he ambled toward the side lot, Daniel vowed to put all thoughts of Andrea out of his mind. He would keep their relationship strictly a professional one and stay focused on the business at hand. His phone vibrated, and Daniel dug it out of his pocket and eyed the display. When he saw Kara's number, he grimaced. He was tempted to ignore her call, refuse to allow this evening to end on a sour note. But he was a businessman, not one for putting things off, unpleasant though they might be. Daniel slid the accept call prompt.

"Hello, Kara," he said, a resigned note to his voice. "What is it?"

"We agreed I was to get Sweet Dreamer!"

Kara's shriek hit him with the force of an open-handed slap, and Daniel recoiled in a futile attempt to dodge the blow.

"You said I could have it, and now your lawyers are waffling. What's that all about, Danny? You can't renege on me at this late date."

Daniel opened the car door and folded himself into the low-slung seat. "Kara, you know, as well as I do that we agreed to a dollar amount." He pressed the ignition, and the engine fired.

"Sweet Dreamer is the one house I'm asking for, you tightwad. And what do you care, anyway? You don't fool me. This is a power play, pure and simple. Hell, you don't even like the islands."

"The Sweet Dreamer property is simply out of the question." Daniel turned the air to max and rolled out to the main lot, only to have to brake to allow a young family on foot to cross in front of him. "Darling, if you insist on the Barbados property, you will receive a much smaller lump sum, and given the lifestyle to which you've become accustomed, I don't think you'd be satisfied with that. Why not trust me? I truly am looking out for you."

"Sure, you are, Mr. Altruistic. My knight… Well, forget it."

The one thing, Daniel repeated silently, plus a ten-million-dollar settlement, plus the Miami property, plus twenty K a month for expenses. And it still wouldn't appease the woman, still wasn't enough to compensate her for seven years of cohabitation, two of which had been happy. No. He wasn't going to budge. Kara was not going to wrest away the Barbados estate.

Daniel took his foot off the brake, and the powerful automobile coasted to the intersection. "The one house?" His voice oozed sarcasm. "What about your domicile, my love? You know… that monstrosity of a residence on Singer Island?"

"I have to live *somewhere*! Do you want me on the streets, Danny? That would come back to haunt you."

As he spun out onto Ocean Drive, Daniel was picturing that very scenario. It was an appealing image. In his mind's eye, he could see Kara—poor, little rich girl, clad only in rags—panhandling the mean streets of Philly in hopes of scoring enough pocket change to purchase a double latte with non-fat cream, maybe a secondhand, consignment shop Versace bag.

"You'll get your blood money, Kara," he muttered. "Just let the lawyers earn their windfalls. We shouldn't have to duke it out. They can do the heavy lifting. You'll be fine. I promise. Good night."

Daniel powered down his cellphone before Kara's shrill reply could further accost him. He tooled a half-block north to the Vero Beach Hotel and Club, vowing to vanquish all thoughts of women. Turning right onto a paver drive lined by towering queen palms, he pulled up to the glitzy hotel entrance. Out of nowhere, a valet appeared. The fellow jogged around the car and deftly opened the driver's side door. Daniel shifted to park, and hopped out, eager for something—anything—to dispel his sudden irritation. On the spur of the moment, he decided to grab a quick nightcap, check out the activity at the bar before retiring to his penthouse suite. The evening was still young, he thought, ruing his former resolve. What the heck? Weren't vows meant to be broken?

~

When Andrea slotted her shiny white Mercedes in next to Margaret's sixteen-year-old silver Volvo, a wave of relief washed over her. In the last few years, her daughter had become self-sufficient, more so than she'd ever imagined possible. But the child's naiveté was a continual cause for concern, and she couldn't bear the thought of Maddy coming home to an empty house. "Hello," she called out, as she entered through the garage door entrance. "I'm back."

Except for the hum of the dishwasher, the house was silent. Andrea crossed through the kitchen in four long strides. A quick look around told her the family room was unoccupied, but then Maddy's high-pitched voice came to her from the back patio, and Andrea's concerns vanished.

"Watch me, Nana."

Andrea stood before the French doors, her eyes drawn to the pool deck.

"Are you watching?" Maddy poised on the diving board, her arms hanging loosely at her sides. In the gloom, the girl's features were indistinguishable; she was but a shapely silhouette cast against a sky awash in the luminous glow of a radiant moon.

"Yes, yes! Go for it, Maddy," Margaret encouraged.

The teen began a series of small jumps, each successively higher and more forceful than the one preceding. Gracefully raising her arms, Maddy reached skyward. Then, with index fingers touching, she sprang off the board, her body forming a compact elliptical arc moments before slipping beneath the water's surface.

Beau had been curled at Margaret's feet, but, at the sound of Maddy hitting the water, he bounded to his paws, barking frenziedly.

"Whoo-hoo!" Margaret cheered as Madison's head broke the surface, a grin splitting her face.

Andrea pushed open the door and was immediately swaddled in a damp blanket of humidity. "Hi, guys." She reached out to pat the terrier on his shaggy head. "Hey there, Beau."

"Hi!" Maddy tread water, beaming. "Did you see my dive?"

"Hello, honey," Margaret cried. "What do you think of our very own fish?"

"I did, indeed, Maddy." Andrea held out a palm. "High five. You rock." She turned to her mother. "Our fish is incredible. You always were the best instructor." Andrea collapsed into a lounge chair beside Margaret. "So, how's it going?"

"Come in, Mommy, the water's great," the teen wheedled.

"Aw, Madison, Mom's so tired. I just want to rest while you dazzle me."

The girl needed no more encouragement. "Okay. I'll practice the butterfly. Watch me," she said, before cutting through the water in rhythmic strokes.

"Thanks, Mom." Andrea turned toward her mother. "I know it was last minute, but…"

"Not a problem, Andy. I'm delighted to help. Anytime with my granddaughter is time well spent."

"What did you have for dinner?"

"We scrounged around in the fridge and pantry to see what ingredients we could come up with. Whipped up some pasta Athena."

Andrea arched a brow. "And just what is that?"

"It's what you concoct when all your scrounging yields is a box of penne, some moldy goat cheese, a bag of wilting spinach, and a jar of kalamata olives."

"Sounds wonderful."

"It was, and Madison was a big help."

Madison swam to the pool steps and clambered out. "I'm beat, too," she announced.

"You should be," Margaret said, offering her a towel. "You had quite a workout."

Madison wrapped herself in the towel and then hunkered down next to her grandmother. "You gotta try the pasta we made, Mom. It's terrific!"

"I see you're not only a fish, but a chef as well, huh?"

"I like to cook," Madison agreed.

"Great. Because tomorrow's Saturday, and we're going to the Farmer's Market downtown to pick up some fresh vegetables from Daddy's garden. We'll have a feast tomorrow evening, but now it's time for you to call it a day, sweetheart. Tell Nana goodbye and then hop into the shower, okay?"

"Okay, Mom." Madison rose and wrapped her arms around Margaret's neck. "G'night, Nana," she said. "Thank you."

Margaret planted a kiss on the girl's damp forehead. "You are welcome, my dearest. Sweet dreams and have fun tomorrow."

"Okay." Madison extricated herself from her grandmother's embrace and then trotted to the French door. Margaret and Andrea watched as the girl let herself in. Then they turned to one another and smiled.

"She is becoming a very attractive young woman."

"I know, Mom. Sometimes I wish she were plain."

Margaret chuckled. "I know the feeling. I felt the same about you."

Andrea gaped. "What? I never heard that before."

"Sweetheart, I don't think it's a unique concept. Mothers of beautiful girls worry about their vulnerability—that they will be beset by predators."

"My sentiments exactly."

"Honey, you've got to loosen the apron strings. Madison has come a long way. It's time you let her fly on her own."

"Come on, Mom. She's clueless. I need to protect her."

"But you can't. You can't be there for her every minute. You need to give her the tools to cope."

Andrea turned her face away, her voice thick with emotion. "I'm trying. You must believe me.

Margaret reached over and took her daughter's hand in hers. "I'm sorry. You have so much on your plate. And you're doing a wonderful job of it. I mean that. Have I told you, lately, how proud I am of you?"

Andrea looked up through watery eyes. "I know, Mom."

"So," Margaret exclaimed, clearing the air. "Tell me about your client. How did it go?"

"Ugh," Andrea grumbled. "I don't know. Daniel's very sweet... but an enigma. I can't seem to get a handle on him."

"Are we talking about real estate or something else?"

"No, no. Strictly business. It's just that... he's very specific about what he wants... and yet all over the place. The man is driving me crazy."

"Not just real estate, then. I get it."

"Mom!"

"What is it he's after? Besides my lovely daughter, that is?"

"Not that. Trust me." Andrea gazed out over a river fast disappearing into the lengthening shadows, and then she dropped the bombshell.

"Actually, I think he'd like your house." She mentally cringed as her words struck home.

Margaret didn't answer immediately. Instead, she seemed to consider Andrea's proposition. "How much do you think you could get for it?" she finally asked.

"More than it's worth, just now. More than you'd ever get on the open market."

"But it's Daddy's place... Papa John's."

"I know. But, Mom, you need a new roof, new windows, four new air conditioners, the kitchen, and baths have to be gutted and completely redone... We're talking a huge amount of cash. In this recession... most clients want to waltz into a turnkey property. They can't see the forest for the trees, and they certainly don't want to have to retain an architect, an interior designer, and a contractor, and then wait for their delayed gratification. I don't care how special a place might be. They want to move right in, and if there are designer furnishings included and the kitchen is fully stocked, so much the better."

"I can understand that—"

"Mom, I think I might have a buyer who would be willing to pay top dollar for a fixer-upper: your place. And this opportunity might never come again. At least not in our lifetime."

"Oh, hell."

Andrea came to her feet. "I'm going to pour myself a glass of wine. Will you join me?"

"Love to."

The moon was at its zenith, yet it still seemed incredibly oversized. The two women sat in companionable silence, marveling at this simple gift. Darkness had descended around them, but the river was striated with reflected golden moonbeams, and a few twinkling lights dotted the horizon, spilling from houses across the causeway.

"What do you think, Mom?" Andrea asked.

"About?"

"Mother…"

"Oh, honey, I don't know. I guess you should show it to him. We'll just go from there, huh?"

"I believe that's the best course. No sense getting all worked up about it until we know if he's interested."

Margaret drained her glass and rose to her feet. "I should go. Set the place to rights. Make sure my underwear isn't festooning the laundry room."

"You don't have to do a thing. Believe me, if Daniel were a woman, it'd be another matter. This guy's going to take one look at the setting, check to see if the foundation's solid, and make his decision. He wouldn't notice your leopard print push-up bra if it were hanging from a chandelier."

"What if it was a thong?"

Andrea choked, and a rivulet of wine ran down her chin. "You are a crazy woman," she snorted.

"Takes one to know one. And you've got my genes."

~

Over the past several years, the Farmer's Market had grown from a haphazardly staged, poorly attended event to a weekly happening. Now, as every Saturday morning, the parking lot across from Humiston Park was bustling with patrons eager to sample the produce and wares displayed in pop-up booths. A carnival-like atmosphere prevailed, and the various purveyors were all doing a brisk trade.

"I never know if this stuff is fresh-picked." A heavy-set woman mopped her brow as she eyed baskets of green zucchini, red and yellow peppers, rose and orange speckled heirloom tomatoes, fragrant arugula, and a variety of leaf lettuces. Andrea arched her brows and kept her own counsel, but Madison wasn't as circumspect.

"It's all fresh," the teen cried in, an indignant tone to her voice. "My dad grows this stuff and it's right out of the ground."

The woman turned toward the girl. "Really? Does he truck it in from Homestead?"

Madison eyed her mother, a question on her face.

"Absolutely not," Andrea interjected. "He owns acreage west of town. As does Seald Sweet, Oceanspray, Becker Farms, and Hale Groves. You've heard of those outfits, I imagine."

"Oh," the woman exclaimed, taken aback. "Of course, I have. The soil's okay, then?"

"The soil's good," Madison said. "Dad farms organic, no chemicals or pesticides."

Impressed, the woman widened her eyes. "I'm pleased to know that. I'll try a little bit of everything he's got here." She gestured toward the produce and then turned to Andrea. "Allow me to introduce myself. I'm the new sous chef at Cobalt, and I'm trying to offer as much local as possible."

"You've come to the right place," Andrea said, shooting her daughter a conspiratorial grin. "Go find Daddy, Madison. Tell him he has an important customer."

The woman pointed with her chin. "I'll take all the peppers you have here—both the red and the yellow." As she made her purchases, Andrea bagged them in paper sacks.

"Hello." Derrick appeared before them. Clothed in bib overalls, a bandana tied around his scraggly mane, he looked, Andrea thought, like an aging hippie. Madison was close on his heels. He thrust an arm out toward the woman.

"I'm Derrick Nelson," he said.

"Esther Grandpierre." The woman took his hand. "Your wife and daughter have been extolling the virtues of your produce."

Esther let go of Derrick's hand, rummaged through her satchel, and dug out a business card. "I'm at Cobalt. I imagine you're familiar with it?"

Derrick's eyes gleamed. "Yes," he said, barely able to contain his excitement. "I've been following you… your blog… and on Facebook. You're pushing the farm-to-table envelope, Ms. Grandpierre."

Esther laughed. "Well, it's nice to be recognized, Mr. Nelson."

"Please, call me Derrick."

"Only if you'll call me Esther. Now, tell me about these lovely greens." She waved toward a bin overflowing with crinolines of dusky green escarole.

Andrea watched the exchange with interest. Derrick could certainly use another buyer, and this woman seemed heaven-sent. She only hoped her ex-husband would follow up, nurture the relationship. Derrick could be charming and personable when he chose to be, but he was a horrible businessman, couldn't balance a checkbook if his life depended on it. Like Madison, he took people at their word, and was the sadder, although not-the-wiser fellow for it. Andrea smiled, indulgently. She still loved him, and she always would. She just couldn't live with him. They were complete opposites. Whereas she was organized and methodical, an A-type personality, he was a total slob thriving on spontaneity. She swore his erratic brain activity gave her a headache. They were as different as chalk to cheese and simply no good together.

"We make pretty babies, though," Derrick had once said, and Andrea agreed.

Esther took her leave, and Andrea and Derrick smiled at one another. "You've got a great potential client there," Andrea said.

"Thanks to you."

"Me, too," Madison cried.

"You, too," Derrick agreed, grinning at his daughter. "So, pumpkin-head, what's up for the rest of the day? Are you two going to hit the shops?"

"Actually," Andrea interjected. "I was wondering if Maddy could help out around here for a couple of hours. I have a showing." She ruffled Madison's hair. "You don't mind, do you, Maddy?"

The teen shook her head. "Can I help, Dad?"

"Sure thing. You go, Andy. We'll be fine. Won't we, sweetie?" He winked at Madison.

"Thanks, Derrick. I'll be back no later than one." Andrea turned to go. "Bye guys. Wish me luck."

She made her way through the crowd and scurried down the sidewalk to where her car was parallel parked in front of the Costa d' Este Hotel, with its dazzling fountain and art deco-inspired facade. If she hurried, she'd be at the office in plenty of time to meet Daniel by nine-thirty.

~

Vagrants often loitered on park benches. Garrett Olson was fully aware of that fact. But today was Saturday, and most working stiffs, himself included, had the day off. So, he didn't feel conspicuous. Just chilling on a metal bench in front of Humiston Park, enjoying the fresh air and watching the tide of humanity swim by. No harm in that. His eyes followed the good-looking older chick as she climbed into her Mercedes, but what caught and held his attention was the dark-haired babe working the vegetable stand. She was as ripe looking as the produce she was hawking. And there was something else about her; she seemed utterly unaware of her beauty, not all stuck-up and snobby like most pretty girls but approachable and sweet. He was long overdue for a girlfriend, had made a mess of his two most unsatisfactory former relationships. His mother was always harping on him to get out from behind the computer screen and live a little. Maybe it was time. He tapped the camera icon on his phone, waited for the girl to turn in his direction, and captured the shot.

~

Andrea pushed through the door at Prestige Realty only to find Heather, the freckle-faced redhead, manning the phones. Expertly, the receptionist cradled the handset between her jaw and shoulder. "Okay, Sally," she said while catching Andrea's eye. Andrea smiled and made as if to zoom past her, but Heather shook her head. Andrea stopped before the receptionist's desk, and Heather tore a message sheet off the steno pad and handed it to her.

Andrea glanced at the note. It read *Nice work at the Ocean Grill last night.* Then she turned a puzzled face to Heather. "What?" she mouthed silently.

"I'll take care of it," Heather said into the receiver, at the same time giving Andrea a conspiratorial wink and a grin. "Now relax, boss, and enjoy your weekend."

Andrea nodded and gave the receptionist a thumbs up before hiking back to her cubicle to collect her briefcase. She'd nearly made it when Margo popped out of her office, barring her way.

Uh-oh. Here we go.

Andrea forced a smile. "Hello, Margo," she said, her stomach souring.

"Hi." Margo's voice was flat, her mouth set in that typically grim fashion she affected. "Got a minute?"

"Uh…" Andrea glanced at her watch. It was nine twenty. "Five max."

"Good." Margo ducked back into her office, rounded her desk, and seated herself in the leather executive chair. She indicated that Andrea should sit as well, and the last vestiges of Andrea's good humor evaporated. She perched on a guest chair, somehow managing to maintain a pleasant expression at the same time tilting her head to one side in a silent question.

"It's come to my attention that you may have more than a professional interest in one of our clients."

Andrea's first reaction was to deny, deny, and vehemently deny. But then she realized that would be playing into Margo's hand. Despite the fact that her blood pressure was spiking, she mustered all her resolve and projected an unruffled exterior.

"Really?" she said. "I can't imagine to whom you are referring."

Margo was not fooled, and she was out for blood. "You know exactly who I'm talking about. We, at Prestige, have an image to maintain…"

Yeah, you humorless wretch. How about pulling yourself up by your bootstraps and working on that one?

"Margo, you're imagining things," she said through clenched teeth. "I am the quintessential professional, and you know it." She rose from her chair. "Now, if you'll excuse me, I have a client. I'm sure you wouldn't want me to keep him waiting."

Andrea strode out of Margo's office without a backward glance, her heels making a satisfying click, click, clicking sound that somehow managed to convey her barely concealed irritation. Too late, she realized she had left her briefcase behind.

To hell with it.

~

Instead of taking the more direct, A1A route, Andrea turned onto Ocean Drive and headed south. Once past the posh commercial district, the road narrowed. As she wended down picturesque, tree-lined lanes, Andrea hoped that Daniel would fall under the enchantment of Old Riomar. "I'm sure you've noticed that some of the streets are unpaved."

Daniel responded with a noncommittal, "Um."

"Don't get me wrong. I like a clean car as much as the next guy. But that's what the residents seem to prefer. Time seems to pass at a slower pace here. I guess there's something to be said for it."

Daniel leaned forward, taking in the gently winding road with its canopy of live oaks wreathed in Spanish moss.

"There's the old St. Edward's Lower School campus," Andrea pointed to the right. "I went to school there as a kid."

"Really? I thought you lived in Miami."

"No. I settled there after college. I had a boyfriend, and his family owned a real estate company. So—"

"You sold real estate," Daniel interjected.

"Yes. Got my license when I was twenty-three, and the rest is history." Andrea angled her head to the left. "There's the newly renovated Riomar Golf and Country Club."

"Nice," Daniel commented.

"Yes. This is a very desirable area, especially for young, upwardly mobile families. It's a quiet neighborhood. There's a sense of community. And you'd be surprised how many people prefer not to live behind walled enclaves."

"Not really."

Andrea turned onto Greenway and headed toward the ocean.

"How did you end up back here?" Daniel asked.

"My love affair with real estate stuck—the man... not so much.

Although he did give me Madison. It just seemed natural to come back to Vero. How was I to know he'd follow me here?"

"Seems like an awfully small town for a girl like you."

"I don't know whether to be flattered or insulted."

"The former was my intention."

"Don't sell Vero short, Daniel. For a small town, Vero Beach is chock full of big city amenities. We have a first-rate professional theater that's been reviewed in the Wall Street Journal, a great art museum that's been featured in the New York Times, a world-class Opera Society, and our own resident opera divas. The list goes on and on."

"I gather you like it."

Andrea glanced at her passenger, her eyes lingering on his sculpted jaw with its barely perceptible dimple. "That's an understatement," Andrea said, thinking the conversation was slipping away from her. She needed to rein it in, concentrate on selling the property.

"Notice how the golf course abuts this parcel," she said, navigating a sharp curve in the road. "What you see now is the Sheridan Estate."

"Impressive." Daniel peered ahead, taking in the lushly planted acreage that rolled toward the glistening blue Atlantic.

Andrea removed a small remote from the ashtray and pointed it at an imposing, black, wrought iron gate flanked by two columns upon which a pair of lion statues perched, guarding the entry. The gate slowly swung open to reveal a paver driveway leading to a sprawling Spanish-style villa with pale yellow stucco walls and a coral-colored, barrel tile roof.

There was a timeless elegance about the residence; it seemed perfectly at home in its surroundings. Two immense oak trees, dripping Spanish moss, shaded the front portico and a tangle of bougainvillea framed the six-bay, side garage with thousands of brilliant magenta blossoms.

Andrea pulled up in the circular drive and shifted to park. "Let's take a look." She hopped out of the car, and Daniel followed suit.

Overhead, a mockingbird was practicing his repertoire, showing off his trills. Andrea rang the bell and waited. "I'm pretty sure there's no one home, but it never hurts to announce. Just in case." When a minute passed, and no one answered, Andrea drew open one of a pair of massive arch-topped, mahogany doors only to be greeted by a refreshing whoosh of cool air.

The large foyer featured a darkly stained, wood coffered ceiling, which presented a textural contrast to the stark white walls and gleaming Mexican tile floors. A pierced, metal sphere pendant was suspended over an antique pedestal center table, and an ancient church pew flanked one wall. The austerity of the room was offset by a boldly patterned kilim rug and a scattering of embroidered pillows embellished with tiny bits of sparkly mirror.

There was a pleasing, minimalist quality to the room, and Daniel nodded his head in approval. "Very nice."

Andrea scurried on ahead into the great room. "The house was built back in the fifties, and it was last renovated about thirty years ago," she said. "It'll need some work to bring it into the twenty-first century. The wood beamed ceilings are sixteen feet high, and as you can see, the transoms over the French doors let in lots of natural light."

"The furniture is awesome."

"Antique, most of it. But the white linen upholstery keeps it from feeling heavy, don't you think? I'm quite sure the furnishings will not be included, mind you." She indicated a side room. "Through here is the kitchen and the not so good news." Andrea led the way into a room, which—after the grandeur of the great room, with its lofty ceiling—appeared drab and cramped.

"The cabinets were replaced in the eighties, but they're hopelessly outdated, and you'd want all new appliances. Unfortunately, the kitchen and baths need total makeovers. I don't know if your client's up for that kind of a project…"

Daniel narrowed his eyes, countenancing the bones of the room. "He could be," he said.

"Back here is the pantry and the original maid's quarters." Andrea disappeared around a corner. "If you did away with these rooms, knocked out the partition walls, you could expand and reconfigure the kitchen. And this closet could be transformed into a combination pantry and wine cellar."

"Seems like you've got it all thought out."

"Oh, I do," Andrea agreed. "I do, indeed."

They toured the rest of the main house, Andrea pointing out the good features and those areas needing improvement. Then she led Daniel out the back door.

"Olympic-sized swimming pool." She extended an arm toward the pool. "It just needs to be resurfaced and a new tile deck installed."

"Perhaps a spa?"

"Yes. Either that or a fountain would be nice." Andrea turned and indicated the pool house. "There's the guest cottage." She set off toward the cabana, but then hesitated before turning back to Daniel.

"The current owner is… How shall I say this?" She struggled for the right words. "In reduced circumstances. Suffice it to say, it, too, needs to be completely redone. Would you like to see it?"

"That's not necessary."

"As I told you from the get-go, the place needs a little TLC."

Daniel's eyes flicked over the main house and then fastened on the expanse of private beach that stretched before him, the long dock jutting out over the Atlantic.

"How much property are we talking about here?"

"Nearly three acres. Like I said, the original structure was built in the early fifties—a family compound. But the children have dispersed, and the current owner is simply unable to keep up with all the expenses, to say nothing of the taxes. Still…"

"I understand completely. This…" Daniel gazed about the property. "This would be difficult to relinquish. I wouldn't if it were mine."

Andrea's heart lurched, and she had all she could do to keep from dissuading him from purchasing her family's property. Instead, she said, "One must face facts. Do what one has to do. Isn't that so?"

Daniel clenched his right hand into a fist and put it to his lips as if to prevent his emotions from spilling over. But then it appeared too much for him to contain. A grin split his face, and he flung his arms wide. "I love it! And I'm sure my client will, too!"

Daniel's elation was contagious, and Andrea couldn't help but be caught up in the moment. Still a small part of her cringed. She needed to make this sale, yet she was dismayed at the prospect of losing her homestead. The transaction would entail forfeiting a part of her heritage. Then Papa John was in her head, all bossy and unemotional.

"Sell it, baby girl," he urged. *"Get you and your ma out from under this."* And Andrea knew she was on the right track.

"It's a very special property, one which could be split up in any number of ways. Naturally, we—that is to say, the owner—would prefer you keep it as a whole. But you could certainly divide it into separate building parcels if you chose to do so." Andrea began the process of disengaging. She was going to do this thing, and she would not get sentimental about it. Still, she felt a heaviness building in the back of her throat. She'd failed; she hadn't managed to preserve the family estate, and now she must act the part of Daniel's agent, to rise to the occasion, and not let her personal life get in the way.

"What is the asking price?"

"Three-point-five million, a cool half mil below its appraised value, back in 2007 before the market tanked."

"But I'll have to put a million or so into it to bring it up to speed," Daniel wheedled, obviously testing the waters.

"Probably," Andrea said, conceding the point. "But it's priced very well. This kind of oceanfront acreage—close to the town center—is rare. Honestly, I can think of nothing else like it in Vero Beach."

"I'll have to consider."

"Certainly," Andrea said. "Shall we walk down to the pier? I need to bring you up to speed about the owner."

They sat with their legs dangling over the side of the dock, gazing out over the glistening ocean. The sun was warm on their backs, but it was still early, and the heat was not yet oppressive.

"Well, this complicates things." Daniel looked hard at Andrea.

"It shouldn't. I would have been upfront with you from the start, but I figured there was no need to get into it until I found out if you had an interest."

"I can't snatch your home away from you. Like some evil Simon Legree."

"Pfft! It's not like that at all. Mother *needs* to sell. The place is too big for her and much too expensive for her to keep up. As for *my* home," Andrea paused for effect before continuing, "I have a very nice little bungalow of my own on the river in Castaway Cove. Of course, I'll be sad to turn over the keys to this place. But, hey, it needs new blood, children scampering down the path to the beach, parties with music, and dancing into the night. Most of all, it needs a conservator who appreciates it—someone seeing to all the maintenance and doing whatever is necessary to preserve the grand old lady as she so rightly deserves."

Andrea turned to Daniel. "Shall I write up the contract?"

CHAPTER FOUR

HOUSE OF CARDS

"Floyd, what's up with my credit cards?" Marcie's strident voice accosted the beleaguered lawyer. He lowered his newspaper to eye his wife. "I was at the Twig, yesterday, buying swimsuits for our cruise, and my American Express was declined. I was so humiliated. I had to pay cash, and now I'm broke."

"I'm sorry, honey."

"Sorry? I have an image to keep up. And so do you. We can't have that kind of thing happening around Vero. No one will trust you."

"Don't worry, babe." Floyd dug through his wallet and withdrew a wad of bills. "Here, take this and go buy what you need. I'll handle the American Express."

Marcie snatched up the greenbacks, seemingly mollified. "Thanks, sweetie." She kissed the air and then spooned a dollop of yogurt into her craw. "Do you want me to pack for you? I can't believe we're leaving the day after tomorrow. You're still good to go, right?"

"Absolutely." Floyd didn't finish his fruit. His stomach was giving him fits.

Probably ulcers. What else is new?

He drained his coffee mug and pushed away from the breakfast table. "Gotta go," he said. "I have an early appointment with Sally Bray."

"Okay, honey." Marcie didn't look up from her crossword puzzle.

"Tonight's Riverside Theatre, and *The Producers*. Remember? We're meeting the Sweeney's at Quail Valley for a pre-show dinner at six."

Floyd's stomach flip-flopped. After what would surely be a trying day of deception, a night of more subterfuge loomed before him. He wanted nothing more than to retreat to his den, slug back a couple of bourbons, and lose himself in some mindless sitcom. But he said, "Great," infusing his voice with an enthusiasm he did not feel. What he felt like was a rat on a treadmill, running and running and going nowhere. But he had no choice, had to keep going through the motions in hopes that no one would catch on until it was too late.

~

It was an old photograph taken with a Kodak Instamatic, and the blacks and whites had morphed into strange shades of pink and gray. Still, the image captivated her. They were all together in another, happier, life—John, so robust and good-looking, the kids, John Junior, Toby, Andrea, and a much younger version of herself—smiling hugely at the camera.

Margaret stared at the photograph and tried to gain a purchase into the psyche of the woman she'd been back then when life had been so full of promise. She sighed, replaced the photo on the bookshelf, and then gazed about the great room, thinking about all the good times she and her family had shared in this space.

The kids were all grown now, each of them successful in their own rights, involved in their own families. She truly believed that she and John would, one day, be reunited, but that didn't make the loneliness easier to bear now. Margaret squared her shoulders. She was stuck here, for the time being, and she had a great deal to be grateful for.

Margaret's eyes fell upon a recent photograph of Madison. She picked it up and brought it to her face to examine it more closely. She loved all of her grandbabies, but Maddy tugged at her heart like no other. She worried about Andrea. Her daughter put up a good front, but Margaret knew she was struggling under too much stress. She was sorry for adding to her burden, but what else could she do? The bills were pouring in, and she was falling behind on her credit cards. "Oh, John," she said, her voice echoing off the plastered walls. "How could you leave me to deal with all this by myself?"

~

"Dad, can we go now?" Madison tugged at Derrick's sleeve. "It's hot. I'm bored."

The Farmer's Market had dwindled to just a few vendors, and the remaining booths were being broken down.

"Mom will be here soon, honey." Derrick glanced at his cellphone display. It was ten past one. He hefted a bushel basket of squash and was carting it to the open bed of his pickup truck when Andrea's white Mercedes pulled up to the curb.

"Mommy." Madison hastened toward her.

Andrea parked and then hopped out of the car, and Madison crossed the difference between them in seconds. "Where were you?" the teen whined. "I thought you forgot me."

"Aw, Maddy, I couldn't forget you. Did you get tired of working for Dad?"

"It was okay," Madison said sulkily. "I got all sweaty."

"I'm sorry. We'll go home, and you can jump in the pool while I fix lunch. How does that sound?"

"Hey there," Derrick cried. "How did it go?"

"Great," Andrea said, a note of irony in her voice. "I think I just sold the farm."

"Wow. That *is* great!" Derrick exclaimed. "You'll be rolling in it."

"Not really." Andrea glanced at Maddy. "I'm not taking a commission on this one, and Mother's been falling deeper and deeper into debt. She's been living on credit cards, and what my brothers and I can throw her way. I've been telling you for years: There's no more money in the estate."

"How can that be? I thought she was set for life?"

"Derrick, let's not go over this just now, okay? Suffice it to say, when all the bills and back taxes are paid, she'll be left with a tidy sum, which will allow her a comfortable lifestyle."

"Is Nana poor?"

"Oh, Maddy, no," Andrea said. "But she's going to have to move out of Casa Rio and get a smaller place."

"I like Casa. Where will she go?"

"To some other nice place that doesn't require so much upkeep. Not to worry."

"Say, who'd like to celebrate over lunch at the Lemon Tree?" Derrick asked.

"Me," Madison cried.

∽

The sun was pouring through the partially raised veins of the plantation shutters, flooding the great room of Casa Rio with light. This Sunday morning, three generations of Sheridan's—Margaret, Andrea, and Madison—were gathered around the game table.

Margaret grinned sheepishly at her daughter and granddaughter. "The sad fact of the matter is that I've got to get rid of a lot of—" she extended her arms. "Stuff."

"I can help, Mom," Andrea offered.

"Me too, Nana," Madison chimed in.

"Thank you, my darlings. But the problem is sorting through all this. I'm ashamed to admit it, but I've been a terrible packrat. Honestly, I'd just as soon pitch the lot of it, but I'm sure there are things you and the boys or the grandkids will want."

"True," Andrea agreed, thinking the task that lay before them was a monumental one. "We're going to have to pick through every drawer and cupboard, huh?"

"I'm afraid so."

"Gosh, this could take forever."

Margaret pursed her lips and nodded her head. "That's why I'm putting it out there. We need a game plan. Otherwise, it's going to be overwhelming." The three women were momentarily silent, each lost in thought.

Madison was the first to break the silence. "We should have a party."

Margaret and Andrea cut their eyes to the teen. "Maddy, what are you saying?" Andrea asked.

"A party," the girl reiterated.

"A party…" Margaret's face slowly lit up.

"I must be dense because I don't have a clue what you two are talking about," Andrea complained.

"A party, Mom." Madison bounded out of her chair. "You know… like a going-away party."

"Right," Margaret said, warming to the idea. "Only this one will be a working party. Madison, you're a genius!"

"Yeah. Everybody has to work." The girl crossed to a console and opened a drawer. "Like, clean this out," she said, indicating the drawer's contents.

"I get it," Andrea said, her mind working in overdrive. They could do this. Not only would it work, but it might bring some closure as well—maybe even prove fun in the bargain.

"We'd have to get oodles of cardboard boxes and plastic bins," she said as a plan began to formulate in her mind.

"To say nothing of garbage bags," Margaret added.

"And food." Madison grinned. "Delicious food."

"I'll put Derrick on it," Andrea said. "He loves to cook, and he could do something organic. It's a super-duper idea, Maddy."

Suddenly, Alicia Key's sultry voice, singing *No One*, erupted from her cellphone. She dug for the phone, pulled it from her bag, and flipped open the clamshell.

"It's Daniel," she mouthed silently to her mother. "Hi, Daniel."

"I was wondering if you had plans for this evening?"

"Not really. I was going to hang with my crib." She bobbed her head while affecting a rapper idiom and gazed at Madison with wide eyes.

Madison snickered at her mother's poor attempt at humor.

Margaret watched the exchange between them. She so wanted Maddy to be a typical teenager, whatever that might be in today's world.

"By that you mean?"

"Stick with my girl," Andrea explained.

"Why don't you both join me? Dining alone at the bar is most unsatisfactory, and I swore I wouldn't do it ever again. If you decline, I'll have no alternative other than to order room service. Now tell me, do you want that on your conscience?"

"Honestly? Room service sounds divine to me," Andrea said. "I think you must be spoiled."

"Come on down, Ms. Biz, and we'll order in."

Andrea strolled to the French door and lowered her voice. "You know I can't come to your room, sir. That would be highly improper." She turned and winked at her mother, and Margaret grinned.

"Nothing of the sort," Daniel protested. "I bet the kid would love it."

"Hmm… Let me see." Andrea returned to the table. "Madison," she said, speaking loudly enough so that her client could hear. "How would you like to join Daniel and me for dinner tonight?"

Margaret nodded her head vigorously in Madison's direction. "Sure," Madison said.

"Okay then. Would you like to dine in or eat outside at the Vero Beach Hotel and Club?"

Madison clapped her hands. "Eat out at the Club!"

"There you have it," Andrea said. "Could we do that, Daniel?"

"Sure thing. I'll meet you poolside at six."

~

It had been a trying day, and Floyd sat stiffly in the dining chair, willing the night to be over.

"Here they come," Marcie hissed, nervously finger-combing her highlights. "Whatever you do, don't talk business." Floyd took a generous swig of Maker's Mark and steeled himself for the encounter.

"There you are!" Clarisse Sweeney's horsey face wore a phony grin that exposed a mouthful of bluntly capped teeth. She turned to her husband and simpered, "Here they are, honey. Come and sit down."

Phil Sweeney had a good twenty years on Clarisse, and she was no babe in the woods. Like so many successful men with an excellent head for business, Phil was clueless when it came to women. As for Clarisse, she'd been marrying up her entire adult life. But her third husband was the prize, and everyone but him knew it. Like Clarisse, Sweeney had no children—no heirs. The gold-digger was sitting pretty, just waiting for the old coot to kick.

Sweeney settled in slowly, his spine's curvature and arthritic joints precluding any vigorous movement, but Clarisse seemed not to notice. Instead, she beamed at Floyd and Marcie, pretending to be having the time of her life. It was clear that Marcie bought it—hook, line, and sinker—always up for climbing the social ladder. But Floyd didn't give a shit. He saw right through the pretense.

"Well, isn't this fun?" Clarisse said.

"Yes," Marcie agreed. "I'm so looking forward to the show. We saw it on Broadway with Matthew Broderick and Nathan Lane—"

"We did, too," Clarisse interrupted. "Ab fab."

"It's nice to support our local theater," Marcie chimed in, thinking of all the money Floyd had invested in advertising, getting his company name on the marquee for having underwritten productions. "Did you know that Riverside is the largest regional theater in the South?"

"No," Clarisse said. "But the shows are first-rate, what with the New York casts. We're certainly fortunate to have so much culture in itty old Vero Beach. Which is why I settled here in the first place."

Right, thought Floyd, bitterly. He'd heard the mean-spirited gossip about Clarisse, that she'd been born and raised in some hick town in the Appalachians. No wonder she thought Vero the cultural capital of the South. But all he said was, "Yes, this place has changed a great deal over the years. When I first opened up my practice, way back in the eighties, they rolled up the sidewalks at six o'clock. Now they wait until at least ten."

A waitress approached the table. "Hello, Mr. and Mrs. Sweeney," she said. "Shall I get you the usual?"

Clarisse eyeballed her husband, and Phil gave an almost imperceptible nod of his head. "Yes," she said. "I'll have a split of champagne, and Phil will have his Chivas—"

"On ice in a tall glass," the waitress said, finishing her sentence. "Coming right up," she said, before sailing toward the bar.

Marcie kicked Floyd under the table, nodding toward Phil.

Taking the none-too-subtle hint, he said, "So, Phil, hitting any balls lately?"

"Oh, yeah," Phil said. "I played eighteen holes yesterday. Unfortunately, my drive is crap."

"It's the weather," Floyd said. "Too damn hot."

"Maybe. But my putting's even worse. It's hell getting old."

"Sweetheart, you're not old," Clarisse protested. "Look around you." She waved an arm about the room, indicating the snowdrift of graying heads occupying the surrounding tables. "You're a spring chicken in God's waiting room." Clarisse laughed too loudly at her mixed metaphor. Marcie tittered as well, but Floyd and Phil merely looked uncomfortable.

The waitress appeared with sparkling wine and a whiskey, and Floyd held up his nearly empty glass while nodding toward Marcie's, indicating they desired refills. He reckoned it was going to be a long night, and liquid fortitude was required to get him through it.

~

Not two miles away, Daniel was laying claim to three lounge chairs set before a blazing fire pit. The fire was unnecessary, but it provided a cheery backdrop. He eased his tall frame into a patio chair and draped his arms around the backs of those on either side of him. It was a mild evening; The heat had seeped out of the day. A gentle ocean breeze kept the no-see-ums at bay, and Daniel gazed toward the steely Atlantic, breathing in the intoxicating fragrance of salt and sea. Vero, he admitted to himself, had cast a spell over him. He was hooked. A skeptic, he'd come here on the advice of his financial advisor and good friend, Nathan McCourt. Nathan was the one person in the world Daniel trusted completely. They'd been college roommates and best friends ever since, and McCourt had never taken advantage or steered him wrong.

"There are up-scale communities all over the country—Chagrin Falls, Montauk, LA, Jolla, Vail, New Canaan—but there's something special about Vero," Nate had said. "Besides, real estate is a bargain here just now. You can pick up a property for a third of its former valuation. Four, five years down the road, these prices are going to skyrocket.

Daniel figured Nate was right about Vero, just as he'd been about so many things. But more than that, he'd been bowled over by the Casa Rio property. The main house looked like a hacienda out of a storybook. With its lush plantings leading down to the incredible stretch of pristine beach, it reminded him of the Breakers in Palm Beach. He'd stayed there during a business trip years ago and been thoroughly impressed by the grand old resort. There was a sense of understated refinement about the Mizner-designed architectural gem; the place exuded a solid sort of permanence, one that said some things —some *good* things—don't change. No, that's not right, he thought, after a moment of reflection. Better put: No matter how the world changes, *some* things are worth preserving. He was about to purchase one of those exceptional properties, and he found the prospect exhilarating.

The hostess, a striking blonde, approached, interrupting Daniel's reverie. And following her were Andrea and a young, auburn-haired beauty, presumably Madison. "Here he is," the woman said, waving an arm in Daniel's direction. "Mr. Armstrong, your girls are here."

Daniel rose from his chair, a welcoming smile on his face. He turned toward Madison, giving the teen his full attention. "Hello, Miss Madison." He extended a hand, taking the teen's in his. "This will be such fun, the three of us dining alfresco. Please, sit."

Daniel indicated that the women should be seated on either side of him, and once they'd situated themselves, he regained his seat.

"What is your pleasure, ma'am?" the hostess asked.

Andrea glanced at Daniel, a question on her face, but he simply shook his head. "I'll have a glass of the house white," she said.

"No, no, no," Daniel remonstrated. He eyed the hostess. "You wouldn't have a 1928 Krug, would you?"

"Unfortunately, no, sir."

"Well then, bring a bottle of Dom Pérignon."

"Daniel!" Andrea protested.

"Shush," Daniel commanded. "This is a celebration."

"It is?" the teen asked, looking confused.

"Yes, Madison," Daniel exclaimed. "Look at that ocean. Heck, look at you! Life's for celebrating, don't you think?"

Madison knit her brows and peered at her mother.

"Sweetie," Andrea said. "He means that on such a lovely evening, we should celebrate the fact that we're alive, and—"

"And enjoying it," Daniel interrupted exuberantly. "What would you like, Maddy, a Shirley Temple?"

Again, Madison searched Andrea's face, but her mother only shrugged. "Could I have a virgin strawberry daiquiri?"

"If that's what you'd like," Daniel said expansively.

"And for you, sir?"

"Bring me a glass, and I'll have some of the bubbly."

"My pleasure." The young woman graced them with an orthodontist's dream smile before scurrying toward the kitchen.

"Ahh…" Daniel gazed out over the ocean. "Isn't this the life?

"Yes, indeed," Andrea said. "This is a real treat for us. Isn't it, Maddy?"

"Oh, yeah."

"I imagine the rooms are sumptuous?" Andrea turned back to Daniel.

"Very comfortable," he said. "But traveling alone... It leaves something to be desired." Daniel suddenly became aware of the fact that Madison was fidgeting in her chair. He pivoted to her, saying, "Madison, what do you say we take a quick run down the beach?

"No," Andrea protested. But it was too late. Maddy had already risen to her feet, obviously eager for the challenge.

"Sure." She craned her neck to assess the dune crossover.

"Which way?" Daniel asked, sloughing off his loafers and rolling up his pant legs.

"Uh, I don't know."

"South?" Daniel pointed in the direction of the Ocean Grill.

"You're on." Madison darted past him and scrambled toward the deck stairs.

"Oh, ho!" Daniel cried.

He cut his eyes to Andrea, and she shook her head and laughed merrily. "What madness!"

"Watch out, wench," Daniel hollered as he closed in on Madison, one stride of his equal to two of hers.

As they tore down the beach, the hostess appeared with stemmed glasses and drinks—a towering pink confection for Madison and a bottle of Dom Pérignon. The young woman uncorked the bottle with a loud pop, poured a small amount into a crystal flute, and offered it to Andrea. "Will you do the honors?"

Andrea swirled the wine in her glass before breathing in the fruity bouquet and taking a sip. "Umm, wonderful."

The blonde filled the glass and then cut her gaze to the shoreline where Madison was charging after Daniel. "They're so cute together. You must be so proud."

Andrea realized the waitress assumed the two were father and daughter. "I know," she said, thinking there did seem to be chemistry between them. How she wished that were true.

∿

Garrett climbed the stairs to his walk-up apartment and unlatched the door. The place was a mess, dirty clothes and pizza boxes strewn about. Maybe he should hire a service. He could well afford one, bring some order to this chaos. But he was too distracted to think about that now. He had other, more important matters on his mind.

Garrett collapsed in his desk chair and burrowed in his back pocket for his cellphone. He searched through his photos, a smile tugging at the corners of his mouth when he came across the latest pic, an image of that cute girl he'd seen at the Farmer's Market. She was so hot! He had to devise a plan and think of some way to introduce himself that didn't come off as dorky. No sooner had the idea occurred to him than Garrett quashed it. What was he thinking? He was a complete and total nerd, had nothing to offer a babe like that.

Garrett tossed the phone onto his desk and powered up his PC. He was ready to escape into Monster Hunter World, to battle Alien's Xenomorph Queen. That was about all the excitement this geek could handle.

CHAPTER FIVE

KARA'S ISLAND DREAM

Kara Armstrong drummed her lacquered fingernails on the Louis XVI desktop while staring pensively out her bedroom window. She surveyed the manicured yard of the palatial Singer Island estate with its splashing marble fountain and white, latticed gazebo beyond. It was beautiful, she mused, yet utterly unsatisfying. Everything was perfect here, so why wasn't she happy?

Kara knew the answer to that question: She was homesick for the diversity Philadelphia afforded, luncheons, concerts, social gatherings. She missed her BFFs, Laney and Becca—their old stomping grounds. And the fact that she couldn't return burned her. Oh, she flew back once or twice a year for a visit to catch up with her mom and her stepdad, hang with the girls. But Philly was Daniel's town. The Armstrong family was, arguably, the most influential of the Philadelphia dynasties.

Rich as Croesus, Daniel's father, Ralph, had his fingers in everything from manufacturing to telecommunications to broadcast radio and television, and his influence didn't stop with media and commerce. He and his wife were fervent philanthropists. They'd endowed the art museum, funded a trust that doled out college scholarships, and made sizable donations to the Homeless Center and the Children's Theatre. Heck, the new wing of the Children's Hospital was named after Ralph Armstrong!

It was one thing to be escorted by Daniel Armstrong to the

Charity Ball or whatever the occasion might be. Wherever they might find themselves, it was sure to be at the center of the Philadelphia society universe. It was quite another to arrive on some lesser mortal's arm—to be cast sidelong glances and know that people were gossiping about Kara, his poor, discarded wife. The thought of it made her blood boil.

To hell with Philly, Kara thought. Before Daniel completely cut her off from the corporate jet or wrested Sweet Dreamer away from her, she might as well organize a trip to Barbados. Suddenly excited over the prospect, Kara reached for her cellphone. She'd call Laney and Becca, see if, in a week or so, they could break away for five or six days. A little get-away was the ideal remedy for her doldrums. Some island time—lazy afternoons spent poolside, open-air dining at the best restaurants in the Caribbean, and dissolute, boozy nights, bar hopping in Holetown. That was the ticket.

When Andrea walked into the Prestige office on Monday morning, the place was in an uproar. Heather sat hunched before the reception desk, the phone pressed to her ear while Sally hovered over her, a look of pained incredulity on her face. Stewart stood next to her, looking stunned. Craig and Jeremy were off in a corner, speaking in agitated whispers. Margo was wringing her hands, more grim-faced than usual.

"Hi, guys…" Taking stock of the situation, Andrea's greeting stuck in her throat. "What gives?" she croaked, cutting her eyes to Margo.

Margo opened her mouth and then clamped it shut as though unwilling to give voice to some dreadful thing and empower it. Sensing something terribly amiss, Andrea suddenly felt weak-kneed, and a feeling of dread washed over her.

"What do you mean they're gone, Carla?" Heather cried. "Where the hell did they go?"

Sally grabbed the phone from the receptionist. "Carla," she barked, "it's me, Sally Bray. Put Floyd on."

Andrea pushed between Craig and Jeremy. "Will somebody please tell me what the heck is going on here?"

"I don't believe it," Sally's voice rose shrilly. "Either you put him on, or I'll be there in five minutes, facing him down in person."

Craig and Jeremy ignored Andrea's question. "I'll drive," Jeremy barked, turning on his heel. The two men cut across the office in tandem and rushed out the door into the parking lot. Moments later, a squeal of tires was heard as Jeremy's black Audi peeled out onto Beachland Boulevard.

"I want my escrows delivered to me in my office no later than two o'clock this afternoon, or there will be hell to pay. Do I make myself clear?" Sally slammed the phone down onto its cradle and sank into a guest chair. Her face took on an ashen hue as she gnawed on her lower lip.

"Can I get you a glass of water?" Margo asked.

"How about a vodka on ice?" Sally said, straightening her spine.

Sally was a well-seasoned veteran; she'd been in real estate for over twenty-five years. Even in the early days of the recession, she'd never lost her cool. Andrea could only guess at what had caused her boss to react in such a fashion, and her mind reeled at the possibilities.

"Take off a few days, and this is what I return to," Sally murmured as her fingers wrapped around the crystal tumbler Margo placed in her hand. She took a long draught and then set the glass on her desk. Gazing about at her handpicked team, she read the apprehension in their faces. "Here's the scoop. Carla says the escrow accounts are gone."

Andrea blanched.

"Gone?" Stewart roared. "Gone where?"

"Good question," Sally said. "I can think of only two possibilities: Either Floyd stole the money. Or someone else did."

"I go with the Floyd theory," Steward said.

"Ditto," Heather agreed.

"The only thing that matters is the fact that they are empty and that we... *I* must get my hands on some cash, pronto." Sally bounded from her chair. "Heather, get Jason Landau on the phone. Tell him it's an emergency, that I need to see him immediately."

"Right-o," Heather picked up the phone and began dialing while Sally hastened to her office to collect her handbag and briefcase. Clutching the glass of vodka, Margo trailed, forlornly, after her.

Andrea crossed to Stewart, who had his head in his hands. "How much are we talking about?"

Stewart kneaded his temples. "I'm not sure," he admitted. "A lot.

Sally and Margo are holding… What? Two-, maybe three-mil? As for me… one-point-five. About the same for Craig. Diaz doesn't have anything moving just now, so he's out of it. Still, that's well over five million. We're not talking chump change."

Just then Craig and Jeremy, their faces grim, burst through the front door.

"What did you find out?" Stewart asked.

"Zilch, nada, zip," Jeremy said.

"That cowardly snake," Craig spat. "The place is locked up tight, a closed sign in the window, but he was in there, alright."

"Oh, yeah!" Jeremy agreed. "His shiny new Beemer was parked in the back lot. He was afraid to come out for fear we'd take him down."

"Just let me get my hands on that creep," Stewart muttered.

Heather replaced the handset on the cradle. "What do we do now?" she asked. Then her face took on a look of horror. "Oh, my God. What'll we tell the clients?"

"Nothing!" Sally swept into the reception area, followed by her ever-present shadow, Margo. "We keep our mouths shut. As far as I'm concerned, the escrows are safe and sound in Floyd's keeping, just like they've always been. If the money doesn't show up by two this afternoon, we move to Plan B."

"Plan B being?" Craig asked.

"I'll think of something." Sally brushed past her associates and made for the front door. Before she was through it, she turned and eyed each of them separately. "For now, everybody pray," she said. "That's an order."

~

"Carla, I need a one-way ticket to Buenos Aires." Floyd pushed away from his desk. "Business class out of Miami."

"Do you think that's wise, boss?" Carla asked, popping a Tums with a water chaser down her throat.

Floyd opened the wall safe. "I believe it's my only choice, Carla." He stuffed bundles of bills into his briefcase. "And I'll need your car."

"What? My car?" Carla nearly stumbled over her own feet. "What do you want with a nine-year-old Honda when you've got that fifty-thousand-dollar powerhouse in the parking lot?"

"Think, Carla," Floyd said, blanketing her desk with stacks of hundred-dollar bills. "Deposit this over time in different banks, and always in amounts of less than five thousand to avoid scrutiny. And believe me, they will be watching you. Or stash it in a safe place, somewhere no one would think to look."

"I… I couldn't, Floyd," Carla protested, eying the silver lining that had magically appeared in this darkest of nightmares.

"Don't give me that crap, Carla. Yes, you can," Floyd contradicted. "You deserve it."

Snapping his bulging briefcase shut, the attorney crossed to Carla. He looked her in the eye, saying, "Listen to me. The shit's gonna hit the fan, sweetheart, and you're gonna be in the thick of it. You can tell them I stole your car. That'll help put them off your trail."

Carla couldn't muffle a sob as Floyd's words resonated. For one insane moment, she thought of fleeing with him, but that was impossible. Who would look after her mother, take care of the dog?

"You've been a wonderful help to me all these years, Carla. I couldn't have asked for a more loyal friend and assistant."

Tears streamed down Carla's face, and she knuckled them away.

"Do what I say, you hea'?"

The distraught woman gave an almost imperceptible nod of her head. Then she dug her car keys from her purse, rose from her desk, and planted a tiny kiss on Floyd's bloodless lips.

"Thank you, Floyd." Carla pressed her keys into his hand. "I'll take care of things on this end. You do what you have to do."

"Bye, Carla." Floyd tossed his car keys on Diane's desk, turned, and scuttled toward the back hallway.

"Wait!" Carla shouted, stopping Floyd in his tracks. "What about Marcie and the kids?"

"No worries." Floyd waved a hand in the air. "Marcie has her own account. The house and her car are in her name. She'll be fine. As for the kids… They've got a whole heck of a lot more than either you or I did when we were their age."

Floyd rounded the corner and disappeared. "They've got their youth," he cried. "What would you give for that, Carla?"

There was the sound of a door being closed with a resounding bang, and then the office was silent.

Wracked by guilt, Carla stared at the stacks of bills on her desk, but it wasn't long before her survival instincts surfaced, and she rallied. By this time tomorrow, the law office would be knee-deep in auditors. She knew she couldn't drive the BMW for long before being apprehended. It was time to bolt and run, she thought while stuffing stacks of bills into her pocketbook. And she'd ride out in style behind the wheel of that big luxury sedan parked outside. But the sun wouldn't set before she'd traded it in for something untraceable. Immediately, thoughts of her nephew, Dillon, flooded her cranium. Maybe, for once in his miserable life, the punk could put his larcenous talents to good use, help his Auntie Carla out of this jam.

She darted about the office, switching off lights and turning up the A/C, never once thinking how foolish it was to conserve energy given her present circumstances. Then, Carla gripped her cellphone with sweaty fingers while searching her contacts for her nephew's number.

Her mind raced as she pulled out onto Ocean Drive. The kid would do whatever she told him to. But what would that be? She had to admit it: she was a lousy criminal.

"Auntie, what's up?" Her nephew's snarky voice came to her from across the miles.

"Hey, Dillon," Carla said, affecting a nonchalance she did not feel. "How're you doing?"

It was half-past three when Sally took a seat at the small conference table in a meeting room on the second floor of the bank. Across from her were Harry Jacoby, a pale, middle-aged fellow with slightly stooped shoulders, and Jason Landau, the slickly handsome new president of The Beach Bank of Florida.

"What can we do for you, Sally?" Harry asked as he and Harry resumed their seats. "Why the urgency?"

Sally took a deep breath before dropping her bombshell. "Gentlemen," she said, "we have a problem."

"We?" Jason furrowed his brow.

Sally met his eyes and then shifted her gaze to Harry. "All of us," she said.

"What exactly is the problem?" Harry asked.

"As you know," Sally said, "Floyd Heller has managed our escrows and those of many other high-end realty firms, for what? The last fifteen years now?"

Landau and Jacoby both nodded.

"Well," Sally said, "our accounts are empty."

"Excuse me?" Jason's smile vanished.

"What do you mean empty?" Harry asked, looking flummoxed.

"Exactly what I say," Andrea answered. "The monies are gone. And Floyd's gone with them."

"Good God," Harry exclaimed, rising to his feet. "How can that be?"

Jason, the new man on the block, remained seated. He scrubbed a palm over his chin, then turned to face the realtor. "Sally," he said, "are you certain the escrows are gone, that the accounts have been emptied?"

"No, Jason," Sally said. "I'm not certain of anything. All I know is that Floyd's paralegal, Carla, said the escrows were no more."

Jacoby pivoted, bent to snatch up a phone from the credenza, and tapped in a number. "Elaine," he said. "Pull up Floyd Heller's escrow accounts and get back to me."

Jason's eyes bored into Harry's. Neither man spoke. Sally fidgeted in her chair. The minutes dragged on until the phone finally rang.

Jason's hand snaked out to grab it. "Yes?" he said.

Both Sally and Harry were laser-focused on Jason's face, searching for any reaction.

"I see," he said, eyes narrowing. He replaced the receiver on its cradle.

"Well? What did she say?" Harry asked.

"There's next to nothing in the escrow accounts. Floyd didn't wipe them out; a few bucks are remaining in each, but for all intents and purposes—"

"Jesus," Harry exclaimed. "I don't believe it!"

Sally squared her shoulders. "So," she looked first to Jason then to Harry, "you see what our problem is."

Jason put a fist to his mouth and considered. Harry looked at Jason. Eventually, the new president drew his hand away from his face and spoke. "Thank you for bringing this to my... to our attention, Sally. How can we help?"

"You're going to have to spot me the cash to cover the escrows, Jason," Sally said. "Duh!"

Harry snorted, and Jason stared off into space, mulling over Sally's extraordinary proposal.

Sally figured the new president was smart enough to realize he had to handle this particular mess with kid gloves. His first obligation was to keep the bank clean and blameless. More importantly, he was duty-bound to aid the bank's clients. She was a big client.

"How much are we talking, Sally?" Jason asked.

"Five point three," Sally said.

"I'll negotiate a very good rate for you."

"No interest," Sally said, her eyes boring into Jason's.

Harry gasped. In all his years, he'd never heard such a demand.

"Why, I don't think…" Jason dithered.

"Absolutely no interest," Sally reiterated. "Or heads will roll. Someone here at the bank should have seen this coming. Escrow accounts being emptied and no one the wiser? You know as well as I do. Don't try playing hardball with me, or I'll make sure this thing comes back to haunt you."

Jason pushed back from the conference table and nodded curtly at Harry, dismissing him. Jacoby scuttled away, but not before bestowing Sally with a toothy grin. Then he scurried out the door with not a backward glance.

Sally rose from her chair, and Jason followed suit. "We'll get through this, Sally," he reassured.

"Yes, we will," Sally agreed.

"But it's a hell of a thing."

"It could hurt a lot of people. First and foremost, me."

"I realize the implications."

"I'm not sure you do," Sally countered. "There's more to it. Something like this could cause a real estate market meltdown in Vero… at a time when property values are at an all-time low, when the stock market and just about everything else is working against us. These are difficult times, and we don't need this extra whammy, Jason. It's up to you to prevent that worst-case scenario from happening."

"I'll take it under advisement," Jacoby said, holding the door open for her.

"And Jason," Sally said, as she crossed in front of him. "I think you're going to be a great asset to the Beach Bank."

"Thank you," Jason said, obviously pleased at the compliment.

"It's too bad you never got a chance to meet John Moore, Sr. Now there was a man."

"I've heard." The bank president escorted Sally down the hall and into the main corridor.

"You can't imagine," Sally said. "He'd a been all over this from the start. Nothing escaped his eye."

"I'm sorry I let you down. It's just that I'm—"

"No! I take it back. It's not your fault, Jason. I really don't believe that. You're going to do a bang-up job. I'm sure of it. It's just that I'm crying fate. Feeling sorry for myself, don't you know? To be truthful, I doubt even John could have seen this perfect storm brewing and forestalled it. Honestly, I'm just grateful you're at the helm, that you can maneuver us through these difficult straits."

Jason paused at the double door exit. "I will do my best, Sally. I promise you that."

Sally darted forward and clasped the bank president's hand. "I know you will," she said, believing that statement would prove true. "In the meantime, I'll put the word out to the other realty firms that do business with Heller and Associates. I'm afraid this might be just the tip of the iceberg."

Jason's face took on a look of horror. "My God," he muttered.

~

Later that evening, Madison balanced at the end of the diving board of Margaret's pool. "Nana, we need to invite a lot of people."

"Why, darling?"

"She's right, Mom. I was against it at first." Andrea lowered herself into a chaise lounge. "Let's face it. You know everyone in this town. If you don't invite all of them, it's at the risk of hurting someone's feelings."

"But, girls," Margaret handed Andrea a glass of iced tea, "we're talking about sifting through my personal things." She took a seat in the chaise next to her daughter. "Who knows what I have stashed away? We can't just let every Tom, Dick, and Harry rummage through my personal belongings."

"Maybe the party's not a good idea," Andrea ventured.

"No. It's a good idea." Madison put the fingertips of her hands together, preparing to spring.

"It's brilliant," Margaret agreed. "But maybe we should do the grunt work before we let every Tom—"

"Dick and Harry," Madison cried, rolling from her heels to her toes.

"Exactly," Margaret agreed.

"Who are we kidding?" Andrea asked. "We might just as well bite the bullet and start sorting through this stuff."

"I like the party," Madison said, taking tiny leaps from the board.

"Me, too," Margaret added.

"Mom! You guys are impossible," Andrea exclaimed. "What'll it be? We need to decide."

"Party, party," Madison chanted. One moment, the teen was hurtling through the air, and the next, she was knifing below the water's surface.

"She's a nymph," Margaret cried, her eyes gleaming.

"That she is," Andrea agreed. "She takes after you, little Miss-Synchronized Swimmer."

"The Water Wonder Girls of Weeki Wachee Springs!" Margaret hooted.

"To say nothing of your stint at the Cape," Andrea said.

"We will not talk about that." Margaret looked chagrined as she cast a sidelong glance toward her granddaughter.

Like a torpedo, Madison sped across the pool. Then she turned and raced back. "Come in," she cried, surfacing for air. "Nana, please!"

"Not now, sweetie," Margaret said. "Nana doesn't have the energy. Another time."

"Watch me," Madison commanded, as she began practicing one of Margaret's old routines. She dove deep and then burst like a rocket out of the water. Arms raised with fingers knit, she treaded water, swaying to-and-fro and affecting a seductive expression.

Andrea raised her eyebrows, shooting her mother a look of dismay. "What have you been teaching her?"

Margaret gazed, transfixed, as Madison performed one of her old routines. "Nothing, honey. Just one of the… water dances."

"Dances?" Andrea cried. "It's like pole dancing in the pool, for heaven's sake. She doesn't know what she's doing."

Margaret felt a twinge of guilt, but she dismissed it. Andrea was too uptight. The teen was a natural. No one else in the family cared a whit about Nana's unique talent. No one—that is—except for Madison. It was gratifying to know Madison inherited her gift. Margaret thought about those halcyon days spent at the Cape—when the astronauts were training, and she was swimming in a tank at a bar on the strip.

Or was that stripping at a bar in a tank?

It was, she decided, all the same. *Let the good times roll.* That had been their motto back then, hers and the other mermaids.

"Way to go, Maddy," Margaret shouted. "Let the good times roll!"

~

Daniel lolled in a slat-backed, teak lounger on his private balcony overlooking the ocean. For once, the shimmering expanse gave him no joy. "What do you mean the jet's unavailable?" Daniel huffed into his phone, scowling. "I've got to fly to the islands the day after tomorrow."

"Sorry, Danny," his secretary said. "Kara booked the plane and paid the retainer. There's no way to stop her that isn't gonna cost you a lot of grief and bucketloads of cash."

"Damn it, Michelle. I'm beginning to feel as though my affairs have run amok."

"I'm afraid they have, Dan," Michelle commiserated. "You need to finalize the terms of the divorce so that you can get on with your life."

Daniel considered his options. "Shit. I guess I'll have to fly commercial."

"It'll be humbling," Michelle chuckled. "Rubbing elbows with the hoi polloi… Just like you did when you were a kid."

"Like I never did as a kid," Daniel corrected.

"Right, Dan. Forgot that. So, it'll be doubly good for you."

"And that is because?"

"I imagine the universe has decided that it's time you see how the other half lives, Boss Man."

"You do? Why's that?"

"It's not for me to say, Danny. That's for you to find out."

"Okay," Daniel said in an aggrieved voice. "Whatever. Book the flight."

~

Floyd hated the Miami International airport. Most people did. "You'd think they'd do something about this dump," he muttered as he followed the overhead signs directing him to the long-term parking garage. "Fix it up like Orlando. Now there's an airport! People flying in from all over the world hop off a plane, take the tram, and step into... Disney World!"

Floyd braked and accepted the token from the dispenser. "Long-term is right," he snickered, imagining how long Carla's car would sit there before someone realized it had been abandoned.

The box-like concourse had all the ambiance of a subway station, but Floyd paid little attention to his surroundings. As soon as he'd checked in and issued his boarding pass, he hiked to the nearest men's room. Sequestering himself in a stall, he rifled through his briefcase and retrieved the black wig he'd purchased on Amazon. It was the same shade as the thinning hair that ringed his partially bald pate. Floyd thought the wig made him look ten years younger, and because his passport was nearly eight years old, he thought he'd have no trouble with the TSA or Customs. He needed the rug to throw off his pursuers, who were, no doubt, searching for a balding gent in his mid-fifties. If the authorities were on to him, already seeking him out, Floyd figured the wig would put them off his trail. If only the media didn't plaster his passport photo all over the newspaper and the internet.

Floyd's stomach was in knots as he approached the TSA agent, a handsome Latino, seated on a stool amid a roped maze thronged with travelers in queues. Struggling to keep the fear from his face, Floyd handed the stern-looking fellow his passport and boarding pass, praying that he would not be called out of line and detained. The agent eyeballed Floyd's wig for a moment and raised his eyebrows.

Then he closed the passport and handed it back. "Have a pleasant flight, Mr. Heller," he said, dismissing him, while extending his hand toward the woman behind Floyd. The man is a machine, Floyd thought, and my get-out-of-jail-free card.

Floyd couldn't keep the smile of relief from his face. He counted his lucky stars as he removed his belt, rolled it up, and placed it in the gray plastic bin. Then he pried off his shoes and placed them on the conveyor line. Just have to get through this, he told himself. He was on his way out of misery and into a new life.

"Laptop and cellphone in the bin," a harried security agent demanded, and Floyd's smile vanished. Hastily, he obliged. Then he was whisked through the X-ray scanner and, in the next moment, retrieving his loafers, belt, and devices. Normally, Floyd would have cringed at the crush of humanity that surrounded him—the meaty naked arms of people clad in tank tops, dressed for yard work rather than international travel. But he was too elated at having passed through security to take much notice.

Might as well get used to it. Where he was going was no country club. He trotted down the corridor toward the terminal, thinking he'd have to lower his standards.

But then he consoled himself with the thought that it was a small price to pay. He had stacks of cash, and given the exchange rate in South America, it should keep him in comfort till the end of his days. No more Marcie carping at him day and night. No more endless worry about the humiliation of being caught and sent to prison, where he'd rot for the rest of his days. He couldn't believe his luck. This was a second chance. A new life beckoned, and he was eager to get on with it.

～

Kara sank back into the buttery soft leather of the swivel lounge chair, smiling smugly. "Cheers, girls," she said, raising her champagne flute. "Sweet Dreamer, here we come!"

"Yay!" Laney, the tall, slender brunette, hoisted her glass.

"To a week of fun in the sun. What's the itinerary, Kara?" Becca asked.

"You know the drill," Kara said. "Same old, same old. Pool, lunch, shopping, pool, dinner, Holetown, shopping."

"Sounds divine." Laney crinkled her plastic surgeon's dream of a nose. "I need to recharge my batteries."

"I need to recharge my sex life," Becca said, eliciting hoots of laughter from her companions. "I'm serious, girls. I need to score. I think I've forgotten how to do it."

"Let's hope we all get lucky," Kara said. "God knows, my sex life has been non-existent for the past two years. Danny and I were living like brother and sister until he finally left altogether. It's been a long dry spell."

Laney cut her eyes to Becca and a silent pact was forged between them.

"Let's not dwell on that, Kara," she announced. "No negativity. Agreed?"

"Gonna get down, get down!" Becca gyrated in her chair, bobbing her head exaggeratedly. "To Holetown, Holetown!"

"Ladies, is there anything else I can get you before we take off?" The clean-cut pilot asked as he emerged from behind the drape between the cabin and cockpit. Becca opened her eyes wide and pressed her lips together, feigning embarrassment at being caught in the act.

Laney snorted, struggling to keep from spewing a mouthful of champagne all over her new Lilly Pulitzer skirt.

"Coffee, tea, or thee, Dave?" Becca arched an eyebrow, gazing at the pilot seductively.

Coming from anyone else, Becca's words might have offended. But the fact that she was teasing—that it was all in good fun—was so openly apparent that the pilot grinned back and played along. "Fly the friendly skies," he quipped.

"We're fine, Dave," Kara said. "Thank you."

"Shall I go over the safety instructions?" Dave directed his question to the woman who was paying for the flight and his fee.

"That won't be necessary." Kara waved him away.

"In the event of an emergency, come get me, Dave." Becca winked at him lewdly.

"Roger that." Dave snapped Becca a salute before disappearing into the cockpit.

"You are so bad, Becca," Laney admonished.

"And that's why you love me." Becca grinned.

The plane vibrated as its engines roared to life, and Becca rose and crossed to the sideboard. "What have we here?" She lifted a cover from one of three silver chafing dishes. "Chicken salad… Oh, and fresh fruit and banana bread. Yum! Lunch, anyone?"

∽

On a much larger but far more plebeian transport, Daniel lowered himself into his first-class seat. Once situated, he closed his eyes and willed himself to ignore the sea of humanity surging around him. When the Boeing 747, its engines rumbling, taxied across the tarmac, the wail of a fretful infant added a note of hysteria to the din. Daniel cringed. The plane roared down the runway, gathering speed and then sprang into the sky. At that exact moment, the baby began wailing. Silently cursing Kara, Daniel steeled himself for a long flight.

∽

They had dimmed the lights in the aircraft that was hurtling Floyd away from all his cares and woes. Most of his fellow passengers were asleep, but Floyd was nursing his third Maker's Mark, gazing out the tiny window at an empty black sky. Several hours into his flight, the lawyer was rueing the wig that itched his head maddeningly. But there was nothing he could do about that now.

A flight attendant paused in the aisle. "May I get you anything, sir?"

"Sure." Floyd tossed off the dregs of his drink before handing her the empty glass. "One more for the road."

∽

It was a somber lot ringing the conference room table at Prestige. Usually, Craig and Jeremy would stir the pot, teasing Stewart about his new trophy bride. But today, the sales team was uncharacteristically glum. Sally sat at the head of the table, her shadow, Margo to her right. All of them had their heads down as though chastened. Andrea felt as though she were in a confessional awaiting absolution. None was forthcoming.

Sally cleared her throat, and heads snapped up as the assembly came to attention. "First, thank you all for doing due diligence and damage control," she said. "You've handled this like the troopers I knew you were, and I'm very grateful."

Margo sniffed and withdrew a tissue from her briefcase.

The gesture was not lost on Andrea. Wasn't Sally's assistant being overly melodramatic?

"So," Sally exclaimed, "here's where we are. The good news is the bank's going to cover our escrows…"

Stewart slapped a palm on the table. "By that, you mean they're loaning you the money. That means *you're* covering the escrows, Sally. It's so damned unfair."

"We do what we have to do, Stew," Sally said, a note of resignation to her voice.

Margo pressed a tissue to her eye.

"Aw, for God's sake," Craig said. "You shouldn't have to cover all our—"

Before he could finish his sentence, Steward cut him off. "I agree," he said.

"Gentlemen, thank you," Sally said. "I appreciate your support, but this is my firm. You work for me. I advised you to escrow with Floyd. The rest is history. I'll… we'll all be fine."

"I feel bad I don't have an escrow," Jeremy complained. "It's like I'm out of the loop."

"Well out of it, my friend," Craig said.

"Chalk it up to survivor's guilt," Andrea added. "If it makes you feel any better, Jeremy, I'm suffering from the same malady."

"Okay, guys," Sally pushed away from the table. "We're not going to beat ourselves up over this any longer. The firm will survive this, and we'll all come out stronger."

"That's right," Heather said, finally finding her voice. "We've got the brightest, most talented broker on the Treasure Coast and the most aggressive sales team anywhere."

"Buck up, me hearties," Sally quipped. "There's still money to be made in real estate."

"Jeez," Jeremy complained. "I'm not sure if I'm getting a pep talk before going out onto the field to be creamed by the three-hundred-pound offensive lineman, or—"

"Or what, Diaz" Craig interrupted, cuffing his friend lightly on the head. "Don't be a wimp."

"Who's the wimp?" Taking the bait, Jeremy bolted from his chair.

Craig scrambled to his feet and dashed out the door with Jeremy and Stewart close behind him.

"Men!" Margo exclaimed. "They're such little boys."

Sally smiled indulgently. "They're just letting off steam, that's all. It beats the heck out of screaming."

No sooner were her words out than the sounds of a scuffle followed by a high-pitched scream emanated from the back offices. The four women exchanged knowing looks and chuckled.

~

The white, linen, cabana curtains were tied back, providing a view of the vanishing-edge pool and a meticulously landscaped yard. Beyond the property line, densely overgrown bush, scrubby, stunted trees, and a tangle of vines terraced for a half-mile down the hillside only to end in a speck of ocean glinting beneath a China bowl sky.

Clad in a skimpy bikini, Kara sat cross-legged on the teak frame sofa, iPad resting on her creamy thighs. Her white-blonde tresses were pulled up in a knot, but a few tendrils had escaped, framing her perfectly oval face.

Becca, her generous curves stretching the confines of a revealing two-piece, pushed open a French door and sauntered out. "Can you grease up this little piggy?" She thrust a tube of sunscreen in Kara's direction. "Gotta fry the bacon."

Laney was adrift in the pool, lounging on a molded float. "Oh, stop," she protested, desultorily trailing her fingers in the water. "You look great."

"Yeah, if you fancy short, fat chicks," Becca countered.

Kara rubbed lotion into Becca's freckled back. "You do, you know. You've lost weight."

"You noticed," Becca said, obviously pleased. "Twenty pounds."

"From you, I don't want to hear a word," Becca said, directing her comment to her willowy friend. "We eat the same food, and I puff up while you remain disgustingly thin."

"It's because she's tall," Kara said.

"It's because she forged a pact with the devil." Becca broke away from Kara and hurled herself into the pool.

Laney raised her arms shielding her face, but she was drenched. Becca rose to the surface and grabbed hold of the float, grinning impishly. Before Laney could repel her annoying pal, a movement from the estate up the hill from Sweet Dreamer caught her attention.

"Oh, look," she said, pointing in that direction. "We have neighbors."

Kara scrambled out from the loggia and peered out over the lush valley to the hilltop estate situated across from hers. There, she could make out several figures on the pool deck.

"Looks like two men and a couple of brats," Becca said. Just then, another figure emerged from the interior, this one dark-skinned and bare-chested.

"Another guy," Laney announced. "Or else the broad's butch and going topless."

"Three males, two kids, no women," Becca said. "What do you make of that?"

Kara hiked to her lot line and peered up the hillside. "This is interesting," she said. "Over the years, I've met a few of my Sugar Hill neighbors, but the multi-acre parcels are separate unto themselves. I don't believe there are any full-time residents. As I understand it, the owners—most of them hailing from Great Britain—fly in for a brief stay only to be gone for months on end. If I had to guess, I'd say those guys are Brits. You know Barbados was formerly a British Colony?"

"Nope," Becca said.

"Yes, until 1961, and to this day, it remains a popular destination for the Anglophile contingent."

The three women continued their perusal of the estate atop the hill. The youngsters had made a mad dash for the pool and were now cavorting in it, and the men were lounging in deck chairs.

"They could be a gay threesome, but somehow I don't think so." Becca hoisted herself out of the pool. "We gotta meet those guys."

Kara nodded, still fixated on the newly arrived neighbors. "That we do, Becca."

Becca snatched a beach towel from a chaise lounge and went to stand behind Kara. "Woo-hoo!" she called, waving the towel over her head.

Kara spun around and tried to wrest the towel from Becca, but the chubby girl persisted. "Hi, y'all," Becca shouted, laying on a phony Southern accent. The distance between them was much too far for Becca's voice to carry. Still, her gesture seemed to have caught the attention of the men she was signaling, for one fellow extended an arm and waved, returning her greeting.

"Becca," Kara snarled. "Stop it."

"Becca," Laney cried, as she climbed out of the pool and crossed to her exuberant friend. "Behave, won't you?"

Instead, Becca dropped the towel and raised both arms above her head while wiggling her hips in a provocative shimmy.

Laney stepped in front of Becca and waved regally like the beauty queen that she was. Kara turned away from the wall and grabbed her boisterous pal by the elbow, hustling her toward the loggia. "What the hell, Becca," she hissed. "I might meet those fellows at a cocktail party sometime. I don't want them to think I'm a wanton hussy."

"Why not?" Becca asked.

Laney pivoted and brought up the rear, exuding grace and refinement in her carriage as she swayed her narrow hips seductively. She knew full well the men were watching her every move; that they were probably just as curious as she and the girls were and trying to gauge what type of women were occupying the house just down the hill from theirs.

CHAPTER SIX

MERMAIDS

Andrea had picked up a bottle of Chardonnay before driving home to lick her wounds. Now, she poured herself another glass and gazed overhead praying for a sign, some inspiration. The moon was an indistinct thumbprint in a murky sky, and it gave her no answers. Try as she might, she couldn't seem to make sense of the events that were unfolding around her. Andrea's musings were interrupted when Madison pushed open the French door.

"Hi, Mommy." Looking fetching in one of Derrick's old college tees that swam on her slender frame, Madison crossed to her mother and plunked down on the lounge chair next to her. "What're you doing?"

"Nothing, honey. Just thinking." Andrea searched the teen's face, noting her lowered brow. "How was your day?"

"Okay." Madison squirmed in her chair. "Um…"

"What is it?" Andrea asked.

"I don't know. It's stupid. I'm stupid…"

"Madison," Andrea exclaimed, setting her wineglass down on the side table and giving her daughter her full attention. "Never say that. You are a lovely and capable girl. And you'll make a success of whatever you put your mind to."

"I know, Mom. But…"

"But what?" Andrea could see that her daughter was troubled, and she was suddenly determined to get to the bottom of it. "Tell me, sweetie."

Madison came to her feet. "It's nothing, Mom."

"Maddy, sit down," Andrea commanded, and to her relief, the teenager complied.

"Now, what's upset you. I'm your mother. You know you can tell me anything."

The girl laced her fingers together and then pulled them apart restively.

"Madison, I mean it," Andrea demanded. "Spill."

"Um… I… Never mind. It's probably nothing."

"Something's worrying you."

"It's just that I feel like…"

"Like what?"

"Oh," Madison furrowed her brow, struggling to put her thoughts into words. "I get the feeling that someone's watching me," she finally admitted.

Andrea considered her daughter's statement before venturing a comment. "Madison," she said, "you are growing up to be a very attractive young woman. Beautiful people draw attention to themselves even when they don't mean to do so," she explained. "Don't you sometimes stare at pretty girls, check out their hair and clothes?"

Madison nodded grudgingly.

"Well, there you have it."

Although she appeared unconvinced, the teen let it drop. "Okay. So, when is Nana's party?"

"In two weeks. I was thinking you and I could go over to Casa Rio tomorrow and do a bit of a trial run to see how it goes. What do you say?"

"Sure," Madison agreed. "Is Dad coming, too?"

"No, Maddy," Andrea said, struck by a pang of guilt over her daughter's transparent desire for the three of them to be a family again. "But he's agreed to cook for the party," she added. "It should be a grand time."

"Cool."

"Honey, it's past your bedtime. You'd best tuck yourself in."

"Okay, Mom." Madison rose from her chair and bent to kiss Andrea. "Night," she murmured.

"Goodnight, baby. See you in the morning."

Andrea followed Madison's retreating figure, noting the teen's shapely figure beneath the oversized tee. Surely, the girl was imagining things. But an unsettling possibility niggled at Andrea's consciousness, and she silently vowed to redouble her efforts to protect her child.

The chiming of her cellphone interrupted her musings. A glance at the display told her it was her mother, and she tapped to accept the call. "Hi, Mom."

"Hello, Andy. How was your day?"

"It was hell. You wouldn't believe it."

"Try me."

"Floyd Heller, you know, the attorney who handles our escrows…"

"Yes. His wife, Marcie, is in my book club."

"Turns out he was embezzling. The escrows have vanished and so has Floyd." Andrea took a sip of her wine.

"You're right. I can't believe it." Margaret exclaimed. "Good heavens!"

"He's been operating a Ponzi scheme for years, somehow managing to stay one step ahead of the game. Apparently, he's been pilfering a generous portion of the escrows to bankroll his lavish lifestyle, using new clients' deposits to cover the deficits in others. But now, with this recession and no influx of cash deposits, his little house of cards has come tumbling down around him."

"I'm…" Margaret paused. "I don't know what to say. This calls for a glass of wine. Okay? Hold on a minute."

Andrea gazed out over the river, feeling the weight of the world on her shoulders. Never had she felt so alone and so afraid.

"Ah'm back. I'm just bowled over, sweetheart. What the heck next?"

"I know, right? And it only gets worse."

"How could it get any worse?"

"Our realty firm's escrows are not the only ones Floyd managed."

"Oh, my God. This *is* terrible."

"It's a scandal that is going to knock our sleepy seaside community on its ear, Mom. No one knows for sure how far-reaching the financial fallout will prove to be. Sally's taken a huge hit, but she's got reserves, and she's tough. She'll recover. Others won't fare as well. I can't believe I am saying this, but I am so thankful I don't have any sales just now. No escrows to speak of."

"I suppose that *is* a blessing in disguise, huh?"

"Yeah, but enough of my woes. Have you come to grips with selling Casa?"

"Surprisingly, yes."

"Really?"

"I love this place, but it's too much house for me. I'm ashamed to admit it, but a small part of me is eager to climb out from this money pit and move on—to travel, see the world before I'm too old to do so."

"Oh, Mom." Andrea exhaled a sigh of relief. "It's all going to work out. You'll see."

"I was just going to say the same thing to you, dearest. We'll be alright. And on that note, this old lady is off to bed. I'd say sweet dreams, but you'd only laugh."

"You got that right. Goodnight, Mom." Andrea tapped to disconnect, and her eyes were drawn to the three-quarter moon above. She remembered her first dinner with Daniel, how the moon had seemed to mesmerize them, casting a magic spell.

There was, she consoled herself, one bright spot in this otherwise gloomy picture. Andrea brought the glass of Chardonnay to her lips and conjured an image of her newest client, Daniel Armstrong. Despite her best efforts to keep business with him on a purely professional level, she was very much attracted to that enigmatic man. Of course, she'd googled him. Not surprisingly, she'd discovered that he was heir to a great fortune—that he had his fingers in lots of pies. But why was he so private? Whatever it was he was hiding served only to heighten her interest, adding fuel to the small fire that was smoldering within her. Yearnings she'd tamped down for a very long time were resurfacing, and for the first time in ages, she felt the stirrings of desire.

She wanted that man in her bed.

∽

Margaret Sheridan cautiously made her way down the pier, wineglass in hand. With considerable effort and much creaking of joints, she lowered herself to the dock, and only a few drops of wine were spilled in the process. The roar of the crashing tide was in her ears, but it was white noise. She'd been inured to the ocean's voice for so many years that it took the howling of a hurricane or a wailing nor'easter to register in her consciousness. She'd spent a lifetime on the ocean's doorstep, she thought, as she extended her still-shapely legs out over the deck and let them dangle. It'd been a good life.

Her dad had been a much-admired physician in what was then a little Podunk town: Fort Walden Beach. Being his only child, she'd been thoroughly spoilt. No doubt about it. Margaret sighed and took a generous sip of wine. Gazing towards the heavens, she didn't see stars. Instead, she saw herself as a girl...

"Maggie, you'd best get in here," Will Nesbitt hollered. "Dinner's ready."

Margaret had just emerged from the sea, dripping. She was climbing the dune—her toes digging into the still-warm sand for purchase—when, at the sound of Doc's voice, she came rigidly to attention. She peered at the clapboard house set back from the sea oats and scrub. In the gathering darkness, she could barely make out his silhouette at the door. "Coming, Dad," she cried, but he'd already disappeared inside.

At the dinner table, Doc picked up the subject that only served to irritate her. "It's time we decided about your higher education, what you're going to do with your life, Maggie."

"Um," Margaret mumbled, chewing a mouthful of one of her dad's improbable culinary concoctions—spam casserole.

"You need to settle on a chosen field, decide what career you want to pursue."

"Dad, I've told you. I don't know. I'd like to swim—"

"Swim?" Will snorted, dismissively. "Swimming's not a profession. How do you propose to make a living?"

Margaret paused, knowing full well that what she was about to propose would meet with pushback. "I was thinking I'd apply for a scholarship to FSU. They're aggressively recruiting swimmers. Female swimmers, Dad."

"Really?" Doc looked skeptical. "And why do you think that is?"

"Because—" Margaret lifted her chin a notch.

"Because men want to see women scantily dressed and doomed to failure?"

"What?" She bolted upright in her chair, bristling.

"Maggie, listen to me. Maybe someday. But not now."

"Dad—"

Doc cut her off. "Mags. Not in your lifetime."

"But—" Margaret wheedled.

"Darling girl." Her father shook his head. "Enroll in a business school or take education classes. What about banking? You could be a teller. Or teach. You love children, Maggie. Don't set your sights on such fanciful pursuits. Be reasonable."

"I've already sent in my application."

Will searched Margaret's eyes, and she knew he saw the resolve there. "Fine," he said, curtly. "But would you humor old Doc? Apply to some other schools, too?"

"Okay." Margaret had all she could do to act the conciliatory daughter, pretending to heed her father's wishes, but she could barely conceal her delight at this small victory.

∽

When the acceptance letter arrived, she did a happy dance with the mailbox. She was going to be a member of the women's swim team at FSU!

The years had flown, and she'd thoroughly enjoyed her college stint at Florida State. Wet more than dry, she'd raced her heart out, accumulating a wall full of trophies to prove it. But when in the spring of 1955 graduation loomed, and Margaret still did not know what her next step would be, her dad's words reverberated in her cranium: "What are you going to do with your life, Maggie?"

∽

"Hey, gorgeous!" The lanky young man caught sight of her at the bar and strode across the room. "How about I buy you a beer?" he asked, resting a palm on her shoulder.

"Champagne, more like." Margaret patted the empty barstool beside her. "It's the least you can do for me after that marathon study session."

Timothy Kerry folded his long-limbed frame onto the barstool and ogled her.

Margaret looked past the leer, taking in Tim's guileless freckled face, his curly copper mop, and she couldn't help but grin. "What's up, Timothy?"

Tim waved a hand in the air, signaling the bartender. Once he'd gotten the man's attention, he raised two fingers and then pointed towards Margaret's empty glass. The bartender nodded and set about filling their order.

In no time, the two were clinking glasses. "Here's to you, Florence," Tim said.

It took a moment for Margaret to get his meaning, but when she did, she chuckled. He was, she realized, referencing Florence Chadwick, who, just last year in 1952, became the first woman to swim both ways across the English Channel. "And to you," she replied, "future scion of business."

"If that's the case, it's thanks to a certain Miss Someone who rides my ass."

"Pfft! You'll do fine. I'll bet you passed your exams with flying colors."

Tim nodded, a begrudging smile on his face. "Yeah, I'm pretty sure. And guess what?" He gazed at her, his eyes twinkling.

"What?" Margaret raised her eyebrows, eager for a bit of good news.

"I'll have you know I scored an interview next week."

"Wow!" Margaret was duly impressed. She had no interviews on the horizon. "Congratulations," she crowed.

"Uh-huh, and guess what else?"

"Oh, c'mon, Timmy, I don't know. What?"

"I've got a lead for *you*."

"A lead?" Margaret pivoted on her barstool and gave him her full attention. "What do you mean?"

Tim withdrew a folded paper from his pocket and placed the advertisement on the bar in front of her. Then with undue theatrics, he unfolded it and pressed out the creases.

Margaret laughed, shaking her head at Tim's dramatics. But then the headline screamed at her—*Weeki Wachee Springs Mermaids* and she gasped. "Mermaids?"

"Yeah, baby, mermaids. And I think you'd be a perfect Siren of the Sea. God knows you've lured me off course."

"Ha!" Margaret huffed dismissively, but her mind was reeling with the possibilities. Weeki Wachee Springs? She'd never heard of the place. But, according to the advertisement, it was fast becoming a popular tourist destination. The enterprising entrepreneur who'd seen money signs in the backwater springs was avidly recruiting attractive female swimmers in their early twenties.

She figured she fit that bill!

~

Newton Perry smiled at Margaret from across a desk littered with mechanical drawings—sketches of air hoses and compressors and underwater waystations. He seemed a simple enough man; his shaggy mane framed a wide face that was dimpled and tanned and in need of a shave. But there was something charismatic about him, too. Or maybe it was just the opportunity to swim that she found so appealing. In any case, she was a mermaid hooked.

"The job doesn't pay much," he said. "Thirty dollars a week plus board and tips."

"What?" Margaret was suddenly knocked out of Mermaid Heaven and back to reality. How could she survive on that pittance?

Newt put his hands in the air, shaking them as if to dispel bad vibes. "I know. Doesn't sound like much. But the tips are considerable. Most girls make so much money, they stay on."

Somewhat placated, Margaret asked, "And what is the board?"

"I've built the cutest little cottages. With all the modern amenities. Two girls to a unit, each with a bath and kitchenette. Plus, there's a camp kitchen that puts out two meals a day. So, you don't have to cook unless you want to."

"Hmm…" Margaret digested this bit of information. She had no other opportunities, but she wasn't about to admit that. "Okay," she finally said, sealing her destiny.

Looking back on it, she had nothing but the fondest of memories of her stint as a mermaid at Weeki Wachee Springs. Not only had those been the most exhilarating years of her life, but it was after a performance there that she'd first set eyes on John. He'd been fresh out of Med School, so tall and handsome and eagerly looking forward to a few carefree days before embarking on his internship. But from the moment his eyes latched onto hers, John's freewheeling days were over, and they'd both known it.

Margaret finished the last of her wine, set the glass down on the raw planks, and gazed out over the fathomless ocean. They'd had a good long run. She only wished her darling boy had stuck around for the golden years. It was hell growing old and doing it alone. She'd never looked at another man. Didn't want one. She'd had the love of her life, and nothing could top that.

"Buck up, old girl. This is just another chapter," she told herself. "It's not the end of the story."

CHAPTER SEVEN

HEISTS AND HIJINX

All the drama and intrigue of the last few weeks— Floyd's sudden exodus, to say nothing of the four bourbons he'd imbibed—had all finally caught up with him. His head grew heavier and heavier until his chin rested on his chest, and he began to snore softly. But no sooner had he entered dreamland—a tropical paradise where nubile young women found him irresistible and anticipated his every desire than his fantasy was rudely interrupted.

Daniel had also nodded off. His dreams were of a lovely, long-limbed creature possessed of delicate features and pale, ash brown hair. He could see the two of them, strolling hand in hand from the Casa Rio main house to the ocean pier. The moon was incredibly bright, a huge, luminous orb that became ever more intense until it blinded him.

Suddenly, the cabin lights came on, and Daniel awoke with a start. "This is the captain," a male voice broadcast from the speaker system. "There is a package on board, which must be returned to Miami." A low rumble of irate voices followed this announcement.

"We're very sorry for this inconvenience. Unfortunately, we have no alternative but to turn back. Passengers are asked to deplane at the terminal and remain there with their boarding passes. We will do everything in our power to get you back in the air as soon as possible."

Floyd was immediately rendered both clear-headed and terrified. Was he the *package*? His wig was itching his scalp, driving him to distraction, and all he wanted was to snatch it off his noggin. But he dared not do so and risk being identified.

When the restive child seated several seats behind him yowled disconsolately, Daniel couldn't help but think of Kara. Having commandeered his private jet, she was off on holiday in the islands, living the lifestyle he'd provided her. For the thousandth time, he cursed her.

~

Second Street in Holetown, Saint James Parish, was where it was happening. A mix of tourists, winter residents, and native islanders thronged the narrow streets and swelled the open-air bistros from which a cacophony of melodies spilled. Rock, reggae, pop, even show tunes combined to create a jumbled mix that fairly pulsed in the air. It was a wild party that occurred with clocklike regularity when the sun went down, and the booze didn't stop pouring until the last reveler either departed or was carried off. There were no loyalties in Holetown. Nobody stayed in one club for any length of time. It was a moveable feast—one that was sampled on the go—a smorgasbord of food, drink, and musical styles.

Kara preferred to start with a shrimp cocktail appetizer and a couple of gin and tonics served up at the Elbow Room—an eating and drinking establishment with no pretensions. There were plenty of tables inside, but the deck was where the action was.

It was a beautiful, mild evening, and a live reggae band provided a calypso beat. The wooden tables and chairs were scarred and discolored from years of abuse, to say nothing of the elements, but Kara wasn't there for the ambiance. On her last jaunt to the islands, she'd had a fling with Ben, the smoldering-eyed bartender whom she'd happily taken to her bed. Naturally, she'd hoped there might be a repeat performance in her boudoir tonight.

Now that didn't seem likely.

Sid, the Elbow Room proprietor, was a squat, rough-looking fellow who, on rare occasions, made an appearance from his tiny back office. Alicia, the perky brunette waiting tables, was Sid's only daughter. Kara couldn't help but notice the chemistry between the barmaid and Ben. What was even harder to miss was the half-carat diamond ring sparkling on the server's finger.

In her three months' absence, Kara hadn't expected Ben to keep celibate while pining away, waiting for her return. But now, the two drinks she'd downed had gone straight to her head, and her former ebullience devolved into pique. Laney and Becca attempted to lift Kara's spirits—to whisk her away to another club—but she would have none of it. Instead, she glared at Ben.

From the bar, Ben smiled weakly in Kara's direction.

Kara waved Alicia over and ordered another round. "What a beautiful ring," she gushed disingenuously, making sure Alicia got an eyeful of the enormous, yellow diamond on her finger. But Alicia remained blissfully unaware of the undercurrents that threatened to unhinge poor Ben.

"Thank you," Alicia said. "Ben popped the question three weeks ago."

"Lucky you," Kara said, archly. "When's the wedding?"

"In October, just a little over five months. I've got a million things to do between now and then."

"Well, congrats," Laney said as Alicia turned to go.

"Make sure I get an invitation," Kara muttered darkly. Just then, a pair of hot-looking men strode into the bar, and Kara forgot about all Ben. Here was fresh meat, and she appraised the two shamelessly.

They were as different as day and night; one was fair and well-muscled, the other dark and slender, but fate had blessed them with movie-star good looks, and the two projected an air of arrogance that bespoke lives of privilege and pricey educations. Laney and Becca exchanged looks of relief. A diversion is exactly what was needed to prevent the evening from turning into a complete disaster.

As if their meeting had been prearranged, the men crossed directly to the three girls. Which came as no surprise, for Kara and Laney were, easily, the most attractive women in the joint.

Kara pretended to ignore the men, feigning a fascination with the lime in her cocktail. But Laney was an open book, and she smiled sweetly at them. Becca grinned impishly, eager for the drama that would surely transpire.

"Hello ladies," the sandy-haired Adonis teased in his clipped

British accent. "Where have you been all my life?" He flashed his perfect white teeth and leaned in toward the women.

On closer inspection, Kara decided he was the older of the two. He was tan, and the white creases at the corners of his eyes told her he was in his early forties.

"Hi yourself," Becca growled. "Anyone care to dance?" She bobbed her head to the beat and widened her eyes, ever the clown.

"Not just yet," the blonde said, dismissing her. He focused his considerable charm on Kara. Thrusting an arm out in her direction, he said, "How do, Luv? I'm Charles Draper." He arched an eyebrow rakishly, and Kara marveled at his boldness. "But you can call me Charlie."

Kara took his hand in hers. "I'm Kara Armstrong," she said, a notable lack of enthusiasm in her voice. "You can call me Kara." She extricated her hand, turned away from Charles, and offered it to his companion. "Hello there."

The slender chap favored Kara with a cocky smirk. "Hello. I'm Trevor." It was obvious this fellow didn't take himself too seriously, unlike the slick Charles. And with his exotic mix of native and Eurasian features—wide, sensuous lips, narrow aristocratic nose, and slightly slanted oval eyes—Kara found him instantly appealing. That he appeared to be a good ten years her junior only added to his allure. It had been a long time since she'd bedded a kid in his twenties. Kara practically salivated at the thought of his stamina between the sheets. She gestured toward her two companions. "And these are my friends, Laney and Becca."

Charles smiled tightly and turned his attention to Laney. She fixed him with a conspiratorial grin, and he responded by giving her a none-too-subtle once-over. Unlike Kara—with her white-blonde hair and a figure that came on like gangbusters—Laney was possessed of quiet beauty. "I think they're playing our song." Charles extended a hand and Laney allowed herself to be led to the dancefloor.

"What do you say?" Trevor asked Kara. "Shall we join them?"

Kara threw her head back and laughed as she rose from her chair.

~

Becca watched her companions dancing with their new partners, and her high spirits plummeted. They hadn't been in Holetown an hour, and everyone was pairing up except for her. Not like that was an unusual occurrence. But this was her vacation, her *Becca gets her groove time*, and it just wasn't happening. She could see it in her mind's eye: They'd all reassemble back at Sweet Dreamer, and she'd be the odd girl out. It was so degrading. Becca let her gaze drift over the dance floor and to the patio beyond. Then finally, her eyes came to rest on a tall, fleshy young man. He was well-groomed and pleasant looking with a mass of wheat-colored hair, and he was standing before a table staring in her direction.

Becca gasped, did a double-take. The dude was checking her out! The sadder but wiser girl, Becca, had no illusions; he was probably wasted. Heck, she was a little tipsy herself, but the two of them could dance, couldn't they?

Becca pasted a seductive smile to her face and crooked her index finger, mustering all her considerable sexual charms into these gestures. The fellow stepped back a pace and put a hand to his chest. "Me?" he mouthed. Becca traced a finger around her lips and arched a brow, and the fellow nodded his head and waved her over.

"Okay, buddy," Becca muttered as she sashayed to him, "the mountain comes to Mohammad."

How was she to know she'd hit the jackpot?

∽

Daniel massaged the back of his neck. This was turning into a nightmare. He closed his laptop and deposited it in his briefcase. The baby was screaming now, and he wanted to add his voice to the caterwauling. Instead, as soon as the passengers seated ahead of him darted to the aisle and collected their things from the overheads, he hustled out of his own seat and hiked out of the airplane onto the jet bridge.

∽

Floyd's brain was soggy, but he still couldn't fool himself into believing that this was nothing more than an annoying, minor setback. Surely, agents had been dispatched to apprehend him at the gate. When he emerged from the jet bridge, Floyd breathed a ragged sigh of relief. No authorities were lying in wait. In fact, no one seemed to take any notice of him. Floyd slithered into a seat in the terminal and snatched up a Miami Herald that some traveler had discarded. He held the newspaper in front of his face and tried to concentrate on the headlines. After a few minutes, he tossed the daily aside, too wound up to read. Might as well find the Sky Miles Lounge, he decided, wait it out with a Maker's Mark to keep him company. Why the hell not? If he *were* going to jail, he should at least enjoy his last hours of freedom.

Floyd gathered up his valise and strode down the concourse. He had nearly reached his destination when a pair of uniformed police officers swept past him heading in the opposite direction. Turtle-like, the attorney retracted his chin into his collar and hiked toward the Sky Mile Lounge.

They were after him!

He slinked up to the bar, took a seat, and hastily withdrew a five-dollar bill from his wallet. As he tucked it into the tip jar, his eyes met those of the bartender.

Like magic, the bartender hustled in his direction. "What'll it'll be, sir?"

"A Maker's on ice." Floyd mopped his brow.

"Coming right up."

Floyd shot a sidelong glance at the man on his right, and his eyes widened when the fellow looked his way. "Weren't we on the same plane? Business Class?" he asked.

"Yep," Daniel said. "Not my lucky day."

The bartender placed Floyd's drink before him. "Here you are, sir."

Floyd took a swig and then swiveled in Daniel's direction. "Nor mine, either. I need to get out of here. I have an important meeting with new clients, and now this. I'll never make it."

"Yeah, same story here," Daniel said. "Lousy luck."

"You can say that again."

"Where're you headed?"

"The Dominican Republic."

"No kidding? I was on my way to Barbados. I have a place there.

But unfortunately, my soon-to-be ex-wife is trying to wrangle it away from me. Anyway, I have some business matters I need to attend to." Daniel tossed a hand in the air. "Divorce," he said, as though that was the perfect explanation. Then he raised his glass and favored Floyd with a wry half-smile.

"I hear you. I'm cutting loose myself." Floyd caught himself. It wouldn't do to reveal his personal history. The less said, the better. "For a few days, that is. But, man, I need to get to my meeting. A potential new client, money on the table."

"Yeah? Well, I just got an update on my cell. Our flight's been canceled. We're not flying out until nine tomorrow morning."

"Oh, God." Floyd mopped his brow with the back of a trembling hand.

Daniel sipped his wine and then cut his eyes to the buffet where a very large, rugged-looking fellow was filling a plate.

"I don't believe it," he exclaimed under his breath.

"What?"

"I know that guy." Daniel nodded toward the buffet. "Small world."

"Yeah?"

"He's a pilot."

"So?" Floyd shrugged.

"Private jet. Charter."

"Ah." Floyd pivoted in his seat to better eye the new arrival.

The pilot glanced around the lounge, looking for a place to sit, and Daniel raised an arm, catching his eye. A grin of recognition split the man's face, and he strode toward the bar.

"Buzz! How are you, my man?" Daniel clapped a hand on the large man's shoulder. "Join us."

"Danny. Long time no see, buddy." The pilot set his plate on the marble countertop and slid his bulky frame into the empty stool on Daniel's right.

The bartender came to stand before Buzz. "Sir?"

"Let me buy you a drink," Daniel said, expansively.

"I believe they're on the house," Buzz smirked. "Clint, how about a Monkey 47 on the rocks?" he said to the barman.

"Come here often?" Daniel quipped, his voice dripping sarcasm.

Buzz raised and then lowered his brows dismissively. "My stomping grounds."

Floyd hung on this exchange. His scalp itched something fierce, and his heart was racing. He knew he had to vanish and quickly, or he'd be spending the next ten to twenty years behind bars.

"What brings you here, like I don't know?" the pilot asked.

"I have to make a quick trip to Barbados," Daniel said, "to tie up some loose ends."

"I figured it was something like that." Buzz wrapped his fingers around the highball the bartender placed before him.

"And you?" Daniel raised his glass in a toast.

"Just flew in from Tobago." Buzz clicked glasses with Daniel. "Have a few days to kill before my next charter."

Daniel nodded, digesting this piece of information. "Say. You wouldn't be up for a quick hop back to the islands, would you?" Daniel asked, as though the thought had just occurred to him.

Buzz took a long pull of gin. "Depends," he finally said. "I might be."

"How soon could we get out of here?"

The pilot withdrew his cellphone from his back pocket and glanced at the display. "It's nearly ten. The good news is, I don't have to file a flight plan, but there's still paperwork, and I'll need to have the plane fueled. That'll take me about two hours." He looked up, mentally calculating. "Add another half hour to grab a cab and drive to Opa Locka. I'd say we could be in the air no later than one."

"What's your price?"

"How many passengers?"

"Two," Floyd said.

"Oh, sorry. This is…" Daniel looked first to Floyd, then to Buzz.

"Fl… Uh," Floyd stumbled. "Frank Hoover."

"Frank and I were on the same plane, and now we're grounded until tomorrow," Daniel explained.

"I need to be in Santo Domingo for a one o'clock meeting," Floyd added.

"I'd be landing at both Saidor and Grantley Adams Airports?"

Daniel looked at Floyd, who nodded. "Guess so," he said.

"Five thousand dollars an hour plus fuel and my return flight…" Buzz did a quick calculation in his head. "Twenty Gs should do it."

"Count me in," Floyd said, barely able to contain his elation.

"Me, too," Daniel said.

"Let's get on the road, gentlemen." Buzz gulped down the rest of his drink and pushed away from the bar. "Or, rather, in the air."

"And get the hell out of Dodge," Floyd mumbled under his breath.

～

The following day, Laney awoke to the sound of laughter wafting up the massive, stone stairwell from somewhere below. Languorously, she extended an arm across the Egyptian cotton sheets, seeking her most agreeable bedmate, but her quest was not rewarded. Laney rolled over and eyed the empty space beside her. Surely, she hadn't dreamt that night of incredible lovemaking. She put a hand to her throbbing head. Anything was possible in the islands, she thought, as her mushy brain scrambled to recall the events of the last twelve hours. Then another peal of laughter—this time definitely male—assailed her ears, and Laney scrambled out of bed and dashed to the perfectly appointed, en suite marble bath. The party was starting without her, and she didn't want to miss out on one moment.

Peering into the vanity mirror, she quickly assessed the damage. Her eyes were bloodshot, but nothing that a dose of Visine couldn't remedy. Otherwise, her night of indiscretion had left no telltale evidence of the debauched lifestyle upon which she'd embarked. Except for her swollen lips, that is. But hey, she thought, she'd have had to fork over eight hundred dollars to achieve the same effect with Botox.

Hastily, she applied eyeliner, a bit of bronzer, and some lip gloss. Then she finger-combed her hair, deciding that the disheveled look would be a good one, given her present circumstances. After donning a white, cotton lace cover-up and a pair of gold-colored sandals, she dashed down the stairs and then cut through the foyer, pausing for a second to eye the two pairs of men's shoes neatly aligned next to the doormat. What considerate houseguests, she thought, a small smile lighting up her face.

Laney followed her ears out onto the terrace. There, she found the threesome enjoying a simple breakfast of fresh fruit and tall glasses of orange juice. Kara, looking dewy as a rosebud, sat between muscle-bound Charles and the winsomely handsome waif, Trevor. The three had their heads together, and Laney felt like an intruder, but she gave herself a mental shove and sauntered toward them. "Hi, guys," she said. "What's happening?"

"Good morning, sleepyhead." Charles pivoted, holding his arms out to her. "Come to Papa, baby."

Laney ducked her head, but complied, flouncing herself down on the brawny specimen's lap. She was more straightlaced than either Kara or Becca, hadn't ever been married, although she'd shacked up with a couple of losers. Manners and good breeding were important in her book. But now, Laney threw caution to the wind. These were the islands, she told herself, and what happens in the islands, stays in the islands.

Charlie's arms encircled her narrow waist, and Laney molded herself against his broad chest. How nice it was to simply be a sexual being, she thought, knowing in her heart she would soon regret this momentary lapse yet incapable of preventing it.

Trevor rose from his perch and gyrated his heartbreakingly slender hips in a poor burlesque. "Hey there, girlfriend, how are *you* feeling this morning?" he sang to Kara.

Kara burst out laughing. Trevor looked like nothing more than a skinny and very comely Geisha.

Charles nuzzled Laney's neck, gently running a hand up and down her bare arm, and Laney felt as though she were about to purr. But in the next instant, her warm fuzzy feeling vanished when she realized something was amiss!

"Where is Becca?" She bolted upright, and the top of her head smacked into Charlie's chin. "Oh, my God, did we leave her in Holetown? With that... that guy?"

"What guy?" Charlie asked.

"She left of her own accord," Kara said, ignoring Charles. "Becca's a grown woman. We can't be expected to run roughshod over her if she doesn't want to cooperate."

"What the hell does that mean?" Laney disentangled herself from Charlie's embrace. "Are you telling me you just let her go?"

"What man?" Charlie asked. "Let her go where?"

"You didn't see him?" Laney asked. Charles shook his head.

"I think you're overreacting," Kara said. "Becca is a big girl."

"A really big girl," Charles added.

Laney spun around and cuffed him playfully, but there was steel in her voice when she cautioned, "Don't go there. She's a splendid girl, and we shouldn't have left her. Who knows? Perhaps the natives have formed a new secret cult or something."

"Not funny on so many levels," Charles confided grimly.

"I wasn't serious!" Laney peered up at him. "What do you mean?"

Trevor had stopped dancing, his expression somber. "I know nothing, but here's my take," he said as he reclaimed his chair. "Becca seems like a… a bigger-than-life kind of personality."

"Right you are," Kara said.

"And a heck of a girl…" Charlie added, eyeing Laney warily.

"True on both accounts," Laney agreed.

"But…"

"But what?" Laney asked.

Suddenly, Charles seemed unable to contain himself. He bounded out of his seat and began pacing. Laney came to stand before him, crossing her wraith-thin arms over her chest and stopping him in his tracks.

"What?" Kara asked, suddenly alarmed.

"It's the islands, for heaven's sake," Trevor said. "Rich girls from the states are fair game."

"Fair game?" Kara scoffed. "I think not. Besides, Becca isn't rich."

"Oh, yes, she is," Charles said. "In the eyes of many a local—someone who may have experienced racism and disenfranchisement—she is that very thing. Don't get me wrong. Barbados has made great strides leveling the playing field with equal opportunities for persons of all races, genders, and faiths. Slowly… very slowly, this island is working through its past. It's a lugubrious process and, for many, one which has not yielded parity fast enough. I'm afraid there are plenty of fellows who would see in Becca—a wealthy gal from the U.S. of A.—a ticket to a better life."

"He's absolutely right." Trevor agreed. "Which leads us to present circumstances. Your missing friend is a well-to-do and extremely vulnerable woman."

"Come on," Kara interjected. "We're talking Becca, here.

Vulnerable? She's a tough broad, and no one can take her seriously. What could possibly happen to her?"

"You know, darling," Charles said, in his crisp British-island accent. "For all your supposed sophistication, you're incredibly obtuse. Kidnappers, outlaws, ne'er-do-wells? I imagine they'd consider Becca—"

"An opportunity ripe for the plucking," Trevor interjected.

"Oh, my God," Laney exclaimed. "What are we going to do?"

～

Floyd had barely been able to mask his conflicting emotions when they'd stocked up on snacks and drinks at a convenience store and then taken a cab to the Miami Opa Locka Executive Airport. His nerves were raw; he was sleep-deprived and drunk. How had he once again avoided discovery and near-certain apprehension? He felt giddy when he bounded up the boarding ramp and into the compact aircraft. The universe had provided him with yet another escape route.

The Cessna 400 single-engine was a model of efficiency. With its six luxurious seats and ergonomic table-workstations, it was the perfect aircraft for short jaunts of five hours duration or less, and, as Buzz had determined, ideal for island-hopping.

Daniel settled into a seat just behind the cockpit, and Floyd selected one kitty-corner and a row back from his. "Not bad, huh?" Daniel pivoted to eye Floyd.

Floyd was giving Daniel a thumbs up by way of response when Buzz emerged from the cockpit.

"You're in luck—no customs, no flight plan. Gentlemen, we're all set to take off. You two all stowed?"

"Yes sir, captain," Daniel said.

"Good." Buzz eyed Floyd. "We'll land at Saidor first, which should take a little under an hour and a half flight time. You'll be first to go, Frank."

Floyd merely nodded, afraid that if he were to speak, his voice would crack.

"Cash up front, my man," Buzz said. "Not that I don't trust you, but we don't have a history like this big oaf and me." The pilot grinned at Daniel.

"Understood," Floyd rasped, digging his wallet from his back pocket. Carefully, he counted out the bills and then handed a thick wad to Buzz, never happier to say goodbye to so much cash.

Buzz palmed the stack of greenbacks and then turned to Daniel. "If you don't mind, I might hang with you for a day or two in Barbados. Maybe take a little rest and relaxation."

"Fine by me, Buzz," Daniel said. "In fact, why don't we just plan on you flying me back to Vero? That is if your schedule allows it."

Buzz nodded slowly, appearing to weigh the pros and cons of this proposition. "That should work," he said.

"Great!"

～

Kara, her pale skin slathered in sunscreen, reclined on the teak settee. "Do you want to go shopping in Bridgetown?" she asked, tossing her Blackberry aside.

Laney, looking sun-dazzled—her eyes unfocused as she drifted in the vanishing-edge pool—shook her head no.

"I'm not in the right frame of mind," she said. "I am *so* worried."

"I know. Me, too." Kara sighed. "I wish there were something we could do."

"Yeah. I feel utterly helpless."

"Me? I feel guilty. So involved with myself, how could I have let this happen?" Kara hugged her knees.

"Don't beat yourself—"

"Hey, girlfriends!"

At the sound of Becca's gruff voice, Laney's head shot up.

"Becca!" Kara jumped to her feet, gaping at the vision of her impish girlfriend returned and, seemingly, none the worse for wear. She leaped up off the settee and rushed to embrace her. "Where have you been?"

Laney paddled to the side of the pool. "Becca! What the hell?" she cried. "You should have called or texted. We were freaking out, figured the natives had abducted you."

Becca laughed, putting a hand to her mouth and affecting a remorseful demeanor, but Laney was not appeased.

"I'm serious!" She climbed out of the pool, all the while shooting daggers at her friend.

"Laney's right." Kara rocked back on her heels and crossed her arms before her. "We were worried sick. What the hell happened to you?"

"I'm serious, too," Becca said, giving Laney her undivided attention. "Because your suppositions weren't far from the truth."

Laney wrapped her arms about the unrepentant reprobate. Then she drew back, balled up her fist, and cuffed her lightly on the shoulder. "Spill, you little twerp."

Kara grabbed Becca's wrist and dragged her to the loggia, and Laney trailed after them. "That's right." Kara sat back down on the settee. "Come clean, and maybe we'll forgive you."

"What were you thinking?" Laney took a seat in a wrought iron patio chair. "We were beside ourselves."

"It's like this…." Becca flopped down next to Kara. "Would you believe it if I told you I hooked up with a wonderful man?"

Laney rolled her eyes, and Kara shook her head impatiently. "Do tell," she said, scowling at her impetuous friend.

"It's true," Becca said. "He seems completely gaga over me. And get a load of this. He's from one of the wealthiest families on the island."

"No way!" Laney cried, scooting her chair closer.

"You're pulling one over on us, right?" Kara asked.

Becca raised a palm. "Scout's honor. You should see his estate." She glanced around, grimacing. "I mean, it makes this place look like Holetown."

"I *do not* believe it," Laney exclaimed.

"Well, it's true. Anyway…" Becca looked smug, "let's just say that Rob Barrow and I *hit it off*."

Kara giggled. "You hussy."

"And who could blame me?" Becca retorted. "He's cute, a good dancer, wealthy, and not snobby in the least. The boy is beyond adorable. So sweet, I could eat him with a spoon."

"Uh-huh," Laney said. "And so loaded, it might as well be a silver one."

"Now, now. Pull in your claws." Becca pretended to scold. "I'll have you know I genuinely like this dude. He's not all snooty and full of himself. A real cutie. You'll see."

Kara shook her head in amazement and leaned back on the sofa. "Well, you deserve all of it," she said, beaming at her girlfriend.

"I'll second that," Laney agreed. "He's one lucky son of a gun."

"Yep. And we're all invited to the Barbados Yacht Club for lunch."

"What?" Kara unfolded her legs. "Impossible."

"Why do you say that?" Becca asked.

"Gauche American chicks don't just get invited to the Barbados Yacht Club. That place is a bastion of patrician, old-island money and tradition."

"Then they must have loosened their standards, for I can assure you, we're invited."

Laney squealed and scrambled out of her chair. "What time?"

"Rob is sending a car around for us at twelve-thirty."

Kara bolted, making a beeline to the house. "I need a shower!"

"Ditto that." Laney followed close on Kara's heels. "What does one wear to the Yacht Club?"

"How would I know?" Becca hurried after her friends. "Boating togs? Sperry Top-Siders?"

∾

The Barbados Yacht Club was an unpretentious looking, low-slung, sun-bleached structure, but the harbor beyond was magnificent—a silver-spangled expanse of blue where vessels of every size and complexion were moored. When the shiny Rolls Royce pulled up in front of the building, the girls tumbled out of the grand automobile only to come face-to-face with Charles and Trevor.

"Fancy meeting you here," Trevor quipped, stepping forward and taking Kara's hand.

Looking dumbfounded, Kara said, "I believe that's my line."

"Hello, beautiful," Charles beamed at Laney.

"Hello yourself." Laney knit her brows, fixing him with a puzzled expression.

In the meantime, Rob had bounded down the steps and come to stand beside Becca. "Surprise, darling." Obviously pleased with himself, he beamed at her.

"I'll say," Kara skewered Trever with a pointed look.

"What gives?" Laney asked Charles.

"It's like this," Charles rushed to explain, "no one mentioned the fact that you—" He broke off to eye Becca.

Trevor interrupted. "That *you* had hooked up with our old—"

"Really old," Charlie continued, "and illustrious school chum, Rob."

"How could you not have seen us at the club?" Becca asked. "We were on the dancefloor, not thirty feet away from you."

"*We* were dancing." Trevor fixed Kara with his dark, almond-shaped eyes. "Slow-dancing. Just getting acquainted." He turned back to Becca. "Sorry, Becca, but you were not on my radar."

"Same here," Charles said. "And I'm not ashamed to admit it: I had other things on my mind." He favored Laney with a wolf-like leer. "Who could blame me?"

～

They were seated at a round dining table next to a window from where they were afforded spectacular views of Port St. Charles. Another couple had joined them, elegantly trim, Jules, a fellow Codrington graduate, and his girlfriend, Sara, who, except for the fact that she was curvy in all the right places, could have been Trevor's twin. They were eight young people in high spirits enjoying their privilege and good looks, to say nothing of the gorgeous day that life had generously bestowed upon them.

"Now, let me get this straight," Jules said, eying Rob. "You and Becca hooked up at the Elbow Room?"

"Yes," Barrow admitted, casting an endearingly hangdog look in Becca's direction.

"Well, that's auspicious," Sara said, her charming accent clearly conveying otherwise.

"I realize you find it crass and common," Rob said. "But it was there, in those humble surroundings, that I found the woman of my dreams." He gazed adoringly at Becca, and she grinned back at him. Rob pivoted to glare at Sara. "So, don't go and spoil it, Miss Hoity-Toity!"

Kara and Laney could barely suppress giggles, while a chastened Sara smiled tightly.

"Lookin' for love in all the wrong places," Kara sang in a small voice.

"Hopin' to find a friend and a lover," Laney chimed in.

"I bless the day I discover…" Rob took up the refrain.

"And there you go," Trevor exclaimed. "Will wonders never cease?"

"But that doesn't let a certain someone off the hook." Charles looked to Trevor for support, a mischievous smirk on his face.

"Oh no." Trevor caught the ball and ran with it. "Our sweet little Becca was a very bad girl."

"Yes," Kara agreed, her brow lowering as she eyed her gal pal. "She put us through untold anguish."

"Pacing the floor, wringing hands." Laney emoted, clutching a fist to her chest. "Not knowing if she were dead or alive."

Becca's gravelly voice cut through the dramatics. "Don't lay it on too thick. I know y'all were too busy pursuing *other* ventures to worry about the likes of poor little ole me." She wrinkled her nose and squeezed Rob's hand. "So don't give me grief."

"Ha-ha," Jules laughed. "What an agreeable story."

"Yes," Rob said. "Let's toast." He raised his glass, and everyone followed suit. "To my American Beauty Rose. To Becca."

Kara and Laney looked at one another and grinned. Could life get any crazier?

CHAPTER EIGHT

MOORINGS

Andrea and Margaret were in the great room boxing up family treasures too dear to part with. "What about this?" Andrea asked, hefting a porcelain heron with bronze accents and stand.

Margaret looked at the piece and raised an eyebrow. "I don't know," she said. "Do you want it?"

"Mom, you can't just give *everything* to me."

"Why not? Your brothers won't want the froufrou stuff."

"Um, I suppose you're right. But we must be practical. Anything that you can part with—that might fetch a price—should be set aside for auction."

"Good plan," Margaret agreed. "Put it on the auction pile."

"Oh, my goodness," Andrea gasped, as Madison tottered into the room on heels too big for her feet. She was dressed in a dated, beaded evening gown and swathed in furs, a tiara of rhinestones crowning her head.

"How do I look, Nana?" Madison giggled.

"My God," Margaret gaped at her granddaughter. "You look like me, sweetheart. Sixty years ago."

"Madison, you're supposed to be helping," Andrea scolded.

"Let it go," Margaret said, shaking her head in Andrea's direction. "I think it's brilliant."

"What now?" Andrea rolled her eyes. "I swear, you two have some sort of silent form of communication I'm not privy to."

"We should play dress-up on the day of the sale," Margaret said. "We could even invite the guests to do the same."

Andrea considered. "Not a bad idea," she said. "People do tend to loosen up when they're in costume."

"And we want them *very* loose," Margaret added. "So much so that they clean out this old manse." She flung out her arms, beckoning for her granddaughter to fill them, "and have a good time doing so." She kissed the girl's forehead. "You're a genius, Maddy."

"Wow. This party is shaping up to be the event of the season," Andrea exclaimed.

~

Nathan McCourt's firm occupied the entire third floor of the handsome 3001 Building, a fact made possible by his long list of moneyed clients. The man who was currently beating a path across his fine silk carpet would be counted at the top of that list.

"So, Danny, how was Barbados?" Nathan asked, eyeing the man who was pacing before a plate-glass window. Blind to the spectacular view of the Atlantic the portal afforded. He appeared oblivious to everything but his insular bubble of misery.

"Great as always," Daniel said. "But, damn it, Nate, I need to finalize this divorce thing and move on."

Silently, Nathan agreed with Daniel. Unfortunately, his friend's assets were proving a hindrance to the dissolution of his marriage.

"I've conceded on every point, agreed to all of Kara's ridiculous terms. Hell, it's not like she gave me an heir. I had a couple of great years with her. And then I married her, and that was the end of that. Now she's out for blood."

"That about sums it up." Nathan ran his fingers through a thick head of hair that was just beginning to gray at the temples. "I've seen it before. She's feeling regretful, wanting to get back to that safe place where she was before… with you and your millions. But you're not having any part of it, and she's striking back at you, her motive: to wound."

Daniel balled up a fist and socked it into his open palm. "It's working." Then the fight seemed to go out of him, and he slumped into a leather guest chair.

"Let's head over to Bobby's Bar and have a few drinks," Nate suggested. "Get shit-faced like we used to. See if you can score a sweet young thing to take your mind off your troubles."

Daniel stopped kneading his temples to gawk at McCourt. "Are you nuts? Isn't that how I ended up here in the first place?"

Nathan reflected on his friend's words. "Yeah. I guess you're right. So, what do we do?"

"That's what I was asking you, counselor."

"I'm not your consigliere, Danny."

"Passed the bar—"

"And chose not to practice," Nathan said.

"Because…"

"Because, as I'm sure you'll recall, there were delicate matters that needed to be dealt with when your dad purchased all that land on the lagoon for the River Mews project. Mixing it up with the Philadelphia mafia… Bring back any memories?"

"I know you've got my back, Nate. It's just so damn frustrating—"

"Danny, Danny…" Now it was McCourt's turn to pace. Suddenly, he was plagued by guilt. He should have anticipated this, done something to prevent the disastrous union that had begun to fall apart the moment it was finalized. Hadn't Kara come on to him—Daniel's best man—on her wedding day? Sure, they'd all had way too much to drink, partying into the wee hours. Still, the woman was much too pretty and too cunning for her own good. Nate loved Dan like a brother, would take a bullet for the guy who'd changed his life and fortune. But Danny had really screwed up with Kara. She was smart and wouldn't go quietly into the night without a messy, knock-down-drag-out. Nathan was afraid Danny was going to pay dearly for thinking with his—

"Argh!" Daniel's snarl interrupted Nathan's musings. "Okay, Nate."

"Okay, what?"

"Let's go get shit-faced," Daniel said.

"Attaboy."

∼

A mere three days had passed since Floyd had gone on the lam. In that time, he'd experienced a lifetime of change. Now, clad only in a sweat-stained tee and khaki shorts, he was relaxing on his tiny balcony and feeling every bit the master of his universe. He mopped his face with a handkerchief, willing himself to chill, and thought about Florida's heat as compared to that of Santo Domingo. Whew! Vero could be steamy at times, but this place was like a Turkish bath. He consoled himself with the fact that the sun was now low in the sky. Soon, the night breezes would cool things down, and he'd venture out to wander the narrow streets on the hunt for a tasty meal.

Floyd gazed down upon the warren of alleyways and crumbling buildings abutting his newfound pied-à-terre. It was a far cry from his posh riverfront estate in Vero, and yet he was content. From this vantage point, he could glimpse an upper turret of the Catedral Primada de las América, which was the heart of the colonial city. Floyd drank deeply from his glass of Mamajuana—an improbable concoction of roots and twigs steeped in honey, wine, and spices. His plan had been to lose himself in some obscure village where he would simply vanish. But in the short time he'd been here, he'd fallen under Santo Domingo's spell. It was only yesterday, his second day in the country, that he'd stumbled upon this walk-up apartment for rent, and after a quick look around, signed a lease.

It was strange, but he felt as though he belonged here. This historic city was alive with culture and music, and he had more than enough cash to live out his days in comfort. His Spanish was passable —good enough to make himself understood. It'd been dicey for a while. But now, he dared to believe he'd gotten away with it! Oh, he suffered twinges of guilt. Not over Marcie. God, no. The kids were another matter. Sometimes he felt despondent for having abandoned them, but he consoled himself with the fact that it was better for him to have disappeared than for them to suffer the humiliation and embarrassment of a deadbeat father languishing behind bars. It had, he decided, all worked out for the best.

Peeking out from behind wooden blinds in a flat across the way, a pair of binoculars was trained on the flabby, balding man who was prematurely celebrating his escape.

~

Andrea's cell vibrated, and she tapped the phone icon to accept the call. Smiling at the sound of Daniel's hello, she said, "Welcome back, stranger. What can I do for you?"

"Plenty."

"Well, that's good, I guess." Andrea glanced at the cell's display. It was after seven. Why was her client calling after hours?

"No. It's most unsatisfactory. I'm starving and alone."

"Go eat," Andrea commanded.

"Not without a dinner partner. Besides, I have something to confess."

Andrea grinned. "Not hearing confessions, Danny," she said in her best brogue.

"Thank goodness. Don't want to give one. Want you."

"What?" Had she heard correctly? Andrea cradled the phone to her ear.

"I know you think I'm self-absorbed, that I'm some jerk who doesn't care about anyone but himself."

"I don't think any such thing," Andrea assured him.

"What a relief. Then come join me for dinner. Won't you?"

"I already ate."

"Ate what?"

"A salad."

"Ah, a cheap date. All the better."

"I'm in my pajamas."

"Fabulous. Don't bother changing. I'm sure you look fetching in your PJs."

"Daniel. What am I to do with you?"

"Please, won't you find something? Anything. Better yet, let's eat."

"I *am* hungry," Andrea admitted. "Honestly, I'm always hungry. I just don't eat much."

"Why the hell not?"

"Don't know." Andrea considered. "Too busy. My stomach's in knots most of the time, what with this damned recession."

"We're going to have to do something about that, pronto."

"Oh, yeah?"

"Get dressed. Although the thought of you in jammies will keep me awake for untold nights. I'm on my way."

"Yikes," Andrea squealed. "Okay. Hanging up now." She tossed her phone onto the coffee table. What was the man up to? And what could he possibly have to confess? She didn't care. She wanted to see him, wanted to be meeting him on a personal rather than a professional basis. Andrea snatched her cellphone back up and keyed in her mother's number.

"Hey there, sweetie?" As always, Margaret's honeyed drawl calmed her.

"Mom, I know it's late, but could you please come and stay with Maddy?"

"Sure. Did something come up?"

"Mm-hmm." Andrea dragged a palm across her face. It was impossible to keep anything from her mom. "Nothing to worry about, though."

"Okay?"

"If you must know, Miss Nosey, Daniel asked me to dinner."

"I'll be there in a flash. Get dolled up, doll."

"Love you, Mom."

"Back at you, baby girl."

～

When the doorbell rang, Andrea was ready. Margaret was in the wings, watching with bated breath, and Maddy was sound asleep and oblivious.

"Go." Margaret gave her a shove.

"Shh, Mom! I'm going." Andrea motioned her mother away. "Get back." She didn't open the door until Margaret was obscured in darkness, and when she did, Daniel's good looks nearly bowled her over. It was as though she were seeing him for the first time. He was so tall and well-built, with those crystalline blue eyes and that jutting jaw that kept him from being downright pretty.

"Hi," Daniel said, thrusting a bouquet of sweetheart roses toward her.

"How did you know? I adore roses." Andrea accepted the flowers, at the same time fixing Daniel with a radiant smile. "Here," she said, back-stepping and handing the flowers off to her mother. "Now, go away," she hissed, angling her head toward the woman concealed in shadows.

"What's going on?" Daniel asked, looking confused. Only then did he discern the figure lurking in the hallway. "Hello?"

Margaret stepped toward him and into the light. "Good evening," she said, holding out her free hand. "I'm Margaret, Andrea's mother." The two shook hands. "I'm meant to be invisible," Margaret explained, a droll smile tugging at her lips.

"Didn't do a very good job of it, Mom," Andrea muttered. Then, in a brighter tone, "Allow me to introduce Daniel Armstrong. Daniel, Margaret Sheridan, aka Mom."

"My goodness." Daniel appeared momentarily flummoxed. "Mrs. Sheridan, it's… it's… What I mean is I am very pleased to meet you, ma'am. I see where your daughter gets her good looks."

"Oh, you're good, Daniel." Margaret made a shooing motion. "Now, get out of here, you two. Have fun. I'll keep the home fires burning."

Andrea didn't need any more encouragement. She grabbed Daniel's arm and pushed ahead of him. "Let's go eat. Suddenly, I'm ravenous!"

~

"Where to, madam?" Daniel asked once they were seated in his automobile. "What's your pleasure?"

"Would you feel emasculated if I said tonight's on me?" Before Daniel had time to reply, she'd placed a palm lightly over his mouth. "Let me explain."

"Bmm woff!" Daniel mumbled.

"Just nod your head." Daniel followed her orders. "It's like this: You're my client. I owe you a great big, honking super night out on my stomping grounds. And tonight's the night." Andrea stared hard at him. "You okay with that?"

"Mmff!" Daniel nodded his head.

"Okay." Andrea removed her hand from Daniel's mouth. "Sorry for that. Just wanted to lay the ground rules."

They wended past the Indian River Lagoon—now streaked in

fiery shades of red and gold—abutting an emerald-green golf course punctuated by towering palms. "Pretty, isn't it?" Andrea asked.

"I'll say," Daniel said. "Shall I turn in here?" he asked as an imposing clubhouse, set upon a rise, came into view.

"No, keep going," Andrea instructed, and Daniel navigated around the massive columned structure. "There, to the left. Pull up there," Andrea commanded. "Yes, right under the lights."

"Your wish is my command."

"Careful, big guy," Andrea admonished. "I could get used to that."

"Where are we?" Daniel eyed the mercury vapor lights overhead, the white fencing that told him they were on the outside looking in.

"We're at the backside of the Moorings Country Club. It's where the regulars park. I know it's not grand and pretentious. But we can walk, and we certainly don't need to pay a valet to park your car. This way, the Moorings can creep up on you, all unsuspecting."

"You're in charge."

Andrea led Daniel up the path, through the gate, and onto the enormous pool deck. To the right of the pool, a three-piece combo was doing a decent job of evoking the islands with Jack Johnson tunes. Children frolicked in the water or played ping-pong at tables set up on the west end of the deck.

"This is great," Daniel said. "I wanna play ping-pong with the kids."

"Maybe later." Andrea gripped his arm and steered him toward the Dockside Grille. "Let's go upstairs." She sailed past the inviting bar where patrons were lined up, chatting with one another and enjoying pre-dinner drinks. "I made reservations for the River Room."

"It looks fun down here."

"It is. And if you're good, we can come back down after dinner, and you can help yourself to a frozen treat from the cooler." Andrea pointed to a glass-fronted freezer tucked back into a corner where a variety of frozen confections were displayed.

"Yay! I like this place."

"I thought you would. Your client should probably join, become a member." Andrea led the way up the back staircase to the upper dining rooms. "This is a wonderful club. Great people, fabulous amenities, no pretentiousness." She stopped in front of a podium, which was, at the moment, unmanned.

"Beautiful room." Daniel's eyes darted about the sumptuously appointed space with its oversized chandeliers, magnificent millwork, and floor-to-ceiling windows affording sweeping views of the glimmering river basin beyond.

"Oh, ho! Look who we have here!" A sophisticated-looking, dark-haired man approached, his arms outstretched.

"Craig," Andrea cried. "How delightful to see you."

"That's my line, Andy." The handsome fellow embraced her lightly.

The moment she was released, Andrea gestured toward her companion. "Craig, I'd like you to meet my client, Daniel Armstrong. Daniel, Craig Lopes, the man who manages this club to such perfection." The two men shook hands.

"You flatter me." Craig winked at Andrea, and then he turned to Daniel. "So, what brings you to our fair city, Daniel?"

"I'm looking at property."

"You found the best realtor to help you in that regard. And I'm hoping you'll decide a club membership is in your future."

"I have to say, I am very impressed with what I've seen thus far."

"You're in luck." Craig crooked a finger, summoning a hostess. "I believe we have a table by the window for you two." He turned to the young woman who now stood before him. "Ami, show our guests to table seven." The young woman nodded and led the way.

"Thanks, Craig," Andrea called, as she followed the waitress to their table.

"Bon appetite, folks."

∾

"I can't believe we've been here four days already," Laney said. "Before you know it, we'll be flying back to reality."

Clad in brightly patterned, cotton sundresses, the girls sat around the kitchen table. They were drinking mojitos and noshing on all the detritus the fridge had to offer—fruit, cheese, doggie bag contents. "Did I ever tell you how grateful I am to count you," she looked first at Kara and then in Becca's direction, "as my greatest gal pals in the universe?"

"Don't think that you did," Kara said, "but duly noted."

"Back at you, Laney," Becca quipped.

"Kara, I want to thank you for making this…" Laney gestured vaguely about, "this wonderful getaway possible."

"Me, too," Becca said. "It's been like a dream…"

"Ha!" Kara chuckled. "A dream at Sweet Dreamer."

"Well, it has," Becca said. "I not only got my groove back, but I also found Rob."

"You got lucky, alright," Laney agreed. "We all did."

"How can I ever thank you?" Becca asked. "You booked the flight and paid for it. You provided the spectacular digs—"

"Ah!" with a curt flick of her wrist, Kara spoke over her friend. "You'd do the same for me."

"Yes, but…"

"Buy me a dinner or two."

Laney and Becca nodded to one another. "You got it," Laney said. Just then, the doorbell rang, and the women erupted in shrieks. "Who could it be?" Laney asked.

"At this hour? I haven't the foggiest," Kara said.

"Well, hell, let's go find out." Becca beat a path to the door.

"Wait a minute," Kara commanded, in a vain attempt to forestall the irrepressible Becca. "We'd better think about this."

"For heaven's sake, come on." Becca pushed past her girlfriend and levered the front door open. "See, it's just…"

And there, standing before them, were three very attractive, very well-dressed chaps. "It's just little old us," the tallest and bulkiest of the three announced in a lilting British accent.

The girls screamed by way of answer. "Oh, my God," Laney cried. "Who *are* you guys?"

"We're not ax murderers, I can assure you," the slender man with the elegant mustache said, backing off a bit.

"Actually," the fair-haired one added, "we're your neighbors." He hitched his head up, indicating the hill beyond, and the three women looked at one another, wide-eyed as the lightbulbs in their brains came on.

"Oh," Kara said, "you're the fellows—"

"That's right." The gorgeous Black gent fixed her with a brilliant Hollywood smile. "We're neighbors." And then he did a girly pantomime of Becca shimmying.

"Oh, jeez," Becca cried. "It *is* you."

"That would be an affirmative, ma'am." He gave her the once-over, his gaze lingering on her generous bosom.

"Well, come on in." Kara gestured for the men to enter.

They sat in the living room, drinks in hand, grinning at one another. "This is *so* bizarre," Becca said.

"Stranger than fiction." The large man raised his glass.

"So, what's your name, big fellow?" They touched glasses.

"I'm afraid that's an international secret."

"We'll get it out of you." Becca narrowed her eyes. "One way or another."

"That's right," Kara said. "We have our methods."

He raised his palms. "Chichester. Michael Chichester," he said, his eyes twinkling.

"Chichester as in… books?" Laney asked.

"One and the same. My family happens to be in the publishing business."

"I'll say." Kara gazed at him with renewed interest.

"And you?" Becca demanded of the buff Black man. "Your name and your relationship to old Chichester here?"

"Ahem… The name's Kent. Jamal Kent. Michael and I graduated the same class at Eton and then we roomed together at Oxford. He's like a brother to me."

"I can see the family resemblance," Laney smirked. "Not."

"And you, Mr. Mustaches?" Kara demanded.

"Me?" The slender gent feigned a look of chagrin. "I'm a nobody, a poor relation."

"I'll bet." Becca snickered. "Tell me another."

"This homely bloke is Neville Lansdown," Chichester interjected. "We drag him along with us because—"

"Because I'm a chick magnet!" Neville waggled his bushy eyebrows.

"Aha. I see it works," Becca said.

"And what of you three winsome lasses? Your names and stories, please?" Chichester demanded.

"I'm Kara Armstrong." The blonde tossed a bejeweled hand in the air. "This is my place, and these are my BFFs."

"Becca, here, hailing from Philly." The chubby young woman feigned a sheepish look. "Alas, just a working gal."

"As am I," Laney said. "We three started out together as pharmaceutical reps in Philadelphia. That's how we got to know one another."

"But Kara bailed," Becca said, "to live the high life."

"Leaving the two of us at loose ends," Laney added.

"Which is why I fly them out here from time to time," Kara explained, "for girl time."

"Not bad," Jamal said. "Can't beat the location."

"I have a question," Laney said. "To whom do the kids belong?"

"My boys, my house," Michael admitted.

"And their mother?" Becca pried.

"We're divorced."

"As am I," Jamal said.

The girls stared hard at Neville, and he put his hands in the air. "Never married."

"Why the heck not?" Becca blurted.

"None of our business, Becca," Laney said.

"I, myself, am in the middle of a nasty divorce," Kara jumped in to smooth over this rough spot. "And I'll tell you, it's enough to make a girl go off men altogether."

"I hear you, but please don't." Michael's eyes fastened on the blonde, and his meaning was clear.

"I'm in Neville's boat," Laney said. "Never married."

"Divorced," Becca admitted. "But ready to get back in the saddle again."

The men guffawed at Becca's boldness while Laney and Kara exchanged pained expressions.

"So, when can we see your place?" Becca asked.

"Becca!" Kara remonstrated.

"No, that's quite all right," Michael soothed. "How about tomorrow? Six o'clock? Cocktails?"

Laney and Becca turned to Kara. "That would be great," she said. "But I have to warn you. Tomorrow, we have reservations at The Cliff for eight o'clock."

"Ah, I love that place," Jamal said.

"Yes, fabulous." Neville agreed. "We know the chef. The food is out of this world."

"To say nothing of the view. Would it be presumptuous if I asked if we could join you?" Michael asked.

Kara glanced at her girlfriends for confirmation, but rather than venture an opinion, they merely shrugged. "Not at all," she finally said, pivoting back to Michael. "But I believe Becca has invited a guest."

"Yeah, my new squeeze," Becca said, her face reddening.

"Becca, you're blushing!" Kara exclaimed.

"Will wonders never cease?" Laney asked.

"You guys!" Becca bounded out of her chair. "Who needs a refill?"

"It's settled, then." Michael held up his glass, and Becca topped it off. "I'll ring up and change your reservation to a table for seven. How does that suit you?"

Laney grinned at Jamal. "What fun," she said. But when his dark eyes latched onto hers, her smile faltered, and she felt a sudden fluttering in her chest.

CHAPTER NINE

CLIFF HANGER

Daniel pulled up next to Margaret's Volvo and killed the ignition. "Thank you so much for a terrific evening." He unbuckled his seat belt. "I can't think when the last time was that someone treated *me*. I could get used to this kind of thing, lady."

"It was my pleasure," Andrea said. "I figured it was time you were introduced to the Moorings. It's a delightful, welcoming club."

"Yes, and the food was excellent." In the next moment, Daniel assumed an aggrieved expression. "Unfortunately, now, I'll… that is to say, my *client*… will have to buy a big freakin' boat."

"I'm sure he can afford it."

Daniel leaned over and casually draped an arm around Andrea's shoulder. "Come here, woman," he said, gently drawing her to him.

Andrea gave herself over to his kiss. "Umm," she murmured when, at last, she released him. "You, sir, are a very good kisser."

"Perhaps because you're so kissable," Daniel said. "Now, I suppose you want to relieve Margaret and send me packing."

"Yes." Andrea levered the passenger door open. "I mean no! Mom is a lifesaver. This single mother doesn't know what she'd do without her. Honestly, that woman would drop anything to help me out. I simply don't want to take advantage."

"You're lucky to have her. But must we call an end to the night so soon?" Daniel bounded out of the car and came to stand beside the passenger door just in time to help her out of the car.

"Let's not." Andrea hiked to the front entrance, motioning for him to follow. "How about a nightcap?"

"I thought you'd never ask."

"Hi, Mom," Andrea called as she let herself in. "We're back."

"Hey, honey." Margaret rounded the corner. "I thought I heard a car." She smiled in Daniel's direction. "Hello, Daniel. How was your evening?"

"Fabulous," Daniel said. "Thanks for letting me spirit the girl away."

"Anytime." Margaret collected her handbag from the hall chest. "I'll see myself out. It was nice meeting you, Daniel."

"What's your pleasure?" Andrea asked when they were alone. "I have just about anything you could wish for."

"I believe that." Daniel gazed at her, his eyes shining.

"To drink, I mean." Andrea crossed to the bar cabinet.

"Hey, let me do that. It's the least I can do."

"Sure. Go for it. I'll just check up on Maddy, maybe powder my nose."

"Your nose is perfect," Daniel said, his back to her. He withdrew two glasses from the glass shelf and placed them on the counter.

"Maybe I'll pee then," Andrea muttered under her breath.

Intent on the contents of the bar cabinet, Daniel gave a backhanded wave of dismissal.

When Andrea returned, Daniel was nowhere to be found, and a bubble of fear rose in her throat.

I knew it was too good to be true.

"Where are you?" she called softly.

"Out here." His voice came to her from the back, and she breathed a sigh of relief.

"On the pool deck."

"Hey." She opened the French door and peered blindly out into the darkness.

A match was struck, and in the next moment, a candle glowed. "Here I am. Your view of the river is amazing, by the way."

Andrea carefully picked her way toward Daniel. It took a minute for her eyes to adjust, to see the demarcation between land and sea, the faint pricks of light piercing the black sky, and the amorphous form in the chaise lounge. "I know. Location, location. That's what they teach us at Bert Rogers Real Estate School."

"I'm sure you were at the top of your class."

Andrea seated herself next to Daniel. "Actually, no. I'm lousy at math. I have to employ a minion to write up the contracts. Oops!" She clapped a hand to her mouth. "Shouldn't have divulged that."

"Love that you did. I want to know your warts and wrinkles."

"No, you don't. Really."

Daniel extended an arm out toward her, and Andrea clasped his hand. "You are an amazing woman."

"True on so many levels."

"Here, try this." Daniel withdrew his hand from hers and replaced it with a squat glass.

Andrea took the proffered cocktail and put a nose to the concoction. "What *is* it?"

"A magic potion."

"Oh, great. Cast a spell on me, would you?" Andrea took a tentative sip and then smacked her lips. "Um. Wow!" she exclaimed. "This *is* good."

"Yep. Thought you'd enjoy it."

"And what elixir are you plying me with, sir?"

"A rusty nail."

"Doesn't sound very romantic. But, gosh, it's delicious!"

"Drambuie and scotch on ice. What's not to like?"

"Mommy?" A small voice came from the open doorway.

"Uh-oh." Andrea placed her drink on the side table. "What's up, sweetie?"

Maddy ambled toward her. "Hi, Mom," she said, lowering herself to the chaise lounge and perching beside her mother. "Hi, Daniel!"

"Hey, Madison."

"Are you okay, kiddo?" Andrea asked.

"Yeah. I couldn't sleep."

"Well, let's get you some milk. Say goodnight to Daniel, baby. And then it's back to bed with you."

"Night, Daniel. Hope we can have dinner again sometime."

"Me, too, Madison."

Andrea arose from the chaise lounge and wrapped an arm about her daughter's narrow shoulders. "I'll just be a minute."

When she returned, Daniel was stretched out on the chaise, eyes closed, snoring softly.

Andrea bent over him, savoring this opportunity for her eyes to linger on his features. He was so good-looking—with his aquiline nose and prominent jawline. But in sleep, he looked like a boy, guileless and vulnerable, a lock of hair tumbling over his brow. She imagined him as a rosy-cheeked boy, how adorable he must have been, and she yearned to brush that wayward lock away from his face and to kiss his sensuously parted lips. "Daniel," she whispered, gently shaking his shoulder, "wake up."

It was no use. He was out cold. "Mm," he muttered, tossing onto his side.

Oh, dear! What now?

"Daniel," Andrea shook him more vigorously, but to no avail. He merely curled into a ball and snored all the louder.

Damn. This complicates things.

"Oh, bother," Andrea muttered, as she went to unearth a comforter.

~

"Wow, look at that." Kara stared out over the precipice at her own property. Sweet Dreamer was situated at least three hundred feet below the wall that delineated Michael's lot line. She turned to her friends, a look of astonishment on her face. "We might as well have been under the microscope!"

"Were. They've got a bird's-eye view, alright." Becca said. "So much for privacy."

"I'll say," Laney added. "Who knew?"

"Hallo!" Jamal bustled from the house. "Drinks are served, ladies!"

"Jamal, you never told us how… exposed we were," Laney chided good-naturedly.

"Honestly, I've only been here twice before, and believe me; there wasn't much to look at on those occasions. But this time…" Neville grinned wickedly. "Well, that's another story."

"We've quite enjoyed the distraction." Michael sidled up next to Kara.

"Is that so?" Kara asked. "And here I was thinking we were always under the radar in this little enclave."

"It *is* a private development, but my parcel features a spectacular view." His eyes roved from her head to her toes before taking hold of her elbow. "Come sit down, won't you?" He hitched his chin toward the palatial house. "We've mojitos and wine inside, whatever's your pleasure."

Jamal lightly pressed a palm against Laney's back and escorted her to the side door, and the others followed behind them.

"Ladies." Neville darted out of the kitchen, a small silver tray in hand. "Sweets for the sweet." He placed the tray of hors d' oeuvres on a cocktail table and indicated that the girls should sit.

Becca flounced down on a sofa and promptly leaned forward, eyeing the snacks. "What have we here? Honest to goodness cucumber sandwiches?" She popped a canape into her mouth. "Umm! I can't believe it," she marveled. "They're scrumptious."

"So," Laney ventured, casting a sidelong glance at Jamal, "look at us, only now getting to know one another, and tomorrow we're leaving."

"Parting is such sweet sorrow." Jamal favored her with a regretful smile.

"Not to worry." Kara said, "We'll be back before you know it." Her eyes fell on the hardcover conspicuously placed on the side table between them. "And what's this? *The Girl with the Dragon Tattoo?*" She snatched up the book, flipped it over, and scanned the back cover.

"Have you read it?" Michael asked. "It was just released, and it's already causing quite a sensation in the publishing world."

"Can't say that I have," Kara admitted.

"Please, take it. It's fantastic. We'll do a book review when you return."

"You're on."

"Mind you, I'm keeping you to it."

"And I'll honor my part of the bargain."

"Oh, my goodness," Becca exclaimed when her eyes fell on her cellphone display. "It's already seven-thirty. We need to fly if we're going to make our reservation."

"You just can't wait to see Rob," Kara said.

"That would be an affirmative!"

∾

Eager for their final island adventure, the girls tumbled out of the Range Rover and stared at the imposing structure situated at the water's edge. "Oh, my God, Kara, I forgot how gorgeous this place is." Laney's eyes gleamed as she took in the magnificent, multi-terraced restaurant hugging the Bridgetown cove.

"No kidding. It's a bit over the top," Kara agreed, linking arms with Michael. "Lead on MacDuff," she said. "It's your party now."

"And we shall make the most of it," Michael said. "I'll just find our host…"

But in the next moment, a compact fellow with a head of dark curls presented himself. "Hello, Michael," he bellowed in an accent that screamed Liverpool.

The two man-hugged briefly. When they broke apart, Michael turned to the others. "Everyone, this is Paul Townsend, chef extraordinaire. He's the reason this joint has been named one of the fifty finest restaurants in the world.

Townsend brushed off the compliment. "We do our best."

"May I present Madames Kara, Laney, and Becca." Michael indicated the women.

"Some place you got here, Paul," Becca said, wrinkling her nose.

Kara and Laney smiled and nodded in agreement.

"And you may remember my mates, Neville and Jamal," Michael said.

"We chartered the fishing boat," Jamal added. "The Miss Barbie?"

"You hooked that enormous swordfish," Neville prompted.

"Ah, yes. That was years ago." Paul nodded. "Nice to see you blokes again. Now, follow me. We have a special table below reserved just for you."

"This is so amazing," Laney said in a stage whisper. "I feel as though I've been transformed to another realm."

"It's like a rom-com movie," Becca agreed.

They were led to the most desired and sought-after table on the lowest terrace, one nestled in a shallow manmade cove that afforded privacy. The only light source was from two medieval-looking metal torches that cast a faintly glimmering illumination on the murky waves lapping at the shoreline.

"Voila, my friends," Paul said, breaking the silence.

Neville whistled, and Jamal sucked in his breath.

"I feel like a pirate," Becca growled, "come to retrieve my booty."

Suddenly, the sheltered space was awash in pinpricks of light that glimmered from thousands of electric fairy lights, only to reveal two unexpected guests. "You already got the booty, babe," Rob exclaimed, grinning widely. "It's the thing I love most about you—"

"We all love about you," Charles interjected, shooting eyes at Laney.

"So true," Trevor added, slipping beside Kara.

"Rob," Becca squealed, rushing to him.

"Baby," Rob held out his arms, and she fell into them. "This," he said, indicating the romantic setting, "is for you."

At that precise moment, a jazz trio filled the empty night with a lazy melody. "Am I good or what?" Rob turned back to Becca.

"You're pretty damned good, mister, but what about your two sidekicks? I mean…"

Chef Paul clapped his hands, and soon the entire party was joining in the applause. "Cheers," Michael said, once more linking arms with Kara, at the same time skewering Trevor with a withering glare.

~

"What the hell was that all about?" Laney watched as Kara shimmied out of her sparkly sequined sheath. "I am *so* confused. Do you have the hots for Trevor or are your sights set on Michael? I was beginning to fall for Charles, but now that dishy Jamal is sending me vibes too intense to be ignored."

Kara crooned her kitten purr while slipping into her silk chemise. "Silly girl," she chastened. "Don't you know what Charles and Trevor are?"

"Rich, gorgeous, intelligent—"

"Gigolos!"

"What?" Laney reeled. "Are you telling me—"

"I'm telling you those preppy island guys are for hire." Kara skewered Laney with a look of concern.

"But then why—"

"Why the hell not? It's fun, a guiltless fling with no strings attached. I don't know about you, but I enjoy being on a handsome fellow's arm."

"Shit!" Laney breathed in an uncharacteristic fit of anger. "I am such an idiot! What was I thinking?"

"Huh?"

"I was starting to feel an attachment." Laney shook her head, mortified at her naiveté. "As though something could actually come of it… a relationship."

"I'm sorry, Laney." Kara loosely draped an arm around her friend. "I should have warned you off. Believe me, what you had with Charles was no relationship. When we're gone, he'll be off on his next conquest. As will my darling Trevor."

"I need a drink," Laney said.

"Come on, then." Kara steered Laney out into the hall and down the stairs to her well-stocked bar. "I'm buying."

Drinks in hand, they sat on the deck, staring blindly out over the yard and murky jungle beyond. But all they could discern in the enveloping darkness was a star-studded sky and the few lights that spilled from windows in neighboring estates. Kara peered up at Michael's estate, but there was no life to be seen there at this late hour. Laney followed her gaze. "They've probably stopped for a nightcap at Holetown," Kara said.

"Yeah. Who could blame them?" Laney agreed. "But explain something to me, will you?"

"Sure." Kara put her glass down and drew her knees to her chest.

"Why would a pair of handsome, entitled preps stoop so low as to pursue lonely females in hopes of financial compensation? Surely Trevor and Charles don't need the money."

"Laney, Laney," Kara clucked, "you are so gullible. They're looking for their one-way ticket out of here."

"What do you mean?"

"Girl, as lovely as it is—as fabulous a holiday destination—Barbados is still a small island with limited opportunities. Despite the airs our friends, Trevor and Charles put on, they, too, want to break out of here, preferably on the arm of some attractive heiress. If matrimony is in the picture—paving the way for US citizenship—so much the better. It's one step removed from the scenario they were touting about Becca's possible abduction, and…" She looked skyward, mulling her words before turning back to her friend. "Unfortunately, the same thing is true of those two."

Laney took a minute to process. "Ah," she finally said, looking chagrined. "I get it. Foolish me."

"Beautiful, normal you." Kara patted Laney's hand. "Don't beat yourself up. Charles and Trevor are nice guys with a lot to offer, but you can't let yourself be taken in by their considerable charms. I truly believe they genuinely like us. But you mustn't ever forget; they have ulterior motives." She grasped Laney's arm. "Enough of that."

Kara rose, unsteadily, to her feet. "We leave at seven tomorrow morning. Best get your beauty sleep, girlfriend."

Laney clutched Kara's hand in hers. "You are my bestie gal pal! Thank you so much for letting me tag along on this wonderful jaunt."

"Are you kidding me?" Kara dragged Laney to her feet. "We're the three Rx-keteers!"

"Really?" Laney scoffed, woozily. "Where's Becca, huh?"

Kara stumbled up the stairway with a suddenly recalcitrant Laney in tow. "Exactly where she should be, with her soon-to-be husband, the incredibly wealthy Rob Barrow."

"We shoul all be shho lucky," Laney slurred.

"I once was," Kara murmured.

"Wha?"

"Nothing." Kara flicked on the light switch and deposited Laney in her sumptuous guest suite. "To bed with you. Big day tomorrow."

~

A rapping on the door pried Floyd from his sleep. Who could be calling at four in the morning? "Damn," he muttered, throwing off his bed linens and lurching toward the front door.

"Mr. Heller," a male voice growled.

Floyd came to his senses. Who *could* be calling at this ungodly hour? "Be right there," he gasped, while madly dashing about collecting his shower kit, the small bag he'd kept packed and at the ready—one that contained his passport and a change of clothing— and an unassuming duffle stuffed with his illicitly acquired cash. Then, possessions in hand, he dangled a white, hairy leg out of his teensy bathroom window, searching for purchase on the slanting rooftop.

Good God, this was scary!

The lights of Santo Domingo momentarily dazzled him. The cathedral was lit up like a Christmas tree. Such a pretty place. He'd always thought Vero was perfection. But here was a more authentic beauty. Neither contrived or perfectly landscaped, Santo Domingo throbbed with red-hot life and was richly imbued with history. Then and there, Floyd vowed to return to Santo Domingo, to become part of this community and to do whatever he could to make amends for his misdeeds.

Floyd skittered down the rooftop like a novice skateboarder, arms alternately flung wide and then lowered and hovering over the tiled rooftop with fingers splayed.

Am I really doing this? It's a James Bond movie!

Before he could reconsider, he was over the eave and plummeting. He landed in an open dumpster brimming with garbage and was, ignobly, branded with the telltale odor of rotting organic material. Still, he hadn't broken any bones. So, he counted his lucky stars, crawled out of the malodorous bin, and hightailed it out of there as fast as his squat legs would carry him.

Floyd's worst nightmare was finally coming true; he was a fugitive.

~

It was a balmy, cloudless day, perfect weather for the Farmer's Market. Humiston Park was inundated with both locals and tourists alike, and all the vendor booths were thronged with eager customers. Oceanside, the playground was crawling with tykes. They were swinging on old-fashioned swings, climbing the jungle gym, and just being kids—unplugged, in the moment, and without the distraction of handheld devices. Garrett would have liked to join them. How wonderfully freeing to be pumping his legs, flying ever higher on a swing! Instead, he sat on his usual park bench, pretending to concentrate on his iPhone. All the while, he was casting surreptitious glances at the pretty brunette working the produce stand across the way. "Damn it," Garrett breathed. "Man up. Go talk to her."

Yeah, but what about her old man? His inner voice goaded. *That dude is seriously over-protective.*

Garrett pocketed his cellphone and rose from the park bench. He was going to do it. He just had to keep his shit together, act normal, non-threatening, not like some stalker. Suck up to the old man and win his trust.

Like you can do that.

Watch me, sonofabitch!

Garrett affected a nonchalant saunter as he strolled toward Ocean Drive. Just as he neared the sidewalk, a white utility van pulled up at the curb in front of him, nearly obscuring his view. He was intent on the shapely teen, wouldn't have noticed anything out of the ordinary, had he not caught a movement from the corner of his eye. Something unusual. Then he turned his full attention to the van, noted the middle-aged white guy with the scruffy beard behind the wheel. He was holding a pair of binoculars to his eyes. Garrett looked first at the driver and then followed the trajectory to where the man's attention was aimed, and his jaw dropped. The dude was focused on the girl. Suddenly, Garrett felt sick to his stomach.

What the hell? What is this? Surveillance or something?

"Shit!" Garrett lengthened his stride, raced to the front of the vehicle, and slapped both palms on the hood of the van, only to be skewered with a maniacal gaze that made him shudder.

This is so not right.

"What are you doing, man?" Derrick shouted.

Startled, the driver let the binoculars fall from his hands. In a split second, he had gunned the engine and was pulling away from the curb. With a squeal of tires, he sped off toward South Beach, but not before Garrett got a glimpse of the license plate. JNX 7 was all he could commit to memory before the vehicle was too far away for him to make out the remaining numbers.

"Holy hell!" Garrett bent at the waist, hands to his knees. Never mind the strange looks the snowbirds gave him. He knew something bad had been about to go down, and that it involved that sweet girl behind the counter in the produce booth. Suddenly, he felt an overwhelming desire to protect her.

He had to let her father know that she was in danger.

No one will believe you, loser.

"Ugh! No one will believe me," he muttered. Garrett ran—full out —across the street and into the pop-up market thronged with shoppers.

"Hey, kid!" a burly fellow shouted. "Watch where you're going."

"Sorry." Garrett's heart was racing, but he willed himself to be calm while sliding to a stop before the produce stand. There was a line of customers. He could hardly cut to the front. The girl was oblivious to him, waiting on buyers. Her father was in the back, unboxing produce.

Now is your chance.

Garrett sidestepped the crowd and ducked around the counter. In a few short steps, he'd covered the distance to the long-haired fellow, who was perched on a folding lawn chair.

"Excuse me?" The man looked up at him, and Garrett could see the emotions that played over his face: surprise, confusion, wariness, and—lastly—fear.

"I'm sorry, sir," Garrett said, making a conscious attempt to slow his breathing and not appear unhinged. "You probably don't remember seeing me."

"No,"

Garrett thrust out a hand. "Hello. I'm Garrett, Garrett Olson."

"Derrick Nelson." The man took Garrett's hand and promptly released it. "Pleased to meet you. But…" Derrick screwed up his face, and Garrett could feel the negative vibe coming off him.

Garrett rushed in to offer assurances. "I know we got off to a bad start, that you think I'm some kind of weirdo—"

"No, no…" Derrick shook his head. "Nothing of the sort. I'm just looking out for my daughter—"

"And I get it, sir. Which is why I'm here to tell you I think she might be in danger."

"What?" Derrick nearly staggered as he rose to his full height. He was in the young man's face when he said, "What do you mean by that?"

"I'm going to be perfectly honest. I'd like permission to see your daughter."

"Ugh…" Seeming to deflate, Derrick collapsed back into his chair.

"I realize this isn't the time or the place, but I just wanted to put that out there, sir."

"Okay? And… you know, the danger part?"

You sound incoherent, buddy. Slow down.

"It's like this. I was sitting over there. See?" Garrett pointed toward the park bench, and Derrick looked in that direction. "And, yeah, I admit it. I was checking out your daughter."

"Argh."

Garrett sat on his haunches, facing Derrick. "It sounds bad, but I have nothing but good intentions. Please believe me on this."

Derrick shook his head as if to clear it. "And how is Madison in danger? Can we get back to that for the moment?"

"There was this white utility van. No markings. I thought it was kind of strange. But you know," he shrugged. "It's Saturday, the Farmer's Market, all kinds of folks turn out on a day like this. Right?"

Derrick nodded.

"So, I wasn't thinking too much of it. It was like… in my peripheral vision. There but not there. Then…" Garrett's face darkened as the recent events replayed in his mind's eye. "I got the feeling there was something strange about it—off—but I couldn't put my finger on it."

"Yeah?" Derrick hung on his every word.

"Uh-huh. And as I got closer, I caught a glimpse of something."

"What?"

"I saw the driver of the van pull out a pair of binoculars."

Derrick waved a hand in the air dismissively. "He's probably a birder."

"No, he was training them on your daughter, sir, on Madison. I'm sure of it."

Derrick's eyes flitted to Madison, and his throat constricted with rising emotion. She was so beautiful. So innocent and vulnerable. "Jesus."

"Would it be all right if I said hi to her?"

"She's busy now." Derrick's brow furrowed, and he eyeballed the young man. "Listen to me," he said. "I'm grateful to you for having brought this… incident to my attention, but we have to face facts. No crime has been committed. We don't know if there was any ill will or ulterior motive."

"But—"

"Hear me out," Derrick interrupted, and Garrett gave an almost imperceptible nod of his head. "I don't want to frighten Maddy," Derrick continued. "This could be nothing. Then again, it's better to err on the side of caution. Wouldn't you agree?"

"Absolutely."

"This is what we're going to do…"

At the word we're, the teen cut his eyes to Madison. Serendipitously, the girl happened to look up and briefly meet his gaze.

For the first time in a long time, Garrett felt a glimmering of hope for his future.

Andrea was dreaming. It was a dream she returned to often—one that was both comforting for its familiarity, yet sinister for its dark undertones. Lost, without a housekey or cellphone, she wandered down a deserted street. She had a vague recollection of where her dorm was, but it was pitch black and all the buildings looked alike. Then, as so often happens in dreams, she found herself in another location. She was walking along a narrow hallway, searching for the door to her room, but she couldn't remember what floor it was on, let alone the room number. On this occasion, however, the script veered from its prescribed narrative. She tossed to her side, flung out an arm, and it connected with a warm body. "What?" Andrea was awake in an instant. Then it all came rushing back to her. Exhausted and slightly tipsy, she'd fallen into bed, leaving poor Daniel on the pool deck with an afghan draped over him.

Daniel! Good Lord. He was here in her bed!

Tentatively, she splayed her fingers, and they found purchase on a rock-solid bicep. "Oh," she gasped. She hadn't imagined it, hadn't dreamt it. He was here, lying next to her.

Yikes!

"Daniel," she whispered, ever so gently poking his shoulder.

"Hmm," was the only response she was given. But then Daniel turned to her and wrapped her in his arms, and the feeling was both exhilarating and welcoming, like returning home after an extended sojourn abroad.

Found.

She had all she could do but to keep from crying out. Human contact! It felt so good, so right.

Don't let him know how needy you are.

"Hey, babe." Daniel nuzzled her neck, and at the touch of his lips on her skin, Andrea did cry out. Slowly, he traced a line from her neck to her collarbone, to her breasts. There, he lingered, ministering to them until she was mewling with pleasure and urgency.

"How did you get in here?" she gasped, trying to sound urbane and at the same time, struggling to keep her wits about her.

"Really? The question is, how do I get in *here.*"

Andrea moaned as Daniel's fingers probed and massaged. "What? Umm. Isn't this happening too fa—" And then she was arching her back, splaying her legs, silently entreating him to enter her.

"Is this okay?" Daniel asked. "Please, tell me now. Before I can't stop."

"Yes." Andrea drew him to her.

"Are you sure?"

"Uh! Damn it…" Andrea's voice came in breathy gasps. "Yes, yes!"

Daniel needed no more prompting, and Andrea felt no shame desiring him. She'd never wanted a man like this. All inhibitions fled, this act reducing her to the most basic human needs: to be held and loved.

When she felt she couldn't endure one more second of pleasuring, Daniel maneuvered her onto her knees and entered her from behind. By this time, she was so sensitive, the smallest move on his part made her cry out in sweet agony, so that when he thrust into that moist chamber inside her—one that she'd nearly forgotten existed—she had all she could do to keep from screaming.

She climaxed in a shimmering explosion like nothing she'd ever experienced before.

So that was the big deal! Sex could be this good. Who knew?

Andrea collapsed onto her side and snuggled next to Daniel. "Oh, my God!" she laughed, throatily.

"And what, may I ask, do you find so amusing?" Daniel asked, stroking her hair.

"You're amazing." She drew her fingernails down his broad back, lightly tracing them to his sweetly rounded buttocks. And then she pulled him to her, for she felt as though she could never get enough of him.

What is it about this man?

~

Andrea reached for him when she awakened, her fingers scrabbling over the bedsheets. It took a moment for her to comprehend, but she soon realized she was alone in bed. Daniel had left her.

I should have known.

"Probably for the best," she muttered, not believing that for a minute. She crawled out of bed, feeling that dull ache between her thighs that only a night of lovemaking could cause, at the same time realizing she'd been a one-night-stand—in Daniel's words: a cheap date. Hell, she'd bought him dinner and then screwed him.

How could I be such a ninny? This is going to mess things up royally.

Silently, Andrea castigated herself as she headed for the shower. How the heck was she supposed to meet him at noon and go over the contract, to maintain her cool as though last night hadn't ever happened?

"Mom," Madison's voice pierced her self-absorbed misery. "You'd better come and look at this."

~

They huddled before the airstairs. "Where the hell is she?" Laney asked. "The least she could have done is give us a heads up. Not leave us waiting in the lurch like this."

"I've stowed the luggage, and we're cleared for take-off. What say you, Ms. Armstrong?" the pilot asked.

Kara fumed on the tarmac beside Laney. Should she give him the go-ahead and fly off without Becca? She was so angry that's exactly what she was tempted to do.

The little bitch.

Kara willed herself to be calm. "We'll wait five minutes longer, Dave," she said, "and then we're out of here."

At that moment, there was a commotion. A silver Rolls Royce careened through the wire-fenced gate, its horn beeping madly.

"Oh, God," Laney cried. "Here she comes."

"And so subtle," Kara said, shaking her head and smiling despite herself.

The regal transport pulled up, and Becca flew out of it, bigger than life. "Hello," she cried, somehow managing to look both ashamed and delighted as she crossed the distance between them. "Making a quick getaway without me, are you?"

"I don't believe it," Laney muttered.

"Ah, yeah," Kara said. "We were. You're late."

Becca wrapped her arms around Laney and Kara. "I've been late my whole life. Just now, I think I'm finally on time."

"What the hell does that mean?" Laney asked, allowing herself to be embraced in Becca's bear hug.

Becca kissed Laney on her forehead and then turned toward Kara, but the blonde backed away, her eyes narrowed.

"Be straight with me, girl," she said."

Becca ducked her head, seeming, for the moment, truly contrite.

Rob emerged from the Rolls, his dimpled smile doing little to conceal his exuberance. "It's all my fault, ladies," he said. "I ravished her, and she's quite lost her mind."

"If she ever had one," Kara muttered.

Laney dug an elbow into Kara's side. "Be nice," she whispered.

"It's true." Becca reached up and draped an arm around Rob's neck, pulling him to her for a quick smooch. When she released him, she said, "I've decided I'm staying." She shot a sidelong glance at Kara. "Sorry for not giving you advance notice. It's just that—"

"These things happen," Laney completed her sentence, at the same time widening her eyes and silently imploring Kara to cut Becca some slack.

Kara made a show of considering before saying, "I assume we *will* receive an invite to the wedding."

"Naturally." Rob threw his arms wide as if to encompass them all.

"Of course, you're to be my bridesmaids," Becca said. "Please, say you will."

"Count on it. Just don't put me in purple voile." Laney said.

"No puffy sleeves or ruffled skirts," Kara added.

"I hate to interrupt this riveting episode of *The Young and the Restless*, Ms. Armstrong." the pilot's eyes twinkled. "But if we're flying out this morning, I suggest we get a wiggle on."

Kara nodded in his direction. "Right, Dave," she said, and he scrambled up the airstairs without a backward glance.

Becca rushed to Kara and Laney, wrapping her arms around them. The three put their heads together, exchanging giggles and goodbyes.

"Okay then." Kara disentangled herself from their mutual embrace. "Here's the deal: We'll all meet back up here in…" She shot a quizzical glance in Becca's direction. "What's the timeframe?"

"Probably a month… month and a half." Becca shrugged. "It'll take me that long to arrange things. But Rob and I don't want a long engagement."

"Not one second longer than necessary," Rob hollered, and the girls smiled at one another.

"Tell me you've met his mother," Kara said.

"Briefly." Becca rolled her eyes.

Laney and Kara exchanged looks of horror.

"No worries," Becca soothed. "It's just so sudden. She'll be fine. She wants our boy happy."

"I'm sure you'll see to *that*," Laney said.

"Duh, that's an understatement."

The girls chuckled and then broke apart. "Love you, girl," Laney said. "How will I survive Philly without my two best buds?"

"You'll thrive, darling," Kara said. "I believe you have a new beau in hot pursuit."

"It does look that way," Laney agreed. "Jamal is not at all what I was looking for, yet so much more."

"With his million-dollar smile and adorable accent," Becca quipped. "Ooh-la-la!"

"Bye-bye, Becca," Laney called as she climbed the air-steps.

"Ciao," Becca cried.

"See you soon." Kara blew a kiss and then followed Laney.

"Well, lovey. It's just us two," Rob said, once the girls had vanished inside the plane and the airstairs retracted. "What shall we do?"

"Let's go plan a wedding." Becca snaked an arm around Rob's waist and grinned at him.

"Sounds good to me, Mrs. Becca Barrow. That has a nice ring, don't you think?"

~

Margaret gazed about the great room, her eyes lingering on the rough-sawn cedar mantle over the stone fireplace where several framed photos of her family were displayed. Then they darted about the room, resting first on an antique side table that she and John had unearthed in a second-hand shop in Winter Beach, next to a mid-century chair with its yellowed oak arms and legs and worn upholstery. She loved it all! These acquisitions were a chronicle of their shared history, each one a minor triumph to be celebrated.

They'd been so young and in love, and this house was a repository of their shared experiences. Now she had to let it all go, to shed the history and move on into the present—a solitary, sexless life without John.

"You stop that, Margaret," John admonished. "Look on the bright side."

"And what bright side would that be, John?" Margaret muttered as she slipped out the door.

She made her way across the lawn and out to the dock, then plunked herself down on the weathered planks. Gazing heavenward, she searched for a sign from John—to get yet another transmission from him—maybe some words of advice. Instead, all she saw was a half-moon with a few scudding clouds ghosting across it. But then wasn't there a wispy cloud taking form, and didn't it look like a stallion with its front legs raised in flight? Leaping off an unseen precipice—isn't that how she felt every day and night since he'd left her—alone and eager to jump into the next existence?

Wait for me, mermaid. John's voice whispered inside her head. *I'll be with you soon.*

"Oh, John, if only that were true."

CHAPTER TEN

EVERYTHING'S COMING UP ROSES

The foyer was awash in roses, as were the kitchen and dining room. There were roses of every hue—pink, coral, yellow, red, white—tender rosebuds, full-blown blooms. "Whoa!" Andrea exclaimed as she rounded the corner into her living room. "It looks like a greenhouse in here.

"Mom," Madison cried, "did you see what's in the front hall?"

"Good Lord," Andrea breathed. "What next?" She raised her eyebrows but couldn't keep the goofy smile from her face. "Seems I have an extravagant suitor."

"There's a note." Madison waved an envelope in front of her. "Here it is. Read it, Mom."

"Okay. Let me see it."

Madison handed her the envelope and plopped down on the sofa. "Come on, Mom," she entreated. "Sit down and read it."

Andrea took a seat beside Madison, dragged a palm over her face, and then took the envelope from her daughter.

"What does it say?" Madison demanded.

"Um," Andrea broke the envelope's seal and then withdrew the enclosure. "Hello, to my two favorite females in the universe," Andrea read.

Madison giggled. "That's funny, Mom."

"Yeah, I guess he likes us,"

"I think so." Madison curled her legs up beneath her and sighed contentedly. "That's nice."

"It is."

"What else does he say?"

"Let me see." Andrea read the missive and then translated. "He says he wants to see us tomorrow."

"Cool. Can we do that, Mom?"

Andrea pursed her lips. Perhaps it would be best to simply put the kibosh on this budding relationship. She couldn't afford to be hurt again, couldn't bear the thought of opening herself up to someone who might disappoint or betray her. And yet..." He'd left her a boatload of flowers. He'd written that he wanted to see her—to see Madison—again.

Maybe you should just trust the guy?

~

Garrett slumped down on his worn futon, thinking about the events of the last couple of weeks—the girl that had turned his life upside down in an instant and was still none the wiser. Sure, he'd wanted a bit of adventure, but this was more drama than he'd bargained for. Garrett felt as though he'd been transported to the action scene of one of his games. It was good versus evil, just up his alley except for the fact that—suddenly—it was all too real. And then it struck him: This is no game, and he was gobsmacked back to reality pretty damned quick.

What did you get yourself into? His ego goaded him.

"I don't know," Garrett muttered. "All I know is that I'm in too deep to bail."

He leaped off the futon and made a beeline to his computer screen. "So, what have we got, huh?" he breathed, as he seated himself before the monitor. Garrett keyed in the license plate number JNX 7_ _and waited for his screen to deliver. It wasn't much, he realized, but it was a start. And a heck of a lot better than aimlessly fuming, waiting around to see what, if anything, developed.

~

"Hey, Buzz." Floyd leaned against one of many large stone columns comprising an eighteenth-century arch-topped colonnade, now swathed in shadows. "It's me, F… Frank. You know, Daniel's friend?" He glanced about furtively, but at this hour, even the late-night bars had closed, and the workaday citizenry had not yet awakened. Except for the cooing and fluttering of mourning doves on the rooftop, there were no signs of life.

"Sorry if I woke you. It's just that I've finished my business here, and I want to take a little side trip before heading back to the states. You interested?" Floyd ducked behind a column when a big, black sedan rounded the corner. He kept his eyes trained on the car, not moving from the relative safety of his hiding place in the recesses of the portico until it was lost from view. "Good, good," he said, keeping his voice low. "The sooner the better." Floyd gathered up his duffle bag and hiked in the opposite direction the car had taken.

"Where am I headed?" He glanced down at the tiny map currently displayed on his cellphone's screen. "Acandi," he said. "Ever heard of it?"

Three hours later, he was comfortably seated in the Cessna when Buzz's voice boomed over the speaker system. "Great view on your left," and Floyd sprang to his feet. He dove across the aisle and took a seat on the other side of the plane. Peering out the window, he gazed down at the swath of green jungle below. It was rimmed with a strip of sandy beach and surrounded by a sea in the most brilliant shade of turquoise he'd ever set eyes upon.

Floyd scrambled down the jet stairs, bags in tow, and Buzz was close on his heels. On the tarmac, they turned to one another, and Floyd extended an arm. "Thanks, buddy." He shook the pilot's hand.

"We have to stop meeting like this," Buzz smirked.

"Yeah, well, you never know," Floyd said.

"You'll want to head in that direction." Buzz pointed. "You can hire transport that'll take you to the boat to Capurganá. It's a bit of a hike, and you look like you could take a load off.

"I'm afraid I'm under the weather." Floyd mopped his brow. This heat…"

"You don't have to explain, pal," Buzz said. "It takes some getting used to. Good luck."

~

Floyd sat astride a study, gray mule. The docile beast plodded, head lowered, over the uneven terrain toward the docks with no urging—as though he'd made this trek a thousand times. And, perhaps, he had. The mule's handler, who trotted alongside, had no idea he was toting a duffle bag containing a fortune.

Floyd tried to see the humor in the situation—he was on an ass, feeling like a horse's ass—fleeing the law. But he couldn't. He eyeballed the bag that contained all his worldly treasure, knowing full well he should be more nervous about that. Suddenly, Floyd realized he didn't give a damn about the money. His sweat-slicked clothing clung to him like plastic wrap, and he was bone-weary and famished. At this low point in his existence, all he required was a hot shower, a warm meal, and a comfortable bed to fall into. Then tomorrow could take care of itself.

~

Please join us for a final soiree.

321 Greenway Drive
Saturday, April 19th
Time: 4 – 9 p.m.
Dress: Retro Fifties to Contemporary Casual

Come prepared to find treasure,
winnow out trash, and celebrate with us as our family bids good-
bye to Casa Rio
and embarks on the next adventure.

Cocktails and Dinner Buffet
RSVP: Andrea Nelson 231-4559

Despite the heat of the muggy afternoon, the double doors to Casa Rio had been flung open wide. A line had formed outside, the would-be entrants laughing and chatting with friends and neighbors while waiting for admittance. The air conditioning was blasting away, keeping the interior cool and dry, and Margaret, clothed in a vintage gown of emerald-green satin, stood poised at the doorway looking regal and self-possessed.

"My word, George," she said, eyeing the distinguished, white-haired fellow standing before her. "You look positively smashing in uniform."

"Thank you, my dear," the elderly gentleman said. "Air Force, the Vietnam War."

He lifted the hem of his jacket to reveal a leather belt tightly cinched over a small potbelly. "I have to admit, it was a bit touch-and-go getting the trousers zipped."

"Well, I hope you've room for dinner. Derrick's working his magic; he's preparing quite a spread."

"First, however," Andrea swooped in and took the man's arm, "there's work to be done." She gestured toward the living room. "Go find Madison, Colonel Morris. She'll have an assignment for you."

"Delighted to do my part, ladies." George nodded stiffly and headed toward the great room.

Andrea turned back to the doorway where a fit young couple, their feet clad in bobby socks and white saddle shoes, were deep in conversation with her mother. "Hello, Nathan." Andrea smiled broadly at the tall handsome fellow, before directing her attention to his partner. "And this must be—"

"Andrea, allow me to introduce my wife. Elissa." Nathan turned to the willowy blonde clad in a red poodle skirt, who stood at his side.

"How do you do, Elissa?" Andrea said. "And welcome. I adore your skirt."

"Thanks. I found it in a consignment shop. Can you believe it?"

"It's classic. Now. if you'll just make your way through there." Andrea gestured toward the great room. "My daughter, Maddy, will get you started on your treasure hunt."

"This is so exciting!" Elissa said, linking arms with her husband.

"I hope we unearth something of value," Nathan added.

"You would be the one for that."

Nathan gazed down at his delicate bride. "I do have an eye." He took Elissa's elbow and steered her toward the living room.

≈

"Here you are." Madison handed the Colonel three plastic shopping bags. "See that chest over there?"

The former Air Force pilot nodded. "Certainly."

"Go through all the doors and drawers. Put anything you think good into one bag. That's the stuff she'll auction. Put the junk in the other. Got it?"

"What about the third?"

"That's for personal stuff. Things that Nana will want to keep."

"I'm on it, Maddy."

≈

"Chef." A young woman, wearing a white apron over black tuxedo pants, her dark blonde tresses pulled up in a clip, indicated a large container by the sink. "How do I wash the truffles?"

"No, no, no," Derrick cried. "Do nothing to them. They're perfect just as they are—two grand worth of exquisite. No one touches the truffles but me."

"Got it. And about the sea scallops?"

"We'll cook up those beauties at the very last second. You can blot them with paper towels until they're very dry. Later, we'll flash sauté them on high heat in equal parts butter and grapeseed oil." Derrick's eyes darted about Margaret's kitchen. His former mother-in-law's normally spare countertops were now laden with a variety of fresh produce—frilly red and green lettuces, purple and orange carrots, fingerling potatoes, onions, fennel, and an assortment of herbs. "Ahh," he breathed, a smile of contentment on his face. "It's showtime."

≈

Margaret was in her glory. The house was alive with people she loved, and she was determined to enjoy every moment. Gracefully, she glided from room to room, stopping to offer directions or answer questions.

She found Sally perched on a vanity stool in the dressing room. "You've discovered those old tortoiseshell combs," she exclaimed, bending over the real estate broker to better examine them. "Beautiful, aren't they? Not plastic like the ones we see today. Mother wore them in her hair."

"Then you'll want to hang on to them," Sally said.

"Yes."

"But what about the rest of this stuff?" Sally indicated the items she'd piled atop the vanity—hairpins, electric razors, boxes of talcum powder, shower caps, worn bath linens, a boar bristle brush that had seen better days.

Margaret's eyes roved over the assortment. "Toss all of it," she finally said. "Unless you think there's something of value here. I leave it to your discretion, Sally."

"Yes, ma'am," Sally turned back to the vanity cabinet and opened a lower drawer.

Margaret wandered into a guest bedroom where two men—one very tall fellow and a slightly built younger chap—were examining a mahogany lady's desk. The pair were nattily attired in upscale fifty's garb, baggy pleated trousers, crisp linen shirts with narrow collars. They'd turned the desk on its end and had their heads together.

"Scottly, what're you up to?" Margaret asked."

The large man glanced in her direction. "Take a look at this, Margaret." He pointed to the carved detail on the apron's front, five thunderbolts tied with a bow knot. "You see that? It's a Duncan Phyfe signature. You've got an original here. I'm sure of it."

"I've always loved this desk," Margaret crossed to them, "but now you're telling me—"

"It's in excellent condition." The younger man's high voice belied his enthusiasm.

"Margaret, you remember Kory, don't you?" Scottly asked.

"Of course." Margaret patted the dandy's shoulder. "So glad you could make it, Kory. I was hoping you two design experts would ferret out the gems."

"You flatter us," Scottly said, carefully setting the desk back on its feet. "But I'm quite sure this is one of those jewels." He beamed at Margaret. "You'll either want to keep this piece and pass it on to your children or sell it at a premium."

"Whoo-hoo!" a male voice hollered, grabbing their attention. "I think I've struck pay dirt!"

In the next moment, Margaret, Scottly, and Kory were charging toward the great room. On their way, they nearly collided with Sally and Andrea, who were stampeding in from the opposite direction. "What's happening?" Sally asked, her eyes wide.

"Haven't a clue," Scottly said.

"Yippee-ki-yay! Oh, happy day."

"Good heavens," Margaret exclaimed. "Who *is* that? My heart can hardly take the excitement."

Scottly clasped Margaret's hand and hauled her into the great room. There, they found Jason Landeau, the new president of Northern Trust Bank, waving an envelope over his head.

"Jason, what is it?" Andrea asked. "Why the hullabaloo?"

"I think we've found the prize, Andy!"

"Why? What have you unearthed?" Margaret asked.

Jason rose to his full height, relishing the moment. With great fanfare, he opened the envelope and withdrew a sheaf of certificates. "Does anyone know what these are?" he asked.

"No!" Scottly exclaimed.

"Tell us," Nathan cried.

"Where did you find them?" Andrea asked.

"In the lower shelf of the bookcase. Don't ask me why, but I felt compelled to rifle through the pages of this volume, *The Complete Works of Shakespeare,* and this fell out. Right onto my lap, I might add. It was like someone from the dead was speaking to me."

"Ooo," Sally said in a quavering voice. "Spooky."

"That *is* strange." Suddenly, Margaret looked apprehensive.

"Yes," Jason said. "I planted a bookmark between the pages from where it fell, *The Tempest, Act 3 Scene 2.*

"So," Andrea said, "what's the significance?" She glanced about the room, a skeptical look on her face. "If there is any."

Jason placed the envelope on a side table and opened the heavy tome. "Aha! Here it is."

An expectant hush fell over the room as all eyes fastened on the banker. Jason inhaled and then struck a pose. "*He that dies pays all debts,*" he recited in his most theatrical voice.

"Come on, Jason, cut the Shakespeare!" the Colonel cried. "What's this nonsense?"

"North European Oil Corporation stocks." Jason grinned.

"What of it?" Sally asked. "Those old stock certificates are worthless."

"I don't believe that's true in this case," Jason said. "I've heard tell that John Sheridan was a savvy investor, and I've read that these particular certificates—NEO purchased in the thirties—could be worth more than two hundred times their original value. Let's do the math." Jason fanned the certificates while calculating. "If I'm right, I believe we're talking in the neighborhood of..." He paused for effect, "three-million dollars!"

There was an audible sigh and then an uptick of breath from all those present. In the next moment, everyone was laughing and clapping one another on the back as though they'd accomplished a great feat.

"Now you won't have to sell," Nathan exclaimed, staring pointedly at Margaret.

Andrea shot him a warning look, and he quickly changed his tack. "But what do I know?"

"Madams and messieurs," Derrick bellowed as he emerged from the kitchen, a white apron tied around his lanky frame, "dinner is served. Please return your bags to Madison in the front hall and then make your way to the patio. There, you shall be wined and dined in exchange for your labors."

The entire company erupted in happy sighs and murmurings. They collected their findings and then surged toward the front hall to do Derrick's bidding, eager for dinner and drinks.

~

Margaret kicked off her heels. "Oh, my Lord, my feet are killing me," she exclaimed, massaging her toes.

"It was worth it. You looked stunning, Mom." Andrea collapsed into a lounge chair opposite her mother. "And the party was a great success."

"Thanks to my granddaughter's brilliant idea!" Margaret beamed at Madison.

"I'm beat." Madison perched on the edge of an ottoman at Margaret's feet and yawned widely. "But I think we did good."

Andrea gazed about the great room. "Jeez," she said. "The place is a mess, huh?"

"It's okay." Margaret's eyes darted over the large, untidy space where drawers gaped open, and books were stacked helter-skelter. "Had to happen sooner or later, and we've taken a good stab at what seemed an enormous task. I, for one, am encouraged."

Derrick hiked in from the back patio, toting a plastic bin piled high with silver chafing dishes and stainless-steel buffet servers. "How about another glass of champagne, ladies?"

"Only if you'll join us," Margaret said. "You've worked so hard. How can I ever thank you enough?"

Andrea snorted loudly, an aggrieved expression on her face, and Margaret pretended not to notice.

Derrick winked at his former mother-in-law. "Don't worry. You'll get my bill."

"I'll have some, Daddy," Madison said.

"Cut hers with orange juice, Derrick." Andrea smiled indulgently at the teen.

When Derrick had disappeared into the kitchen, Margaret leaned into her daughter. "So, about those railroad certificates…"

Andrea nodded. "That was a surprise, alright."

"Do you think they're worth anything?"

"Who knows? I did a quick google search, and most of those old stocks have no value whatsoever."

"But not all," Margaret pressed.

"No. Some, as Harry said, are worth plenty. We'll just have to wait and see what Nathan determines. He's the financial guru. He'll get the real lowdown. Until then…"

"We don't count our chickens—" Margaret said.

"Until they're hatched." Madison finished her grandmother's sentence, looking pleased with herself.

∼

Floyd was dog-tired, but the donkey driver took his job very seriously. "Hey, mon," he said, jiggling the slumped attorney's shoulder when he started to doze off. "Nearly thar."

"Umph!" Floyd grumbled. "So hungry."

"Not to worry. Bes' food on di island, coomin riight up! Stay awake, mon. Doon wan to miss iit."

"I could eat a horse."

The donkey balked and craned its neck, giving Floyd a hard look before braying in protest.

"Just kidding."

Josefina's was nothing more than a ramshackle, hole-in-the-wall joint hugging the coast. But the laughter and enticing aromas wafting to the weary traveler were enough to hearten him, and his flagging spirits revived. No matter that he hadn't secured lodgings. There'd be time for that. Never had he had a more harrowing day. Floyd had been at his rope's end. Now he was ready to be fed and embraced.

"Hallo, straan-jaar!" The voice that welcomed him was warm and mellow, drawing out vowels in ways he'd never imagined possible.

"Hello, yourself," Floyd sniveled, peevishly, as he perused the menu. He was famished and dead on his feet.

"Whhaat kaan I get choo, sweethaart?"

Floyd looked up only to encompass a female with impossibly high cheekbones and a ready smile, and it was as though a volcano erupted in his consciousness. He'd awakened. She was as lush and ripe as the island itself, and her lively eyes seemed to bore into his soul.

All that had been dead in Floyd seemed to come alive again. He felt a long-forgotten yearning, and his pants were suddenly too small to accommodate what had been dormant so long. It was all so confusing yet exciting at the same time. "What are the specials?" he rasped, and the waitress answered with a throaty laugh.

Had he said something funny?

"I wood recoomand the shreemp cer-vaychee. But whaat ehvah you waant, ees spee-cial!" She raised an eyebrow and blew a kiss in his direction. "Diahhna, dat's me," she said, "I bring you whaat ehvah you need."

~

Floyd pushed his plate away and belched softly. The Cazuela de Camerones—fresh prawns simmered with vegetables in a hearty broth —had more than met his expectations.

"You laik?" Diana asked, scooping up his empty plate.

"Delicious. I'll have another Presidente," Floyd indicated the empty green bottle.

"Coomin raaht up. Dahsurt?"

"No, no! Just a refill, and then I'll be on my way."

The waitress turned as if to go, but Floyd's voice stopped her in her tracks. "Tell me, can you recommend a place to stay?" he asked. "Long term."

Diana set the plate back down on the table and slowly folded herself into the chair opposite his. "Nah thaat I caan," she said, clasping her hands in front of her jutting breasts. "My seestah has a plaace cloose into tawn. Klan. Reahl naace. Shaal I raang hah?"

"Yeah. And can you get me a bottle of this most agreeable elixir to go?"

~

Benita beamed at Floyd, and for a moment, he thought she might have been Diana's twin. Except for the fact that she was ten years older and thirty pounds heavier, she could have been. She possessed the same warm manner and sweet disposition. "You see, thaa's a view. Raaht here tru dis window."

Dutifully, Floyd bent and peered out the tiny bathroom portal. "Ah," he said, taking in the bird's eye view of the wharf. "Very nice." He straightened and pushed past her, eager to escape the cramped space. "You mentioned a terrace?"

"Yaas! Dis way," Benita said. "You calm tru heah." She led the way through the cramped living room into a small passageway. "Up thaah." Benita nodded toward a narrow stairway, indicating that he should climb up. "Ah'm afrd of haats. You go. Ah stah heya." Floyd arched a brow but said nothing. He doubted Benita was afraid of heights. He figured she was reluctant to squeeze her corpulent frame up the narrow corridor.

When he reached the tiny landing, Floyd pushed open the door and stepped out onto the terrace. "Oh, my God," he gasped, gazing about in wonderment. The rooftop enclosure was plebian, no more than twenty feet by twenty with a stick-built railing on three sides to prevent from tumbling over the edge, but the view of the harbor it afforded was magnificent. "This will do," he murmured.

Back in the kitchen, the two of them faced off. "Fahve-huundrad COP a moont, plaws eggstra foh laundry suhvace," Benita said.

"Seems a bit steep."

"Dat's ma finaal oofah." Benita pretended to glare at him, but she only managed to look like a pleasant-faced matron doing a bad job of acting.

"You drive a hard bargain." Floyd struggled to keep his expression impassive.

"Humph." Benita narrowed her eyes, a smug smile creeping over her face.

"I'll take it." Floyd made a show of slowly selecting bills from his wallet and presenting them to Benita. "There are three hundred and fourteen U.S. dollars for two month's rent," he said, "and an additional eighty-something to cover my laundry and God knows what else."

"Wahlcomb to da naybooh-hood," Benita said, palming the cash.

"Thank you. And where, pray tell, can I buy some decent furniture for this place?"

CHAPTER ELEVEN

THE ENEMY OF THE GOOD

"You should have been there." Andrea drew her knees to her chest and stared out over the gleaming black river while replaying the evening in her mind's eye. "It was crazy and sad and wonderful all at the same time. I have to give it to him, Derrick put out an amazing spread: shrimp cocktail, seared sea scallops with champagne reduction, beef Wellington with truffle Madeira sauce, to say nothing of the spinach-escarole salad and garlic roasted veggies. It was incredible."

"All of which is precisely why I didn't come." Daniel reached over and clasped Andrea's hand.

"Huh?"

"Andy, do you have any idea how I feel about all of this? I'm literally throwing your mother out of her home and depriving you and Madison of your inheritance."

"But—"

"No, hear me out. I am well aware of your reasoning, and I fully understand your circumstances. Still, do you think I could stomach seeing you sad, knowing full well that I was the reason for your unhappiness, all the while drinking your champagne, eating the meal your ex-husband prepared and pretending not to be a callous cad?"

Andrea let go of Daniel's hand and jumped to her feet. "You listen to me, Mr. Armstrong," she said. "I may be a bit tipsy, but I will have no more of that drivel. Do you understand?"

Daniel peered up at her, a confused expression on his face. "I—"

"You must swear to forget everything I am about to say. No memory."

"Uh…"

"I mean it." Andrea plopped down on Daniel's lap, straddling his long legs. "You," she said, while cupping his well-defined chin in her hand and bending to brush her lips against his, "are my knight in shining armor, come to rescue me."

Daniel made as if to protest, but Andrea covered his mouth with her fingers. "I will have no more crying-in-my-beer talk about how you've displaced Mom while robbing me of my familial home. We *have to sell*. Do you understand me?"

"Mmph!"

"I'll take that as a yes."

Daniel wrapped his arms around her and drew her to him. "What am I going to do with you, woman?"

"Whatever you like." Andrea's tongue circled her lips as she reached for his fly. "Please sir, may I have more?"

∾

Andrea awoke to the annoying buzz of a leaf blower. A glance at her alarm clock told her it was not yet seven o'clock in the morning. "Dang it!" She threw off the covers and scrambled out of bed, moaning, "The price of paradise." Slipping her arms into a terrycloth robe, she sprinted out the front door to retrieve the newspaper only to be greeted by the whining din of lawnmowers and hedge trimmers.

A yardman, his head covered in a wide-brimmed straw hat, waved to her from over the hedge that separated her yard from the neighbor's. She yelled, "Don't you know that the perfect is the enemy of the good?" Not surprisingly, he didn't appear to be familiar with Voltaire. Besides, he couldn't hear a word she said. The poor fellow merely smiled by way of answer.

Once inside, Andrea crossed to the kitchen, withdrew the rolled paper from its plastic sleeve, and tossed it on the table. The paper unfurled of its own accord, revealing a headline that screamed at her: *Local Attorney Charged with Embezzling Escrow Accounts.*

"Oh, my God!" Andrea pulled out a side chair and sat heavily. She unrolled the paper, her eyes immediately drawn to the feature article.

It wasn't but a moment after she'd finished the first speed-reading when her cellphone clamored. A quick look at the display and she knew it was Jeremy Bell calling. Andrea brought the device to her face, muttering, "And now all hell breaks loose."

"Hi, Jeremy." She propped an elbow on the table and cupped her chin in hand. "Yeah. I saw it," she said, her eyes once more scanning the news article. "Yep. It's bad, alright."

The realty office was pandemonium. Heather and Margo were at the front desk manning the landlines, and everyone else was jabbering away on their cellphones, fielding questions from anxious sellers and buyers. Andrea's eyes met Jeremy's, and he shook his head, a doleful smile on his face. She answered with a shrug, then made a beeline to Sally's office where the harried broker was similarly occupied.

"I understand your concerns," the curvaceous blonde soothed. "But I assure you, there's nothing to worry about. Your escrows are fine. Trust me." She raised her eyebrows, acknowledging Andrea's presence, and waved her toward a chair, indicating that she should sit. When the call ended, Sally turned to Andrea.

"We're up to our necks in it now," she said.

"What can I do?" Andrea asked.

"Sell a property."

"I'm on it."

When Andrea swept into Nathan McCourt's inner sanctum, he rose from his desk and strode toward her. "Andy, so great to see you!"

"You, too, Nate."

"Please," Nathan indicated a lounge chair by the window, "have a seat."

Andrea settled herself, and Nathan perched on the divan opposite her.

"Lovely party the other night," Nathan said. "Elissa and I thoroughly enjoyed it."

"Thank you for coming. And about those stock certificates…"

Nathan folded his arms and sat back down. "I did my due diligence, Andy, and I have to say—"

Before he could continue, Andrea cut him off. "Unlike everyone else, Nathan, I didn't get my hopes up."

"Yes. As I was saying, I thought the certificates might be genuine. As it turns out, they were."

"Good enough to warrant framing, I imagine."

"Um." Nathan nodded. "My initial guesstimate—as was Harry's—was that they'd be worth somewhere in the neighborhood of two to three hundred times their purchase price."

Andrea's eyebrows shot up. "And?"

"My research leads me to believe the lot of them are worth only about one-point-five mil."

Andrea's jaw dropped. Suddenly, all the paradigms had shifted, and she struggled to make sense of this new reality. "You're sure?"

"Absolutely. I imagine this changes things, huh?" Nathan leaned in toward her, his palms on his knees.

Andrea gazed out the window, her eyes unfocused. Then she turned back to the financier. "Yes and no."

"What do you mean?"

"Nate, the real estate market has tanked, and no one knows when we'll recover. Sally has had to front all the escrows that damned thief, Heller, embezzled. With borrowed money, I might add."

"Sally will be fine," Nate interjected.

"Maybe." Andrea tossed her head dismissively. "But we need sales. Desperately. Honestly, a million and a half isn't nearly enough to pay the back taxes on Casa Rio, make the necessary renovations, and maintain the estate. I love the place, but it's a money pit."

"Perhaps I could help."

"Nathan, I appreciate the offer, but no. Mom and I had resolved to sell. As you know, we've already started packing. You can help by cashing in those certificates for us and investing them wisely.

Nathan paused briefly to consider Andrea's proposition. Then he said, "That I can do, ma'am." He came to his feet. "And it'll be my pleasure." He extended a hand to Andrea and helped her up.

"Thanks again, Nathan." Andrea allowed herself to be led to the door. "One more thing. Could we keep this stock certificate thing under our hats for the time being?"

"Mum's the word."

. . .

Downstairs in the lobby, Andrea pushed open the large, plate-glass door, and the humidity smacked her like a steaming towel. Her mind was awhirl. Yet she knew what she had to do. She withdrew her phone from her handbag and tapped in Daniel's number.

~

The bus wheezed to a stop, and the door fan-folded out like an accordion with no melody. Madison, her backpack strapped to her shoulders, rose from her seat and trudged to the front of the bus. Her head was lowered, eyes downcast as though she were fending off imagined insults—a result of having fielded her fair share. She tripped down the rubber grip-lined steps, and as her mother had instructed her to, canvassed the area. Nothing seemed out of the ordinary; the usual line of late-model SUVs parked on the shoulder, moms or dads behind the wheels waiting to pick up kids, and one white utility van. She ambled toward Castaway Cove, humming softly to herself.

Madison ducked beneath the arm of the unmanned security gate and headed toward the river. She didn't notice that the gate swung open almost the moment she'd passed beneath it, and was startled when a voice called out, "Hey there. Wait up!"

The white van pulled up next to her and braked. Madison thought nothing of it. There were always workmen on the island—carpenters, plumbers, electricians, painters—and more than half of them drove utility vans.

A man with a gray-streaked beard, his eyes obscured by black sunglasses, leaned out the driver's side window. "You live here?" he asked, a smile on his face.

"Yes." Madison was not programmed to lie.

"Cool. I'm Jack, by the way. You've probably seen me around."

Madison nodded, although she didn't recognize him.

"What's your name?"

"Madison."

"Right. Madison." He nodded. "I'm working on that big house under construction on Olde Doubloon Drive. You know the one I'm talking about?"

"Sure." Madison felt the first twinges of regret. "I gotta go." She turned away and resumed walking.

"Oh, yeah. Sorry." The man shifted into drive and slowly released the brake, and the van coasted along beside her. "It's just that I lost my contact lens."

"Huh?" Madison stopped walking and gazed at him, bewildered.

The man lowered the shades from his eyes and peered out over the rims. "Can't see worth crap. Could you help me out?"

"Uh…" Madison hesitated.

"I mean, it's pretty dangerous driving like this. I'd be beholden to you."

"Maybe. How long will it take?"

"Not more than a few minutes." He leaned over the center console and levered the passenger side door open. "Hop in. You can direct me there. I've got a pair of prescription glasses in my carpenter's apron. Once I've got them—my eyeballs—I'll be fine." He snorted in a self-deprecating sort of way, shot Madison a goofy grin, and she giggled obligingly.

Alarm bells clanged in Madison's cranium, but she rounded the van anyway.

"Just throw your backpack on the floor," Jack said. Ever the obedient girl, Madison shrugged out of her backpack, tossed it inside, and then climbed aboard.

"That-a girl." As soon as Madison was seated and the passenger side door closed, Jack jerked the wheel to the left and drove around the security gate to the exit.

"Doubloon is back there," Madison protested.

"It's okay. I'm taking a shortcut."

"Let me out." Madison gripped the door handle with her right hand, preparing to open the door and jump.

But Jack wrenched her left arm, yanking her sideways, and put his face in hers.

"Chill," he snarled. "I'm taking the back way."

"Let go of me. I want to go home," Madison wailed.

~

Garrett was stopped at the light on Beachland Boulevard, waiting to turn right onto the Seventeenth Street Causeway. He had the radio's volume turned up to the max while grooving to Viva la Vida by

Coldplay when a white utility van breezed past him on its way from south beach to the mainland. His eyes fell upon the license plate, and his jaw dropped: JNX769. "Shee-it!" Eyes glued to the van, he prayed for the light to turn.

When it did, the chase was on.

"Hey, Mr. Nelson!" Garrett held his cell in his right hand. "Yeah, it's me, Garrett. Sorry to bother you, but believe it or not, I'm on the tail of the white van."

At the end of the bridge, the utility vehicle turned left onto Indian River Boulevard, and once again, Garrett was cooling his jets at a red light. "Damn it," he cursed softly. "I'm going to lose him, sir, but the tag number is JNX769. Yeah, like jinx. Go figure. You might want to write it down."

The light turned green, and Garrett stomped on the gas, his eyes searching the lanes of traffic up ahead, but the utility van had vanished. "I lost him," he groused. Unconsciously, he slowed, unsure of his next move, and the driver of the car behind him tapped his horn, urging him forward. In the next instant, Derrick was in his ear, rattling off instructions. Garrett sped up, all the while concentrating on Derrick's words. "Oh, okay," Garrett said, "Second Street Southwest. It's as good as an off-the-beaten path as you can get. I'll start there and work my way back toward town. But jeez," he complained, "he could be anywhere."

～

The sun was low in the sky, the air alive with the unearthly screech of tree frogs and cicadas in the bush bowing an atonal accompaniment, but Madison was deaf to all but her captor's voice, her brain having veered off into a panicked jumble as she began to shut down. "Get out, I said," Jack commanded, holding the passenger door open. "Now!"

The bearded man grabbed her ankle and yanked. Madison did as she was told. She bounded down, and as soon as her feet hit the ground, her abductor grabbed her shoulder roughly. "Over there," he said, prodding her toward a ramshackle trailer squatting on the overgrown lot. "You and I are going to get better acquainted."

Madison cut her eyes to the trailer, and muscle memory from her martial arts training was suddenly in her head and limbs. She had no other choice. She knew what she had to do. "No!" Madison squirmed out of the scruffy fellow's grasp, pivoted, and kicked him hard between the thighs. She didn't wait to assess the aftereffects of this maneuver but tore out of there as fast as her legs would carry her.

Jack was bent over double, his breath coming in labored gasps, but he raised his head and, through narrowed eyes, marked her passage. She was heading north. "Get back here," he wheezed, lowering his head again. But by the time he'd recovered from the crushing blow to his balls, Madison had vanished.

~

Madison had no idea where she was. All she wanted to do was get as far away from that horrible man as was humanly possible. She turned left on Thirty-fifth Avenue, her legs pumping like pistons, all the while praying she was going in the right direction. Wherever that was. Here, the traffic was heavier, and suddenly it came to her: She should have kept off the road! A car horn blared, and she zigged off the shoulder and cut across a well-tended yard. She was completely out in the open, and that creep would surely be trying to find her.

"Hey, kid." A male voice accosted her. Madison's heart was in her throat, but she'd been reared to respect her elders. She stopped up short and gave the pudgy, bare-chested guy her full attention.

He was standing in the driveway of a modest, one-story cinderblock ranch, a thick-jowled, dark-complected fellow, garden hose in his hand. "Why the hurry?" he asked, turning away from the bushes he was dousing.

"Uh!" Madison put a knuckle to her mouth and staggered.

A lanky teenager darted out from the garage. "Dad," the boy cried, "Mom says it's time for—" Cutting his eyes to Madison, he stopped up short. "What the—"

Madison's mind reeled. She opened her mouth to answer, but no words came to her. Instead, her brain finally did shut down. Slowly, she crumpled, would have smacked her head on the cement driveway had not both the teen and his father rushed to her side and caught her before the lights went out.

～

Floyd sat at a table at Josefina's beachside eatery, smiling sagely. It was crazy he knew, but never had he felt so relaxed or more at home. His belly was full of coconut lobster and rice, and he had a sweating Presidente at hand. Diana, the voluptuous waitress—his angel—seemed prepared to cater to his every need. Thanks to her, he had taken possession of a great little flat with a view of the harbor. More Diana favors seemed implicit, and he dared hope they'd be forthcoming.

"Hah waas youh dinnar?" Diana trailed her index finger across the back of Floyd's neck, and he came to attention.

"Fabulous, Diana." He reached up and clasped her hand in his. "When are you free? I'd like to buy you a drink."

"I'm off in half an houah, silly mahn. Oof coorse you caan buy me ah drink. But the liquah is free at mah place." Diana winked as she placed the check before him, and Floyd thought tonight he might get lucky.

A glance at his new cellphone—one that couldn't be traced—told him it was after ten. He leaned back in his chair and crossed his feet at the ankles while gazing about at the other tables dotting the beach. Most of the dining patrons had moved on, but there were three middle-aged men seated several tables away, and their coarse laughter caught his attention.

It had been days since Floyd had stopped looking over his shoulder, but he was still cautious; he knew disaster could strike at any minute. Yet just now, he'd downed two beers, and a feeling of contentment washed over him. Diana posed a pretty development, so it's no wonder he was feeling as if he'd finally gotten it right. His troubles momentarily forgotten, he let his guard down and withdrew his billfold from his back pocket. From the wad of cash nestled within, he peeled off two twenties and set them on the chit. No credit cards now, or ever, he'd decided. No paper trails leading to him. It was cash on the barrel from here on in. Clean, simple, untraceable.

When Floyd looked up, it was to find three pairs of hostile eyes staring at him.

He sucked in his breath.

Who are those guys?

They were natives, obviously—sunbaked, dressed in jeans and cotton shirts—nothing out of the ordinary. Except for eyes that seemed hardened and inured to violence. Under his scrutiny, two of the men averted their eyes, concentrating on their beers, but the third held his gaze and nodded a greeting. Despite the smile on his face, the man's reptilian eyes sent another message. Floyd flinched as a tingle of fear ran up his spine, but he locked eyes with the fellow. Then much to his relief, Diana returned, and the brief encounter ended.

She came to stand at the table occupied by the three men, and Floyd relaxed, knowing he was off their radar. They spoke in Spanish, but he could make out a phrase here and there.

"¿Qué le sirvo?" *What would you like?* Diana asked.

The evil-looking fellow snaked an arm around her back, his hand coming to rest on her ample bottom. "Solo usted, cariña," he said, shooting Floyd a taunting grin.

Floyd made as if to rise from his chair, but then thought better of it. Instead, he tossed his head and snorted, playing along rather than falling for the dare. Three men against one? He knew his limits, and they looked in much better shape than he. Best to ignore them, he decided.

Diana laughed and wriggled out of the man's grasp saying, "No, del menu, amor," immediately diffusing the tension. She set their check on the table and sashayed over to Floyd. "What about you, hon?" she asked.

Floyd pointed his nose toward the three men. "Do you know those guys?"

"Bandidos." Diana shrugged, glancing briefly at their table and then looking away.

"Who knows? Delincuentes, pandillas, or sindicato, de grupos armados Organizados. Perhaps, Pince Gringo."

"Gangs?"

"Si, secuestro, robo, lo que caiga. Whatever cooomes their way."

"Kidnapping? Robbery! And you're not afraid of them?"

Diana shook her head. "I am too old for trata de personas. Human traffic. And I have no money, nooothing dey want."

"Let's get out of here." Floyd glanced back at the three men. They were tallying up the bill, dividing it between them, and they paid him no mind.

. . .

Later, the two sat in plastic chairs on Diana's small front porch batting away mosquitoes and drinking rum on ice. Her tiny house was on a narrow street backing up to a dense tangle of jungle and, unlike Capurganá proper and its beaches, quiet except for the occasional barking dog or cackling rooster.

"Diana," Floyd said, "I want to thank you for everything you've done for me."

"Yoou, walcome." Diana rose from her chair and reached for Floyd's empty glass. "But now, it's time for dis workin' gal to go to bed."

Floyd grabbed her wrist and pulled her to him. "I want you, Diana."

"Not yet, Floyd. I want you to coome to church wit me."

Floyd released her. "Church!" he scoffed, coming to his feet. "Why?"

"It would mak me happy." Diana leaned into him, her eyes gleaming.

Floyd was mildly inebriated, and the sweetness of Diana's flawless skin combined with the remains of her perfume overwhelmed him. He wrapped his arms around the generously endowed woman and nibbled her neck.

Diana tilted her head to him and brushed her full lips across his cheek. Floyd moaned, bringing his lips to hers. Diana laughed softly, breaking the spell as she drew away. "Coome to church wit me," she demanded.

"Oh, alright." Floyd knew when he was defeated. If that's what it took, he'd accompany her to Mass. What could it hurt? "When and what time?"

~

"Wake up," a woman's voice coaxed her back to consciousness. "Are you okay?" Madison's eyelids fluttered before finally opening. When they did, she found herself sprawled on a sofa in unfamiliar surroundings and staring into the compassionate eyes of a petite Latina.

Where am I?

"Huh?" Madison's eyes darted from the woman to the middle-aged fellow who'd interrupted her flight, to the skinny kid so intently fixated on her.

She cringed.

"It's okay," the woman said. "I'm Sophia. Sophia Menendez." She turned to the bare-chested man beside her. "This is my husband, Carlos." Madison made no reply. "And you are?" The woman peered at her, waiting for a response.

Madison looked first to one face, then another, her eyes finally coming to rest on the boy.

"Hi," he said, "I'm Tyler."

He was so nonthreatening, so openly eager for her to respond, she couldn't help but comply. "I'm Madison," she said in a small voice.

Sophia and Carlos exchanged brief looks of relief and then focused back on the distraught girl. "Good," the woman said. "And what were you running from, honey?"

Madison compressed her lips, and the boy nodded encouragingly. "A bad man," she finally said.

The boy's eyes darkened, and Sophia stiffened, once again eying her husband. Then she turned back to Madison and resumed her questioning. "What bad man? You can tell us. You don't have to be afraid anymore."

"I don't know. He said his name was Jack."

Sophia took a deep breath, seeming to process Madison's words. "And how is it you were with this… this, Jack?"

"He said he'd lost a contact, that he couldn't see. So, I thought I'd help him. But then he drove me away from there. When he stopped and opened the car door, I kicked him hard and ran."

"Oh, Madison!" Sophia put her hands on the girl's shoulders. "You were very brave." She glanced at her husband, and he stared back hard at her. Then she leaned in close to Madison. "You're safe now, sweetie. We won't let anyone get to you. Do you hear me?"

Madison bit her lip as tears welled in her eyes.

"We should call the police, Mom," the boy said.

"No," his father countered. "Madison, we must call your parents. Do you have a phone?"

Madison nodded. "It's in my backpack." And then her face took on a look of anguish. "Oh, no," she wailed. "I left it in the van!"

Sophia squeezed Madison's shoulder. "It's all right, dear. You did exactly the right thing. You vamoosed and lickety-split. Good for you."

"What's your mom's phone number, Madison?" Carlos withdrew a cellphone from his back pocket.

"It's 231-5222," Madison said.

"Area code 772?"

"Yes."

Carlos punched the numbers into his phone. After a few seconds, he frowned, mouthing to his wife, "recording." Then he spoke. "Hello, this is Carlos Menendez. Please don't be alarmed. Madison is here at our house. We're on the corner of Thirty-fifth Avenue and Highway Sixty. She's fine. I'd be happy to drop her to you, or you can come and pick her up. Call me at 559-0700."

Menendez disconnected and turned his attention to Madison. "I'm sorry. No one answers. Is there another number I can call?"

"Call Mom's cell," Madison said, "231-9298."

"We need to finalize the contract," Andrea snapped into her phone. "I have to know whether you're serious. If not, I've got to do more advertising. Mom needs to sell."

Daniel listened to the agitated female on the other end of the line, and a lazy smile inched up his face. "Andrea," he said, "are we a teensy-weensy bit stressed?"

"Yes," Andrea shot back at him. "Totally."

"Take a deep breath. And no, I'm not patronizing. I just want you to come back to planet Earth. Alright? Where I live, too."

Andrea breathed deeply, briefly putting her head in her hands before speaking evenly. "Okay, I'm back."

"I was thinking about an early dinner."

"What?"

"I'd like to take you out for a bite to eat. You haven't eaten. Am I right?"

"Hmm. You're getting to know me too well."

"I want to know everything about you, woman."

Andrea snorted, but then her voice took on a serious note. "Madison's bus must be late. I'm expecting her to walk through the door any moment."

"Great. She can join us. I'll be there in fifteen minutes."

Andrea's phone vibrated. "Okay. I need to take an incoming call. I'll see you soon."

～

Daniel arrived at Andrea's house in Castaway Cove, only to find her in a state of panic when she met him at the door. One look at her was all he needed to know that whatever had gotten her into such a state was no trifling matter. "What is it?" he asked, suddenly grave.

All the color had drained from Andrea's face, and when Daniel held his arms out, she fell into them.

He wrapped his arms around her. "Hey, baby," he soothed, patting her shoulders. "What's this all about?"

"We have to go pick up Madison," Andrea said. "I was on my way, was headed out just after you called. But I was so flustered; I didn't trust myself. So, I figured it would be best to have you along. Let's go."

"Ah, not so fast." Daniel held Andrea at arm's length. "First, you need to fill me in."

Andrea pulled away, meeting his eyes. "Something happened to Madison."

Daniel went rigid, his eyes searching Andrea's. "What are you saying?"

"I have no idea. Come on!" Andrea grabbed her keys from off the foyer console. "We have to go fetch her." She brushed past him, and despite his misgivings, Daniel followed.

"I should drive." Daniel reached for the keys.

"No. You don't know where we're headed. At least I have a vague idea."

Daniel's only answer was a frustrated sigh.

They drove for a few minutes in silence. But as Andrea approached Indian River Boulevard, Daniel could contain himself no longer. "Please, be straight with me," he implored. "My mind is conjuring the most lurid of scenarios. What the hell is going on?"

Andrea kept her eyes on the road. It was late in the day, and she hated driving across town during rush hour when the bridges were thronged with traffic. "I got a call from a Carlos Menendez."

"And?"

"He seemed a decent sort."

"That's good. So?"

"Apparently, Madison tore across his front yard, running for all she was worth, and then collapsed."

"Collapsed? From what?"

"I don't know."

"My God!"

"Yeah. So, that's where we're going."

~

They were seven thousand feet above the ocean drinking Bloody Marys and recapping the events of the past week. "That was a total blast, Kara. Thank you." Laney swiveled in her luxuriously soft captain's chair, eyeing the perfectly painted toenails that were peeking out from her strappy sandals. "Island time," she murmured, "a time out of time."

Kara fished for the pimento-stuffed olive in her glass. "We definitely got our mojo back on, girlfriend." She popped the olive in her mouth, smiling at the memory of Trevor in her bed.

"I guess, we'll be returning before you know it. For Becca's wedding."

Kara narrowed her eyes. "Umm," she said. "Sure. That'll be fun. But who shall we ask as our dates? Huh?"

Laney sat up straight and eyed her friend. "Oh! I hadn't thought that through. Well, I guess I'll ask Jamal. I'm certainly not going to ask Charles. What about you, Kara?"

"I believe I have no option other than to invite Michael. He's interesting, smart, rich. *Did I say rich*? And I actually like him. So, why the hell not? Maybe if Jamal agrees to go, Michael will pop over, too."

"I love that idea. Besides, Chichester's a hunk and a half."

"He has his charms. On the downside, I may have to rent a place to stay. It doesn't look like Daniel's going to let me have Sweet Dreamer."

Laney's face clouded. "Oh, gosh. Shame on me. Naturally, I just assumed we'd stay at your place." She swiveled her head to gaze, unseeing, out the tiny oval window at her side. "Well, that is a bummer," she said, turning back to Kara. "But heck, between the two of us, I imagine we can swing a decent VRBO rental, even if it is in high season. Let's not sweat the small stuff. We're two capable gals; we'll manage just fine."

All the elation Kara had felt over the promise of a meaningful relationship with Michael quickly vanished. She was not returning to the mansion in Philadelphia but rather to her place in Singer Island— the soon-to-be-divorced castoff of Daniel Armstrong—and the bitterness of it rankled.

"Come on." Laney raised her glass. "Cheer up, Kara. We've got new men in our lives, and it looks like Becca's found a real keeper. If that's not worth celebrating, I don't know what is."

"You're right," Kara agreed, shaking off her ill humor. "Here's to the future, one that is filled with lovely, wealthy men."

"And to more island adventures." Laney clinked glasses with Kara and coaxed a smile out of her. "Many, many more."

CHAPTER TWELVE

REVELATION

Floyd and Diana sat shoulder to shoulder on the crude wooden seat of the panga—a small, outboard-powered fishing boat. It was not yet nine o'clock in the morning, still relatively cool. They, and the eighteen other passengers with whom they shared the modest vessel, gazed about at the coastline, its verdant jungle rising from a crystal clear, turquoise basin.

A short jaunt of twenty minutes found them disembarking on the wharf at Sapzurro, and Floyd's first impression of the town was of a sleepy village that time had forgotten. As much as he wanted to explore, there was no time to waste. Diana gripped his hand and hurried down the main street. She appeared single-minded of purpose, and Floyd allowed himself to be manipulated. This was her deal, and he was resolved to do whatever it took to make her happy.

The Catholic Church Sapzurro was a tiny, one-story building painted white with Copenhagen-blue trim. Unassuming, except for a peaked roof crowned with a small white cross, it perfectly reflected the sea and sky of Sapzurro. It was like a little gem tucked away in this backwater, and Floyd could not suppress the smile of delight that lit his face upon catching sight of it. As they neared the entrance, a young male acolyte, clad in a billowing white robe, tugged on a rope attached to the small bell mounted above the entry. The bell's clamor cut through the moist air, summoning the faithful.

The sight that greeted Floyd's eyes upon entering the church was even more resplendent for its austerity—white stucco walls, more blue trim, a ceiling laced with slender, mahogany beams, and a single, massive, bronze wheel-chandelier that had been converted from gas to electric. They walked down the center aisle where the red tile floor had been painted in traditional patterns rendered in shades of white and black. Twelve plank-constructed pews flanked the center aisle, and Diana hustled him into one of them before falling to her knees on a wooden kneeler. That was just fine with Floyd. Now, he could sit back and take in the rest of the church's accouterments: the suffering Christ on a simple wooden cross, an altar draped with a lace cloth—so simple and soothing. He sat next to an older woman; her gray hair draped in a black mantilla. She was praying the rosary, mumbling the prayers to herself while the clacking of her rosary beads provided a faint, percussive accompaniment. Floyd had visited the splendid cathedrals of Italy and Spain with their massive stained-glass windows, gilded ornamentation, and priceless art treasures. Yet none of those places of worship touched him as did this modest chapel nestled within a wild tropical forest.

There was no music. Instead, the chirruping of hundreds of birds announced the priest, a wizened dark-skinned man trailing behind the sole acolyte. When he swept in from an alcove to the left of the altar, the thirty-some parishioners rose to their feet. "En el Nombre del Padre, y del Hijo, y del Espíritu Santo. Amen," he intoned, and the devotees crossed themselves and prayed along with him.

Floyd was familiar with the Catholic Mass. He'd attended the baptisms, weddings, and funerals of his Catholic colleagues, and he was prepared to rise, sit, and kneel when the liturgy demanded. Now, he fell into a somnambulistic kind of trance. The burgeoning heat and accompanying humidity, the communal prayer, the charming church —they all worked on him, and he gave himself over to the moment. Floyd figured he was having an out-of-body experience. Whatever it was, it was exceedingly pleasant. He felt as though all his troubles had suddenly vanished—that he was being washed clean by the brilliant island light that was streaming through the unadorned windows.

"Hermanos: Para celebrar dignamente estos sagrado misterios, reconozcamos nuestros pecados," the priest intoned, and Floyd thought about his sins. The universe had gifted him with a second, and now, a third chance. He regretted his sins and was genuinely sorry for all the misery he'd undoubtedly caused. Images of his children suddenly filled Floyd's head—his son and daughter, so young and beautiful. He'd been asleep all those years they were growing up, so intent on making a success of his career, trying to provide a life for the wife and kids. When had it all gone so wrong?

"Jesucristo, el justo intercede por nosotros y nos reconcile a con el Padre." The priest uttered the familiar prayer in a singsong voice, but his words struck a chord, and a single tear leaked from Floyd's eye. He wanted to repent and atone, to be free of this burden that had brought him here, to feel absolved and whole again.

Suddenly, that seemed possible.

The priest held the chalice over his head. "Tomad y bebed todos de él, porque éste el Cáliz de Mi Sangre," he intoned. Floyd knelt on the unpadded kneeler and bowed his head, and when Diana rose to take Holy Communion, Floyd, too, came to his feet. Diana shot him a pleased smile and nodded, and Floyd followed her. Slowly, he processed in the line of parishioners toward the altar to receive the sacrament. When it was Diana's turn to receive, he watched her closely. Then he stood before the priest as she had done. Making the sign of the cross, he held his cupped hands before him to accept the host, saying, "Amén" as it was placed in his hands.

Back in the pew, Floyd knelt beside Diana. Feeling infused with the Holy Spirit, an inexplicable joy welled up within him. The thought occurred to him that maybe everything in his life had led him to this moment in time.

One thing Floyd knew for certain: he was a changed man.

～

Garrett was freaking out. A glimpse of a slight figure sprinting down Thirty-fifth, then stuck at a light and losing her. Could it be the girl he couldn't get out of his mind? There was no way of knowing. The briefest sighting from the corner of his eye, yet he figured it was her. Suddenly, Garrett knew what it meant to be coming out of one's skin. Jeez!

Gotta get in better shape, man! No more pizza.

Garrett's heart was in his mouth when the light changed. He stomped on the gas. Whatever he'd gotten himself into was terrifying and thrilling at the same time. His pulse quickened at the thought that he might rescue the defenseless girl—for once, do something noble in his life.

Hell, maybe reap the rewards.

Shut up, loser!

Out of the corner of his eye, he saw something. A house set back from the road, people in the driveway. But there was a car on his tail, and he had to keep his eyes on the road. Still, he kept casting surreptitious glances over his shoulder, struggling to make sense of what was happening back there.

By the time Garrett managed to turn around, backtrack, and pull up into the drive, everyone had vanished. He had no idea what he was doing. Should he knock on the door like some crazy man? Nah, that probably wasn't a good idea. What would he say? The girl didn't know him from Adam. They'd probably call the authorities and have him thrown in the looney bin. It didn't matter, he finally decided. He had to find out.

He knocked on the door, and when it opened a crack, swallowed hard. "Hello, sir," he said, meeting the cold, hard eyes of the Mexican American who was eyeing him suspiciously. "I'm Garrett Olson."

"Si?"

"I just want to make sure everything's okay here."

An attractive, dark-haired woman came to stand behind the man. "What business is that of yours?" she asked, looking none too happy to see him.

"I'm not sure. A friend of mine might be in trouble, and I thought I might have seen her in your driveway."

The woman turned away from him. "Madison, is this a friend of yours?"

She and her husband separated, and Madison came to stand between them. The woman put a protective arm around the girl's shoulders. "Do you know this person?"

The girl shook her head, and Garrett knew he'd blundered badly. He opened his mouth to explain just as Derrick's Jeep Safari pulled up into the driveway.

In one fluid motion, Derrick cut the ignition and hopped out of the vehicle, his long legs covering the distance between them in a matter of seconds. "Maddy," he exclaimed, "are you okay, baby?"

Madison broke away from the couple, burst out the doorway past Garrett, and threw herself into her father's arms. "Daddy," she cried.

Andrea's Mercedes wheeled in behind Garrett's Honda and Derrick's jeep, a moment later.

"What the hell's going on here?" the man at the door muttered.

~

Madison was seated between Sophia and Andrea on the Menendez's living room sofa. "I'm still not clear on this guy," Andrea said, looking confused as she eyed the young man with the wild mane of hair who was standing next to Derrick.

"I've seen him at the Farmer's Market, Mom," Madison said, smiling shyly at Garrett. "He's a regular." Garrett returned her smile.

"I can vouch for him," Derrick rushed to explain. "He's a good kid. He came to me when he suspected that someone was stalking Maddy."

"And you didn't do anything about it?" Andrea's voice rose shrilly. "What were you thinking?"

"What could I do, other than be vigilant? I had no proof of anything."

"He's right, ma'am," Garrett said. "I was suspicious, but heck, looking at someone isn't a crime. So—"

"So, the creep kidnapped her," Tyler piped in. "Jeez! This sucks, man."

Daniel leaned against the doorframe and addressed Andrea. "You need to call the police," he said. "Now."

"He's right," Carlos agreed. "That guy," he scrubbed a palm across his chin, "he's probably changing his license plates as we speak."

"Shit!" Garrett cursed softly.

Derrick dug his cellphone from a back pocket and punched in 911.

Andrea turned to Carlos. "I can't thank you enough for looking after my daughter." Before he could reply, she pivoted to face Sophia. "And now, to have to involve you in this... I am *so* sorry."

"No, no." Sophia shook her head vehemently. "It's what anyone would do." She glanced at her son. "I'm sure you would have done the same if it had been my boy who was in danger."

Andrea followed Sophia's gaze, taking in the eager young teen who had eyes only for Madison, and she smiled. "Well," she said, "I see what you mean. But I don't even want to imagine what might have happened if it weren't for your quick thinking."

～

Once the Mass had concluded, the final benediction given, Diana was eager to be on her way. But Floyd insisted they linger outside the church, and his ploy paid off; when the priest swept past him, he called out, "Padre, por favor," and the clergyman whirled around to face him.

"Si, mi'jo," the old man said. He turned to Floyd, a benevolent expression on his lined face. "¿Como le ayudo?"

he asked. "What can I do for you, my son?"

"Le pido un favor," Floyd said. *I have a favor to ask of you.*

"¿Si claro?" *What is it?*

The weariness in the old man's eyes was hard to miss. Padre was ready for his lunch and a nap, but Floyd knew he must persist. "Senor," he said. "Tengo algo que deseo confiarte" *I have something I wish to entrust to you.*

At those words, Diana tugged at his elbow, attempting to maneuver him down the path, but Floyd resisted. "No, Diana," he muttered, breaking free. "This is what I need to do."

The priest gave Floyd his full attention, and this small victory was so exquisitely rewarding that Floyd had all he could do to keep from weeping with joy. Somehow, he knew that every step of his life had led him to this one defining moment. He was going to give away all his plundered treasure, to divest himself of the very thing that was weighing him down. Never had he felt such conviction.

～

The panga was even more crowded on the return trip to Capurganá than it had been on the outbound journey. Throughout the short boat ride Diana remained tight-lipped, but every time Floyd met her eyes, he found hers upon him, a puzzled look on her face. The heat and humidity had settled in, but the open-air vessel was cutting across the sea at a good clip, creating a freshening breeze that made the crossing a pleasant one—all the more so given Floyd's buoyant good humor. The Caribbean-blue water sparkled like diamonds and the verdant jungle coastline made him think of Bali Hai, the island paradise in South Pacific. He'd always loved that musical. Now here he was, thrust into a romantic locale every bit as exotic. He was living the high life!

No sooner had they set foot on dry land than Diana grabbed his arm and peppered him with a barrage of questions. "Floyd, whaaat has gotten into yooou?" she asked as she hustled him away from the docks and down the main thoroughfare. "You're acting sooo strange. What was dat nonsense all abooout? What is it you waaant to give to the priest?"

"Not to worry. I'll explain everything, Diana," Floyd said, "over lunch and an El Presidente. I'm famished. Please say you have more of that delicious prawn stew you served last night."

Later, they sat on Diana's minuscule front porch, nursing cold beers. "That was delicious," Floyd said. "You are an amazing cook."

"It's Josephina's reeecipe."

"Superb."

Diana leaned back in her chair and eyed Floyd. "Now you tell me, huh?"

Floyd's face darkened. The sublime joy he'd experienced that morning had faded, and he was having second thoughts about giving away all his cash. "I'm afraid I got caught up in the moment. Such a sweet church... the Mass. I feel as though I should make a donation."

Diana smiled at him. "Dat wooould be nace. Maaaybe we go to church next Sunday, huh?"

"Yes, maybe." Floyd reached out and patted Diana's hand. "But after that wonderful meal, I'm feeling sleepy. Why don't we take a siesta?"

"We?" Diana's eyes twinkled.

"I did go to church with you, after all..."

Diana rose from her chair. "I bring you another beer while I see to the dishes. Dan maaaybe we lie down for a little while."

〜

Andrea and Madison were on the front porch saying goodbye to Sophia and Tyler while Carlos, Derrick, and Garrett stood beside the police cruiser parked on the street. "Officer, thank you so much," Derrick said to the cop, who was now seated behind the wheel. "This has been…" He sighed and looked away, seeming to struggle with his emotions.

Carlos clasped Derrick's shoulder. "Hey, man," he said, releasing him, "it's all good. No es? Isn't it? All's well that ends well…"

"Mr. Menendez," the deputy interrupted, "I commend you for your intervention. Good citizens, like you and your wife, give me hope for the species."

Carlos gave a brief nod of his head. "Thank you, sir. But we only did what anyone would do. No?"

"No." The officer directed his attention to Garrett. "And you, son, I strongly advise you against any more car chases. Trust me. You don't want to mess with the likes of this creep. We'll take it from here. You got that?" He gave Garrett a hard look.

"Yes, sir." A sheepish smile flitted across the young man's face.

The cop focused back on Derrick. "Mr. Nelson, I'll need to see you, Ms. Nelson, and your daughter tomorrow at headquarters. Shall we say ten o'clock? It shouldn't take more than a couple of hours."

"We'll be there, officer." Derrick lightly smacked a palm on the hood of the cruiser, then hopped to the curb when the engine roared to life. As the car pulled away, he put two fingers to his forehead in an informal salute.

As this was transpiring, Madison and Tyler left the porch and went to join their respective fathers, while Daniel, having distanced himself from the family drama, leaned against Andrea's Mercedes, staying well out of it.

He was checking the messages on his cellphone when Andrea came up behind him and tapped his shoulder. Spinning around to face her, he said, "Hey there. Ready to go?"

"In a minute," Andrea glanced at the police car pulling away from the curb. "Madison's just saying goodbye to her father and Mr. Menendez."

Daniel nodded. "No rush."

"Thanks for coming with me. I know it's been awkward, but I appreciate your being here."

"Please," Daniel said, "I'm glad I was able to lend my support."

"I'll go get Maddy, and then we can leave." She turned away. "I won't be but a moment."

"I'm not going anywhere without you."

~

When the patrol car zoomed down the street, Carlos turned to face Derrick. "So, my sister-in-law has a little mom-and-pop restaurant out near the mall, Carmelita's."

"Sure. I've seen it. Never eaten there, though."

"She's always looking for new sources. Maybe I should make an introduction?"

"Yeah. I'd appreciate that." Derrick said. "Let me give you my card." He dug a business card out of his wallet and pressed it into Carlos's hand. "Have her call me."

Carlos glanced at the card before depositing it in his back pocket.

"Hey, Daddy." Madison was suddenly behind Derrick, pulling on his shirtsleeves and demanding attention.

"Hi, darlin'." Derrick took one look at her, and his eyes welled.

"Madison," Carlos said, noting Derrick's distress, "your old pop is feeling pretty fragile right about now."

Sophia came to stand beside the girl. "Which is probably the way you're feeling, too, huh?"

Madison ducked her head. "Mm-hmm. I feel kind of… wobbly."

"Wobbly. I get it." Sophia rested a palm on Madison's shoulder.

Carlos nodded. "Well, listen. We're celebrating Tyler's birthday on Sunday with a picnic at Riverside Park."

He gestured toward the huge pontoon boat trailered beside his garage. "I'll be putting that leviathan in the river. So, there will be boat rides."

"That's right." Sophia grinned at her husband and then turned to Madison. "Tyler's asked me to prepare my world-famous enchiladas. The food will be great. You and your family should join us."

"What do you say?" Carlos squinched up his face, teasing a small smile out of Madison.

"That sounds wonderful," Andrea said, crossing the distance to her daughter and putting an arm around Madison's waist.

"Sure." Madison looked at her father. "That is if Dad says it's okay."

"Dad says it's a great idea, Maddy," Derrick said. "And I'll contribute a big garden salad."

"Awesome." Tyler sidled up next to Madison and flashed her a smile.

"Yeah, cool." Garrett pushed past the gangly teen. "I'm invited. Right?"

"Certainly," Carlos said. "Riverside Park, Sunday at noon down by the docks."

"Great," Garrett said, sending Tyler a warning look.

Carlos clapped Derrick on the back. "See you then."

∾

"I'll drive," Daniel said as Andrea and Madison drew near. Uncharacteristically subdued, Andrea offered no resistance. Instead, she fished the car keys out of her purse and held them before her. Daniel took them and slid in behind the wheel.

"I'm going to sit in back with Madison." Andrea didn't wait for a response. Instead, she opened the rear door and motioned Madison inside. Then she rounded the vehicle and climbed in next to her daughter.

"Strap yourselves in, girls," Daniel said. "We're going to Bobby's to eat and rehydrate."

"Sounds good by me," Andrea said. "Maddy?"

"Whatever."

Andrea turned to Madison and took her hand. "Are you alright?"

Madison's face crumpled, and the tears that she'd held in check now flowed freely. "I'm tired," she admitted with a ragged sigh.

"Oh, darling, of course you are." Andrea dug through her bag for a tissue. You've been through such an ordeal." She pressed the tissue into Madison's hand. "You've held it all in, so composed. It's no wonder you're at your rope's end."

"I'm sorry, Madison," Daniel said, peering into the rearview mirror. "It was insensitive of me to think we could go out for a bite to eat as though nothing out of the ordinary had happened. You've had a terrible fright, and you've handled it remarkably well. Cry it out if you must, dear. It just might help."

"I'll order a couple pizzas when we get home," Andrea said. "You can take a nice, hot shower and change into your PJs. We'll find a movie on Netflix and eat in front of the TV. How does that sound?"

"Good." Madison blew her nose with a loud honk.

"You're welcome to join us, Daniel." Andrea reached out and tapped him on the shoulder.

"Another time." Daniel pivoted to glance at Andrea. "Truth be told, I'm flagging myself. I think we could all use a good rest."

"Yes, I believe that's best." Andrea gazed, unseeing, out the passenger window. "It was nice of Carlos and Sophia to invite us to their picnic." She turned and searched Madison's face. "Wasn't it, honey?"

"I guess."

Andrea straightened and studied Daniel's profile—his prominent jaw, eyes obscured by sunglasses—and her heart expanded. He was so impossibly good-looking, and he radiated calm strength and toughness—attributes she found extremely attractive just now. "You'll come to the picnic?" she asked.

"We'll see." Daniel turned right onto Wave Drive and nodded at the cop behind the wheel of a police cruiser conspicuously parked beside the gate. "Good," he said, nodding in the car's direction. "It didn't take them long."

When he depressed a button on the rearview mirror, the Castaway Cove security gate hitched up, and Madison cringed. "Oh!" she cried, a stricken look on her face.

Andrea squeezed her daughter's hand. "It's okay, Maddy. You don't have to be afraid anymore."

"But he's out there—that man, Jack. He's been watching me."

"Listen, Madison," Daniel said. "We're going to find that sick bastard, and believe me, when we do, we'll make sure he rots in prison. Until then, you are perfectly safe. If he has any sense at all, he's already out of the county and headed for parts unknown. He wouldn't be foolish enough to come around here again. The sheriff has authorized extra patrols all along this stretch of the island."

"Daniel's right," Andrea said. "You are safe, and you're going to stay that way."

Her eyes bored into Madison's. "Do you understand?"

Daniel pulled up into Andrea's driveway, and Madison answered with a slight nod of her head.

"Here we are, ladies." Daniel cut the ignition, bounded out of the car, and then opened Madison's door. "Come on, Maddy. Let's get you inside." As they made their way up the drive, Daniel tossed the keys to Andrea, and she caught them easily.

The three bunched at the front door while Andrea unlocked it. "Go ahead, honey," Andrea said, once the door was open. She reached out and flicked on the light switch. "Into the shower with you. I'll just have a few words with Daniel, and then I'll order those pizzas."

Madison turned to Daniel. "Thank you," she said. "I do feel safer now."

"As you are. Good night, princess. Maybe, if you're up for it, we'll have dinner tomorrow at my place, huh?"

"Okay." Madison turned away and headed down the hallway.

Andrea and Daniel marked her passage until she disappeared into her bedroom. Then they faced one another. "So, what do you really think?" Andrea asked when Madison was out of earshot.

"What do I think? Jesus, Andrea, this is a hell of a thing!"

"I know. It's just starting to hit me. I could have lost her!" Her hands flew to her mouth.

Daniel clasped Andrea's shoulders. "But you didn't."

"Do you believe she's safe now?"

"I do. The police are going to be a very real presence. They'll keep the house under surveillance until they apprehend the guy. But hey, if you want me to stay here, I will."

"I would love that, Daniel. I sure as heck would feel more secure having you under our roof." Andrea sighed. "But it just wouldn't look right. Besides, Madison must be my number one priority. I think, for now anyway, it'd be best to maintain the status quo. Let's not throw anything new at her."

"As usual, you're right." Daniel drew her to him and held her close. "Is there anything else I can do for you?"

Andrea chuckled softly. "Oh, how I wish." She wrapped her arms around his neck, and Daniel kissed her long and hard.

"Maybe you should stay," Andrea said when he released her.

"Madame, I'm taking my leave before I am no longer capable of doing so."

"Will I see you tomorrow?"

"If Madison's up for it, we can have dinner at my place. If not, I'll have something delivered here and join you for a meal. Just let me know what works."

"Mom…" Madison's voice floated down the hall.

"Coming," Andrea cried.

"Go to her." Daniel brushed his lips against hers. "I'll call you later. Alright?"

"Yes."

Daniel made as if to go, but before he'd crossed the threshold, he turned and eyed her somberly. "Lock up," he said.

Andrea met his eyes and nodded before closing the door. Only after locking it and setting the deadbolt did she scurry down the hall to tend to Madison. "Coming, sweetie."

~

Daniel sat on his small balcony staring out over an ocean that, with the onset of dusk, had taken on the look of beaten pewter. Dark clouds bunched on the horizon. It was a fitting backdrop for his black mood as he pondered the events of the last weeks. He'd thought, once he made the break with Kara, he'd be rid of all the drama that had plagued him, but recent events proved otherwise.

How the hell did this happen?

Suddenly, the image of Andrea appeared in his mind's eye—her lissome dancer's body, gold-flecked eyes, and silken ash-brown hair—and he knew he was in too deep and past the point of no return. There was nothing for it; he was in love with that woman. As for Madison… Well, the teen presented an entirely new dynamic. He'd never fathered a child. Madison wasn't his, but there was no denying the paternal bond he felt toward her.

Daniel leaned forward, cupping his chin in hand. The little beauty —a combination of heart-wrenching innocence and wily pluck—had gotten under his tough, alligator skin. He reached for the bottle of bourbon on the side table and poured himself a generous draught. The alcohol hit his empty stomach like a rock, reminding him that he should eat something, but the thought of food made him nauseous. The girl was in danger! Never mind his reassurances to the contrary. Imagining her as some madman's captive made his blood boil. He needed to fix this.

But how?

Daniel came to his feet and gripped the balcony railing. It was nearly dark, and a peek-a-boo moon shone softly between sheets of ragged clouds. He was reminded of that magical night—his first dinner with Andrea—when he'd fallen under the moon's enchantment. And hers. Then his mind veered off onto another track as his brain grappled for a solution. Briefly, he entertained the idea of hiring a security service for Madison. It wasn't unusual for his company to retain WPG—a VIP protection firm—when he or one of the execs traveled to third-world hotspots where the chances of being kidnapped for ransom was an ever-present danger. No sooner had he thought of it than he nixed the idea. He doubted that Andrea would approve, and the girl would probably be intimidated by a bodyguard hovering over her.

Damn it!

There had to be something he could do to keep her safe. Then an idea sparked. He withdrew his cellphone from his back pocket and tapped in Andrea's number.

"Hi, Daniel." Her greeting came to him from over the miles, but now Daniel detected a new, tremulous quality to Andrea's voice. He knew the reason for it, and it infuriated him; this capable, self-sufficient woman was wracked by fear, and who could blame her? "Hey, babe," he soothed, "how's Madison?"

Andrea sighed before answering. "As good as can be expected, given the circumstances. We're watching *Star Wars, The Revenge of the Sith.*"

"The one where the Jedi Council dispatches Obi-Wan Kenobi to eliminate General Grievous and puts an end to the war?"

"Yes, when Anakin Skywalker is sent to spy on the Supreme Chancellor."

"Ah," Daniel stared out over the vast, empty sea, "and Anakin is turned to the dark side. Plenty of good versus evil there! I commend you on your selection."

"I thought it would cheer her up, but at this moment, Madison resembles nothing more than a frightened girl whose faith in humanity has been shaken."

"I'm sorry. That is a lesson she did not have to learn."

"Maybe. But you know what? I've realized I won't always be around to watch over her… that she's going to have to learn to be very cautious and to keep her guard up… and that makes me incredibly sad."

"Look here," Daniel said, infusing his voice with a lightheartedness he didn't feel, "I have a proposition that'll lift us all out of our doldrums."

"I'm all ears."

"This is too good to divulge over the phone. It'll have to wait until I can see you."

"That's a heck of a thing. I could use a bit of cheering up."

"And you shall have it. Good things come to those who wait, missy."

"Don't make me wait too long, buster."

Andrea's tone was playful, but Daniel thought she meant it. "Tomorrow then."

CHAPTER THIRTEEN

OUT OF THE FRYPAN

From the moment the excruciating pain in Jack Cramer's balls eased, he'd been a perpetual motion machine gone haywire. There'd been no time to waste. He'd made a mess of it, and now he had to do everything in his power to cover his tracks. The first order of business had been to switch the license plates on his van, which was an easy fix, for he had an old set of plates in the shed out in back. He realized that that minor alteration would buy him but a modicum of time.

Before long, the authorities would be running down every white utility van registered in the state of Florida and then coordinating with Indian River County to narrow the search. Worse yet, the girl could identify him, maybe even lead the authorities to his place. He had miles to go and much to accomplish before he'd rest easy. The one ray of light in this otherwise bleak picture was that his domicile was mobile; it seemed a no-brainer to move the damn thing off the property. Once it was gone, this weed choked plot would be merely a vacant lot, which is not how the girl would remember it.

It had been no small task disconnecting the hookups—displacing the cement blocks that had kept the tires high and dry, and hitching his trailer to the van—but sheer terror seemed to imbue him with superhuman strength, to say nothing of determination. It was insane to try to move a fully equipped mobile home without first securing all breakables—dishes, glasses, TV—but he hadn't the luxury of time to do so. His hastily devised plan was to head south on Interstate

Ninety-five. Sure, he'd be taking his chances with the state police, but he figured it'd be safer out on the expressway, where he'd blend in with the convoy of snowbirds making their way down the coast. What choice did he have? It was only a matter of time before the cops would be all over this neighborhood.

The sun had set, and the light was quickly fading. That would provide him some cover, and it wasn't more than eight miles to the RV park in Fort Pierce. He'd be safe there, hiding in plain sight. That thought sent him scuttling back out to the shed, where he retrieved fishing poles and gear. Might as well make the most of it, take a little holiday. If nothing else, it would provide him an alibi for the immediate future until he could devise a better plan.

One thing was for certain: either he had to disappear, or the girl did.

~

Andrea awoke to the jangling of her cellphone. She sat up in bed and retrieved it from the nightstand. "Hello, Daniel."

"Good morning."

"That remains to be seen."

"I'm just checking in. Everything all right?"

Andrea yawned and stretched. "Um-hmm. At least I think so," she said as she climbed out of bed. "Just a minute, Danny." She traipsed down the hall, stopping at Madison's doorway. Then, as quietly as possible, she turned the doorknob and opened the door a crack. Madison was lying on her side, and Beau lay curled against her hip. The cairn terrier raised his head and peered at Andrea, and she closed the door and then retreated into the kitchen.

"She's fine," she said. "Sleeping like a baby, and Beau's keeping watch." Andrea plugged in the coffee pot and then went to gaze out the French door at a view of the sun-spangled river she never tired of.

"Good. Do you want me to drive you to the police station?"

"That's not necessary. But I'd love for you to join us tomorrow at Riverside Park for Tyler's birthday party." Andrea could almost hear him grimace.

"You know, I just don't feel comfortable doing that."

"Why not?"

"That's going to be a family affair, and I would be the odd man out. You and Derrick need to be there. I don't."

"Danny—"

Daniel cut off her protest. "I'm sorry. That's my final word on the matter. You and I are going to have plenty of one-on-one time with Madison. I promise you that."

"Oh, alright." Andrea was annoyed, but she couldn't fault Daniel's logic. He'd only be uncomfortable in that situation, and why should he subject himself to such torture? What was his role, after all? Wannabe boyfriend?

"I'll call you this afternoon about dinner."

"Fine. Bye-bye."

~

They'd assembled in a tiny windowless room, its walls painted a tepid green, the only furniture, a table, and four straight-back chairs gathered around it. Andrea, Madison and Derrick occupied three of those chairs, and Officer Campbell sat at the fourth. "Are you sure you can't remember what street you were on when you got out of the van?" he asked.

Madison shook her head.

"Do you remember how many streets you crossed before getting to the Menendez house?"

"Like I said, two? Maybe three. It all happened so fast."

Andrea glanced at her cell. It was twelve forty-five, her stomach was growling, and she was getting antsy. They'd gone over and over the circumstances of Madison's abduction, making little headway. Maddy's expression told her she was stressed, that a total meltdown was imminent.

"I'm sorry, officer." Andrea pointed her chin toward the girl. "Are we nearly done here? I'm afraid my daughter's told you all that she can."

Campbell glanced at Madison, suddenly noting her distress. "Good job, Madison," he said, coming to his feet, "you've been a wonderful help. I think we can wrap this up now. At least for the time being."

"Thank you, officer." Derrick pushed away from the table and stood. "If there's anything else we can do—"

"No," Campbell interjected, "I believe we have all the information we need, Mr. Nelson."

Andrea rose and came to stand behind Madison. "Come on, honey." She extended a hand toward the teen. "Let's go." But Madison, her brows knit, seemed incapable of moving. "Sweetie," Andrea coaxed, "what is it?"

"Umm... something else."

Campbell's eyes latched onto Madison. Slowly, he pivoted to face her. "Maddy," he said, "what have you got for us?"

"Madison?" Andrea gripped her daughter's shoulder.

Derrick fell to his knees beside the girl. "Sweetheart, tell Daddy."

"There was a trailer," Madison said in a small voice. "Old... horrid looking. That's where he was going to take me." She stared off into space, focused on another dimension—one that was almost too ghastly to revisit. "I'd... forgotten. I had to kick him and get out of there. But that's where he was taking me. The trailer..."

Andrea gasped, and Derrick put a fist to his mouth. Campbell crossed to the girl in two long strides and leaned into her. "That's very good, Madison. You remembered. What else can you tell me?"

∾

Eighty miles and a world away, Kara was ensconced in her Palm Beach Shores lanai. Every surface that was not glass was painted white and—with its three walls of floor-to-ceiling windows and airy cathedral ceiling—the room was awash in light. Her Blackberry vibrated, and she tossed her book aside. A glance at the display told her it was Michael Chichester calling, and a smug smile crept over her face. "Hello, Michael."

"Hello, doll. What are you up to?"

Kara laughed prettily. She adored Michael's oh-so-proper English accent, and she could see him in her mind's eye, with his tousled head of hair, so ruggedly good-looking. "I'm reading your book, *The Girl with the Dragon Tattoo*. It's a page-turner."

"Told you."

"And pining away for the islands."

"Don't give me that drivel. It can't be all that bad in Palm Beach in April. Sunshine, ocean breezes. It beats the hell out of dreary old London town."

Kara surveyed her lushly landscaped yard with its splashing fountain and latticed gazebo. "I suppose you're right," she conceded. "But you know as well as I; there's something about Barbados."

"I do, indeed. Which is why I'm calling."

"Oh?" Kara straightened on the divan.

"Yes. What's the status of your divorce, if you don't mind my asking?"

"Why on Earth would you ask such a thing?"

"Because I'm thinking of flying down there in a couple of weeks, and I hoped you might join me."

Intrigued, Kara asked, "And what does my marital status have to do with *that?*"

"Darling, I have an ex-wife who'd stop at nothing to keep my boys from me. If we're going to have a relationship—"

"Stop right there." Kara rose to her feet and crossed to the windows. "A relationship?"

"I'd like to think that's possible."

Kara arched a brow. Everything was falling into place. "Anything's possible."

"Don't toy with me, Kara. I'm serious. I cannot afford the mere scent of a scandal."

"My divorce will be final within the week."

"Good. Then I'll make plans."

Kara's mind raced. "Michael, you might as well know—"

"Know what?"

"It's looking as though I may have to give up Sweet Dreamer."

Michael's snort of derision was music to Kara's ears. "Take the money and let the damn thing go," he said. "What do we need with two houses in Barbados, especially when mine is twice the size of yours?"

At the word *we* Kara tossed her head and breathed a happy sigh. Still, she was not about to let her defenses down. "Well," she said, putting a pout in her voice, "when you put it that way…"

"Right-o. I'll be in touch."

Kara disconnected and then, unable to contain her elation, danced around the room. But her victory celebration was short-lived. Suddenly sobering, she flopped back down on the divan to plot her next move.

"Oh, Danny," she breathed over templed fingers, "you're one lucky fellow, alright."

∽

Daniel lounged beside Nathan McCourt's saltwater pool, a bottle of beer in hand.

"You've come a long way, done well for yourself, Nate."

Nathan chuckled. "You mean from rags to riches?"

"You could say that." Daniel waved a hand toward his friend's enormous manse. "Pretty cushy life you've carved out here."

"You're one to talk. I'd say life hasn't treated you too badly." Nathan clinked bottles with Daniel and then seated himself in the chair beside his friend.

"It's not the same. I was guaranteed a spot at the table... the Armstrong legacy, a fat inheritance. I didn't have to prove myself the way you did. I'm proud of you."

"Ah," Nathan brushed off the compliment. "And am I correct to think that you'll be wintering here?"

"That was the plan, but who knows? Maybe I'll make Vero my permanent residence."

"As I've told you, it's a damn fine little town with all the trappings of the big city but without the pollution or traffic."

"Yeah. Vero's growing on me. I have to admit."

"Uh-huh." Nathan's eyes gleamed. "And so, I presume, is a Ms. Andrea Nelson."

"Guilty as charged." Daniel shook his head at the absurdity of it. "My divorce isn't even finalized, and here I go again."

"Don't beat yourself up over it. Andrea is a great girl—pretty, smart, genuine... Did I say genuine?"

"I hear you."

Nathan leaned forward in his chair. "I'm telling you. Andrea's the real deal, the whole enchilada. And Madison's a sweetie. I know it's a package deal, but any man would be lucky to have those two."

Daniel raised his beer bottle in a toast. "Thank you for the off-the-cuff. I do believe I needed to hear that." His cell sounded, and he withdrew it from his back pocket. When he glanced at the display, he scowled. "Jeez! Speak of the devil. It's Kara."

Nathan rose to his feet. "Take it," he said. "I'll give you some privacy. Then we'll go have lunch at the club." He hiked toward the house as Daniel tapped the phone icon to accept the call.

"Hello, Kara." Daniel girded himself for the inevitable squabble.

"Danny," Kara spat, "I want to get past this divorce as soon as possible."

Daniel bounded out of his chair and immediately began pacing. "My sentiments exactly."

"You can have Sweet Dreamer."

Daniel raised his brows. Was he hearing properly? "In exchange for what?"

"The original terms: a ten-million-dollar settlement, the Palm Beach property, twenty thou a month for three years."

"I'll have my attorneys prepare the documents. You'll have them in the next day or two."

"Great… and Danny…"

"Yes?"

"Thank you." Kara's strident tone softened. "I'm sorry it didn't work out between us. I really am. You're a good man."

Daniel shook his head as if to clear it. He could hardly believe his ears. "Me, too," he conceded. Hell, it was the least he could do. Might as well stay on amicable terms. What else did he have to lose? Besides fifteen mil, give or take?

"Thank you, Kara." He tapped the disconnect and then sat heavily in his chair. His mind was awhirl. This was a gift from the gods, and it couldn't have come at a better time.

Out of the frypan into the fire!

❧

"Oh goody, Madison," Daniel exclaimed as he parked the car in the Moorings' back lot. "Your mom says we're eating downstairs, tonight."

"Yeah. I like downstairs better." Madison clambered out of the car. "More fun."

"More fun. Yay! And we can get an ice-cream from the freezer, right?"

"Yes," Madison agreed, "but only if you eat all your dinner."

Andrea burst out laughing and clasped Madison's hand. "That's right, honey. So, you and I will have to keep a close eye on Daniel and make sure he licks his plate."

Madison rolled her eyes. "Mom…"

"Just kidding, kiddo. Come on, let's find a table."

"Hello, there." The strikingly handsome club manager appeared out of nowhere and hiked toward them. "How nice to see you, Andrea." He swooped in, brushed a kiss against Andrea's cheek, and then turned his attention to Madison. "As for you, Miss. Madison, are you swimming tonight?"

Madison hefted her beach tote. "I brought my suit."

"Great," Craig said. "Maybe you could do a routine for us?"

Andrea looked pointedly at Madison, but her daughter refused to meet her eyes. "Maybe," Madison said.

Noting the sudden tension between mother and daughter, Daniel rushed in to diffuse the situation. "I, for one, would love to see one of your routines, Maddy."

His innocent statement was met with a scowl from Andrea and a distressed look from Madison, and he figured he'd better shut the hell up and quit while he was ahead.

"Here we are," Craig said, indicating the last unoccupied table on the patio. "How's this?" He pulled out a chair. "Madison, you have a clear view of the pool. I would think that's about perfect, huh?"

Madison averted her eyes and blushed. "Mm-hmm," she mumbled, flouncing down into the chair. "It's good. Thanks."

Daniel held out a chair for Andrea. "You remember my client, Daniel Armstrong?" she asked.

As soon as she was seated, Daniel turned to Craig and extended an arm. "Mr. Lopes—"

"Please," the manager shook Daniel's hand, "it's Craig. Mr. Lopes is my father." He turned to the women at the table. "Ladies, chef has prepared a feast. Be sure to check out the raw bar. It's fabulous." That said, he turned on his heel and headed back inside.

≈

Having inched low on the horizon, the sun was painting the lagoon with garish strokes of crimson and gold, and as daylight fled, the illuminated swimming pool gleamed a brilliant lapis blue. Strings of fairy lights—strung around planters and suspended from eaves—twinkled merrily, and a waning moon poked an oblong hole in the sky. The table had been cleared, and Andrea sat at it alone, nursing a glass of white wine. During dinner, a guitarist had set up next to the pool house. Now he was singing the last refrain to a Joni Mitchell song.

Don't it always seem to go
That you don't know what you've got
Til it's gone?
They paved paradise
And put up a parking lot.

As the last chord faded into memory, Andrea applauded heartily. That song always got to her. She thought about the transformations that had occurred in Vero Beach in her lifetime. Andrea's reverie was interrupted by gales of laughter coming from the gaming area where a sole ping-pong table was occupied. Daniel was on one end of it, valiantly holding his own against a very determined and gleeful Madison and some giggling classmate she'd attached herself to. The teens were furiously beating back Daniel's assault, and it was comical to see him trying so hard, and yet seeming to be having the time of his life. Could she let this gorgeous man into her life, and if she did, would he break her heart? She didn't know the answer. All she knew was that she was falling for him in a big way.

The next morning, Madison sat at the breakfast table, picking at her eggs. Andrea glanced up over her newspaper and noted her daughter's sulky expression. "What's the matter, honey?" Andrea set the paper aside. "No appetite?"

"Can I be excused? I'm not hungry." Madison made as if to push away from the table.

"Sit for a minute. I want to talk to you."

Madison slumped in her chair and sighed. "Oh, brother."

"Look, Maddy, I know this has been difficult for you—"

"I'm fine," Madison interrupted.

"No, you're not, and that's perfectly normal. You've had a real scare, a very close call. It's natural to feel…" Andrea struggled for words, "off-kilter. Which is why we're seeing Doctor Dean next week."

"A shrink." Madison crossed her arms before her. "I'm not crazy, Mom."

"No, you're a level-headed teenaged girl who's suffered a very bad experience, and you need to work your way through it. Dr. Dean will help you do that."

"I'm not going."

"Yes, you are. End of discussion. Heck, Madison, every pop and movie star sees a therapist. There's no shame in it. In fact, it's kind of cool."

"Humph," Madison huffed, obviously unconvinced.

Andrea rose from her chair and came to stand behind her daughter. "Look what a beautiful day it is." She gestured toward the French doors and then placed her palms on Madison's shoulders. "Aren't you looking forward to this afternoon?"

"No."

"What?" Andrea pulled out a chair and sat down next to Madison. "Why not? A birthday party and a boat ride? Since when are you not up for a fun day in the park?"

Madison turned away, scowling. "It's just…"

Andrea clasped her daughter's hand. "Madison, what's eating you?"

"Garrett, Tyler… boys. Ugh!" Madison blurted.

Andrea took a moment to process this information before responding, "Ah! Do those two make you feel uncomfortable?"

Madison nodded sullenly.

"How come? They seem to like you. A lot. I'd think you'd find that flattering."

"It makes me embarrassed. I don't know how to act."

"Oh, Maddy. You're a beautiful young woman. You might as well get used to boys' attentions. So long as they're honorable. And I'm convinced Garrett and Tyler want nothing more than your friendship." Andrea looked away and grimaced. "At least I hope so," she muttered.

"But what do I do?"

"You know the answer to that question: Just be yourself." Andrea gained her legs. "Come on. Carpe diem! Let's seize the day. What do you say?"

"Okay." Madison came to her feet. "But Mom?"

"Yes, sweetheart?"

"What should I wear?"

Andrea smiled. At last, they were back in familiar territory.

Madison had decided to take her mother's advice. She wasn't going to worry about the boys. Either they liked her, or they didn't, but she was pretty sure they did. Tyler was puppy-dog cute but way too immature. Garrett was older and, with his intense blue eyes and wild hair, so dreamy.

Once Carlos had put the boat in the water, they'd left their picnic trappings on a table near the docks and clambered aboard with beach bags and coolers in hand. Andrea sat in front with Sophia. Carlos stood at the wheel, and Derrick leaned against the railing beside him. Madison had taken a seat in the back, and when Tyler slid in beside her, Garrett promptly plopped down on her other side.

"Wedged in tightly enough there, Madison?" Derrick teased. "All safe and secure?"

Carlos glanced back at the kids and guffawed, and Madison's cheeks burned, but when Garrett loosely draped an arm across the seatback cushion, she suddenly felt empowered.

Mom had been right. This was going to be fun.

Propelled by its monster 250-horsepower outboard, the ungainly boat cut effortlessly across the moderate chop. The sun was warm on Madison's face and shoulders, and beads of perspiration popped out on her brow. With not a trace of self-consciousness, she unbuttoned her coverup, stood, and shrugged out of it, and Garrett and Tyler made no secret of watching her every move.

Andrea held out her hand. "Here, honey. Give it to me," she said, and Madison balled up the terrycloth sheath and carried it to her.

Andrea stuffed the garment in her tote and fished out a tube of sunscreen lotion. "Turn around and let me do your back."

Once she'd been appropriately slathered, Madison made her way back to her seat. Suddenly aware of Garrett and Tyler's eyes on her scantily clad body, she managed to sashay toward them with her shoulders back and head held high. Andrea watched her daughter with mixed feelings of pride and concern. Madison was coming into her own, and God help them all!

Garrett caught Madison's eye and grinned, and she flounced down beside him. "Nice bathing suit," he said.

"No kidding," Tyler agreed.

When Carlos had navigated to a wide spot in the river—one where no other watercraft were bearing down on them—he turned to the kids, hollering, "Who's up for water-skiing?"

"I am, Dad." Tyler jumped to his feet and strapped on a lifejacket, and Carlos cut the engine. Once the boy was in the water, skis affixed to feet, he signaled to his dad, and Carlos gunned the engine. Like a bottlenose dolphin, Tyler popped out of the water in one graceful motion. Then, seemingly in defiance of gravity, he skimmed over the water's surface with effortless ease.

Garrett and Madison swiveled in their seats, their eyes trained on the slender youth. "Man, he's good," Garrett said.

Tyler made a circular motion with his hand, and Carlos jerked the wheel to the left, executing a sharp turn. Tyler flew by the stern, grinning widely. When Carlos righted the boat, Tyler pivoted, skied backward for a moment, and then flipped back around.

"Whoo-hoo, Tyler," Madison cried. "You rock!"

Eventually, Tyler made a slashing motion, dragging his thumb across his throat, and Carlos cut the engine. When the boy was hauled aboard, he was greeted with much fanfare. "You are terrific," Madison said, her eyes gleaming.

"Not bad," Garrett said, clapping Tyler on his narrow but well-muscled back.

"Okay, enough for now," Sophia said, pressing a can of beer into her husband's hand. "Would you like one, Derrick?"

"I wouldn't say no," Derrick admitted.

"I brought mimosas—fresh-squeezed orange juice and

champagne." Andrea opened her small igloo cooler. "How about it, Sophia?"

"Yummy! Count me in," Sophia said. Then she turned and pointed to a large, built-in cooler up front. "There are sodas on ice over there for you kids," she said, motioning for the young people to help themselves.

"I'll anchor the boat just offshore," Carlos said. "Then I'll fire up the grill. We'll take her out again after lunch."

"Not to mention a birthday party," Sophia added, smiling at Tyler.

~

The kids stayed behind on the boat while the adults went ashore—Andrea and Sophia to set the table, and Carlos and Derrick to stoke up the charcoal grill. The boys lingered on the pontoon's swim platform, Garrett, legs hanging over the side. Tyler stood next to him, casting a line out beyond the mangroves in hopes of hooking a snapper.

Having spread a beach towel out on the upper deck, Madison was sunbathing. Small waves lapped against the side of the boat, and the sun worked its magic; she drowsed.

Tyler's line zinged out, the hook landing with a plop, and Garrett watched as ever-widening concentric rings on the water radiated out from the initial point of contact. "You are quite the hotdog," Garrett said, his voice full of admiration.

"Why, thank you." Tyler's face split in a sardonic grin.

"I mean that as a compliment. How did you learn to water ski like that?"

"Pfft," Tyler snorted. "That was nothing. You should see me dry-start slalom."

"What's that?"

"That's when I stand on the dock on one ski, and Dad guns it. I fly. It's cool."

"I'd like to see that."

Tyler jiggled his pole. "Maybe someday."

Garrett pivoted to glance at Madison and then swiveled back to face the water. "It's a shitty thing... what happened to her."

"It sucks. You think that guy will come back for her?"

"I don't know, but I'm afraid he might. She can identify him, right?"

"Damn. That's what I was imagining, too."

"Well, I'll let you in on something. I've got a plan."

Tyler turned to Garrett, giving him his full attention. "A plan?"

"A way to beat the pervert at his own game. You interested?"

"Are you kidding me?" Tyler said. "Count me in."

Sophia stood at the water's edge. "Come on, birthday boy, it's time for your party," she cried.

"Okay, Mom. Coming." Tyler tossed his pole aside, and Garrett came to his feet.

"I'll get Maddy," Garrett said.

Tyler grasped the older boy's arm. "I like her, too. You got that?"

Garrett snorted. "If I die trying to save her, you can have first dibs, kid. But let's face it, you're in the junior league, here. And I'm in the majors. Honestly, you need to fall in line if we're going to do this thing." Garrett put his face in Tyler's. "Can I count on you?"

Tyler's jaw clenched, and he looked away. Then his eyes found Madison. She was awakening, rising slowly from her berth, and she was so beautiful as she looked around wide-eyed, seeming a bit disoriented.

Garrett followed Tyler's gaze, and his face hardened. "She's not stupid."

"I know that!" Tyler shot back hotly. "But she's probably the most vulnerable chick I ever met."

"Yeah," Garrett agreed. "Like she was born without... I don't know... the caution gene."

"A freakin' sitting duck," Tyler muttered. "So, what do we do?"

∽

A rooster crowed, jolting Floyd out of a most delightful dream. He'd been flying—on his own power—rising higher and higher over the Catedral Primade de las Americas, and the view was spectacular. The ancient city was lit with a thousand lights. So that now, the transition was jarring. He could see nothing in the dark, and it took a moment for him to get his bearings. Then it all came back to him. He realized he was in Diana's bed, and memories of the best sex in his miserable existence flooded his consciousness. The mere thought of his unbridled prowess was enough to bring a blush to a face that had never blushed before. Had he actually done *that*?

Yes, he had, and he looked forward to a repeat performance soon.

"Floyd? What's the maaataar?" Diana reached for him in the darkness.

"Nothing. Go back to sleep," he muttered. In response, Diana nestled closer to him. It wasn't long before her breathing slowed, but Floyd lay awake for a long time pondering the events of the last several weeks. He'd thought beautiful Santo Domingo would be his home, but he'd had to flee that UNESCO city with only the shirt on his back and a valise stuffed with cash. He'd been reduced to a man on the run. And yet, somehow, fate had not abandoned him. Instead, she'd led him to Capurganá and Diana.

What luck!

He could easily lose himself in this jungle paradise, spend his remaining days in the arms of the sweetest, most voluptuous woman on the planet.

Not a bad life.

Eventually, Floyd succumbed to exhaustion, and he, too, slept.

When he awoke, it was to the mouth-watering aromas of bacon sizzling in a pan and freshly ground coffee percolating. "Ahh…" Floyd stretched his limbs, languorously savoring these few moments between repose and wakefulness. Then the sound of an unfamiliar, taunting voice caused his hackles to rise, and with the vigor of a teenager, he shot out of bed. Shrugging into his clothing, he crossed the short distance to the kitchen, only to be waylaid by the sight of Diana's generous backside. Which, inevitably, conjured images of last night's wanton performance.

She was leaning out the front door, exchanging barb for barb with the three malevolent-looking men they'd encountered the previous evening.

What the hell?

"Diana, what's going on? What are those men doing here?" Floyd grabbed the woman's arm.

She turned a guileless face to him. "Is noothiing. No woorries."

Floyd's brow creased. He took in the men—their transparently phony, good-natured smiles—and was not mollified. Instead, alarm bells clanged in his belfry. It didn't take a rocket scientist to figure out what they had come for. They were after his money!

He recalled last night's dinner, could picture himself in the continual loop that was his brain, fat cat, and careless. Like a fool, he'd pulled out his cash-stuffed wallet to pay for their dinner. That thoughtless action had been his undoing. He'd realized it too late when he'd raised his head only to find the three gangsters staring at him as though transfixed.

The apparent ringleader, the man who'd met his eyes, did so again, this time openly smirking at him. "Senor." He touched two stubby fingers to a sun-creased brow in a salute, which was not deferential.

Floyd saw it for what it was: a challenge, and that infuriated him. He hadn't come this far, endured all the hardships and humiliations of his exodus, to be foiled by these three low-level hoodlums. In a split second, Floyd realized he needed to buy time, to diffuse the situation, get these bozos off his ass, and then rid himself of the cash. Otherwise, he and Diana would live in constant fear.

Damn!

"Diana," Floyd hissed, "tell them we'd love to stay and chat, but that we have to catch the panga to Sapzurro. We're going to church."

CHAPTER FOURTEEN

INTO THE FIRE

"So, how did it go?" Andrea was so tightly wound, her mother's warm contralto failed to calm her nerves.

"Fine," she said, holding the cell to her chin, her eyes closed.

"Fine? Excuse me?" Margaret's voice took on a strident tone. "Is anything fine just now? Do not trifle with me, Andy. I have a vested interest in this, you know."

Andrea exhaled and settled herself. Her mother didn't need another teenager sulking. "Sorry, Mom. I'm a mess."

What is the matter with me?

"No, no," Margaret hastened to placate. "That was out of line. It's just that I'm... so worried."

"I know, Mom. We all are."

"Tell me, what can I do?"

"Honestly, I don't know what *I* can do." Andrea's voice hitched, and she held back tears. "I'm lost. This is uncharted territory. On the one hand, I'm told that Madison is perfectly safe, that there are police patrols, surveillance, that the madman wouldn't dare show his face here again. Yada yada yada. And the fact that Madison can identify him..." Andrea paused, allowing for that last bit of information to resonate. "So, you get my drift."

"My God!"

"Yeah." Andrea's cell vibrated, and she glanced at the display. "Say, can I call you right back? Daniel's trying to get through."

"Sure thing."

Andrea tapped to accept Daniel's call. "Hi."

"Hey there. How was the big birthday bash?"

"It was nice. I think it was a good diversion for Madison. Garrett and Tyler kept her occupied, and she seemed to relax and enjoy herself, which is probably just what the doctor ordered. What about you?"

"Nothing much." Daniel hesitated before continuing. "I puttered about, contacted a couple of the architects you suggested and set up interviews."

"Great." Andrea's brow furrowed. "About the closing…"

"Tell me you're not getting cold feet."

"Not at all. I was just wondering if we could finalize a date. Get this show on the road. Mom's already packing up, so…"

"Absolutely. When were you thinking?"

"The sooner the better."

"Fine by me. How about we talk about it over dinner?"

"I couldn't leave Maddy."

"I wouldn't expect you to. You and Madison are welcome to come here. We could dine out by the firepit. Or I could order something and bring it to you."

"You have no idea how much I'd love coming to you… to pretend —if only for a few hours—that everything was normal, but I'm afraid our girl's not up for it."

"Say no more. I'll be there at six."

Andrea had set the patio table for three—linen napkins, her second-best china, crystal waterglasses, and a floral centerpiece comprised of freshly picked hibiscus blossoms surrounding an oversized, flickering candle. It was a typical South Florida evening— the air wrapped in a veil of humidity and redolent of citrus and gardenia, the darkening sky glittering with faraway stars.

When the doorbell rang, Andrea called out, "Maddy, would you get that, please? I'm not quite dressed."

"Okay, Mom." Madison darted from her bedroom and loped to the front door. When she opened it, it was to find Daniel laden down with bags of takeout.

"Hey, kid!" he said. "I'd say long time no see, but I can't really see you."

Madison couldn't suppress giggles at the sight of the typically unflappable Daniel struggling as he juggled so many packages. "Come in," she said, attempting to relieve him of some of his burdens.

"No, no, no," Daniel cried, tripping past her. "If one is removed, the lot will surely tumble, and we do not want that." He staggered over the threshold.

Madison erupted in gales of laughter.

"What's so funny?" Daniel grumbled.

"Here, let me help," Madison said, following on his heels. But Daniel continued on his way into the kitchen. There, he nearly tripped over the dog, who was suddenly yipping at his feet, eager for a handout.

Madison grabbed Daniel's elbow and steadied him. "Beau! Go away," she cried. Despite Daniel's objections, she began unloading his tower of offerings, setting bag after bag on the kitchen table. "Gosh, this smells good, Daniel," she said. "What's for dinner?"

"I didn't know what your favorites were, so I ordered everything I could think of."

"Like?" Madison leaned into the table and put her nose to a container. "Umm…"

Daniel shooed her away. "Wait until your mother comes to sort out this mess. I will tell you this: We have sushi from Siam Orchid, pizza from Diavalo's, stone crab from the Ocean Grill…"

"What?" Andrea exclaimed as she sailed into the kitchen. "Daniel, you're spoiling us.'

"Nothing's too good for my two favorite ladies on the planet," Daniel said, slipping an arm around Andrea's waist.

"Unhand me, sir," Andrea squealed, but Daniel drew her to him and planted a chaste kiss on her lips.

In the meantime, Madison had pried open a cardboard container and was eating from it with her fingers. "Maddy, stop that." Andrea dashed to her daughter and snatched the box from her hands. "Be useful. Drag Daniel over to the bar and help him uncork the wine while I set out the buffet. What a feast!"

The detritus of their takeout dinner had been cleared away, and Andrea and Daniel sat at the patio table watching Madison cut through the pool, swimming laps. "That was a wonderful meal, Daniel." Andrea raised her wineglass in a toast. "You brought food for an army."

"I enjoyed ordering out so that we could dine in," Daniel said, bringing his glass to hers. "It was great fun."

"You have been so kind to us." Andrea grew somber. "I don't know what I would have done without you these last few days."

Daniel shook his head. "Not at all. I wouldn't have had it any other way. I only wish there was more I could do. Are you sure you wouldn't like me to retain a security service?"

"I'm sure. But thank you for the offer."

"Well then…" Daniel set his glass down, a look of determination on his face. "I've got a proposition to run by you."

"Oh?" Andrea cocked her head.

"Isn't Madison's Spring Break next week?"

"Yes."

"That's what I thought. How about we fly the coop for a couple of days?"

"What do you mean?"

"I was thinking of flying the three of us someplace where we could just kick back, get Madison out of her element for a little while, and let her be a kid—a kid with no worries."

"That's sweet of you, but—"

Daniel cut her off. "Don't nix the idea before you've heard me out. The place I have in mind is a magical getaway for all ages." He arched a brow, letting that sink in. "But it's especially geared to teens."

Intrigued, Andrea propped her elbows on the table. "I'm listening."

"Good." Daniel withdrew a brochure from his breast pocket, unfolded it, and placed it in front of Andrea. "Atlantis. Paradise Island. What do you say?"

Andrea snatched up the brochure, taking but a moment to scan it. "I've heard of Atlantis. Who hasn't? But I never thought of it as a vacation destination for me."

"And why not?"

Andrea tossed the brochure onto the tabletop. "Because I'm living smack dab in the middle of paradise. Why would I want you to spend ridiculous amounts of cash so that we could hang out in some tropical tourist trap?"

Daniel dug his heels into the deck and pushed back from the table. "Why? Are you kidding me? Because, my dear, you are always *working* in paradise. I truly believe I need to get both of my women out of Vero for a few days to—"

"What?"

"Chill? To forget about work, school… kidnappers."

Andrea dropped her head to her hands, but then Madison was behind her, wrapping a damp arm around her shoulders. "Hey, Mommy, what's this?" The teen leaned in, examining the brochure that now lay open on the tabletop. "Atlantis?" she breathed. "Cool."

Madison reached for the leaflet. "I always wanted to go there." She was dripping but seemingly unmindful of the fact, and she pulled out a chair and plopped into it. Unfolding the brochure, she gazed at the images, raptly. "Wow. Aquaventure! Robinson Crusoe Shipwreck!" She turned an eager face to Daniel. "Can we go there?"

Daniel pivoted to Andrea and shrugged before turning back to the girl. "It's up to your mom, kiddo."

Andrea glared at the back of Daniel's head. He'd put her on the hot seat, and she didn't feel obliged to defend her position. No sooner had that thought crossed her mind than it struck her: he was merely offering his support. Surely, he had only the best of intentions, and not just for her, but for Maddy as well.

She took a deep breath, and her objections died in her throat. "Humph!" Andrea reached out and stroked her daughter's auburn hair. "You *are* a minx."

"I'd say she was a mink," Daniel said. "Sleek, luxurious, *expensive*, and an amazing swimmer." He turned to Andrea. "So, what about it? Do I have your permission to book us a couple of days on Paradise Island?"

"Yes, yes!" Madison jumped to her feet and hopped up and down. "Say yes, Mommy. Please."

Andrea narrowed her eyes and focused on Daniel. "You, sir, are a troublemaker."

Madison put her face in Andrea's, capturing her gaze. "No. He's not, Mom. He's a good guy." She turned and grinned at Daniel. "This is a great idea. When can we go?"

∾

A little over an hour after his latest encounter with the three hooligans, found a freshly showered Floyd back at Diana's. He was wearing a clean shirt and Bermuda shorts, toting a bulging valise and directing traffic. "Hurry, Diana, we need to be at the panga in fifteen minutes."

"Whaat's da big hurry, Floyd?" Diana protested while washing a glass at the kitchen sink.

"I want to go to Mass," he said. "And I need one of your enormous handbags." Diana looked at him askance, and he gave her his full attention. Putting a palm on her shoulder, he looked into her eyes and said, "Trust me on this. Okay?"

"Humph!" Diana glowered, lowering her brows and slowly shaking her head.

"Now go." Floyd took the glass from her hand, set it on the counter, and traced a finger down her impossibly high cheekbone. "Please." He brushed his lips against hers and then gently turned her in the direction of the bedroom. "Prisa!" He lightly smacked her fanny, speeding her on her way.

∾

Father Enrique Ramos donned his vestments as he had a thousand times before, although now, in his advanced years, there was pain involved. Lifting the white alb above his head, his rotator cuffs screamed in protest. Arthritis had settled in his joints years ago, and his range of mobility was limited. Still, he mumbled the prayers that were as familiar as was his pain, "Limpiame, oh Señor, y purifica mi corazón, para que, lavado en a sangre del Cordero, alcance el gozo eterno." *Cleanse me, oh Lord, and purify my heart, that washed in the Blood of the Lamb I may attain everlasting joy.*

The words rolled from his lips, one tumbling over the other, a meditative litany that allowed his mind to soar. He tightened the cincture about his waist. "Cíñene, oh Señor, con el conturón de la pureza..." *Gird me, O Lord, with the cincture of purity...*

How many years did he have left? It had been a good life, he decided, living out his days in service to the Lord—tending to his little flock. But try as he might, self-recrimination niggled. He'd always thought to accomplish grand things. There was so much need in his little parish of impoverished souls. If only he could do more for them...

~

The scenic boat ride from Capurganá to Sapzurro had lost its allure. Instead of feeling enthralled at the sight of the tropical foliage ringing the crystalline, turquoise waters, Frank brooded the entire way, lost in his own torment. "Floyd, whaats da maater?" Diana reached for his hand.

Floyd jerked away. "Nothing." He eyed her critically. "Please, would you hold that bag closer to your chest?"

"Whaat?"

"Diana!" She responded by clutching the tote to her breast.

Soon, they were docking at Sapzurro's rickety wharf, and Floyd steeled himself for the business at hand. As a deckhand looped a line over a piling, he thought about what he was about to do, and it burned him. Everywhere he turned, it seemed someone was after him —either on his tail or conspiring to rob him of his ill-gotten gains. Perhaps he should have anticipated this development, but he hadn't, and the stress of it was taking its toll.

He extended an outstretched arm to Diana, and she took his hand, allowing herself to be helped off the boat. The two made their way up the main thoroughfare leading to the church, and when it came into view—so white and pristine, framed by a fringe of palm fronds—all Floyd's doubts fled. He was infused with such a sense of wellbeing that his heart seemed to lift in his chest. He knew what he had to do. Once again, Floyd clasped Diana's free hand, and the two joined the small group of parishioners outside the chapel. He was so focused on his mission, that it took a moment for Floyd to realize that something was amiss. A sudden commotion from a side street grabbed his attention, and like the others gathered there, he turned to stare. Diana's face took on a look of horror, and Floyd's mouth gaped open. A crudely constructed, four-wheeled cart, pulled by a large gray donkey, was barreling toward them! Even more bizarre was to find that the three brigands of his nightmares were sprawled on the flatbed cart! Their ringleader had the reins in hand, while the other two miscreants passed a bottle between them, alternately drinking and singing lustily in Spanish.

To add to the confusion, the acolyte began ringing the church bell, which so surprised one of the drunken men seated atop the cart that he pulled a pistol from his belt. In the next moment, the conveyance bounced over a rock in the road, and the pistol discharged.

Perhaps it was the bell that startled the poor beast of burden or, more likely, the crack of gunfire. Whatever the reason, the donkey reared up and then bolted. Charging, full steam, he made a direct line toward the congregants! The worshipers cried out and scattered. Upon hearing the ruckus, Father Enrique Ramos hastened from his cramped robe room to the nave of the church to see what the fuss was about. When he emerged into the brilliant sunlight, it was just in time to witness the spectacle of his lifetime.

~

On this sun-shiny morning, Jack Cramer's mood was anything but bright. He was seated outside the trailer in a folding lawn chair—flimsy chrome struts supporting fraying, green plastic-coated material—his scrawny, white legs sprawled before him. He took a long drag from his cigarette, thinking he'd made a botch of it, that he hadn't thought things through. Otherwise, he wouldn't be cooling his jets in this shitty RV park. And the girl? He shook his head, rueing his own stupidity. Abducting her had been a dumb-assed, hare-brained, spur-of-the-moment lapse in judgment that sure as hell had landed him in pretty damn hot water.

But then he cut himself a little slack. She was some sweet morsel, alright. He could see her in his mind's eye, doe-eyed, ripe, and innocent. Hard for a man to resist. Maybe, if he'd been a little more adept, the risk would have been worth it. Jack took another long pull from his Chesterfield and then tossed the glowing butt into the weeds. No use thinking about what could have been, he chided himself. Better to concentrate on what lay ahead. The girl had gotten a good look at him, could easily pick him out in a lineup of possible suspects.

"Mornin'," a chubby, middle-aged, bleached blonde called out to him as she passed by on her way to the pool.

"And to you," Jack answered, his eyes latching on to an ass that jiggled and strained beneath the confines of skintight capris. Damn, he was horny! Had to be if he could rise to *that* bait. Then he thought about what he might do to little Miss Madison when next they met, and a twisted smile crept up his face.

Soon.

❧

It was eight-thirty in the morning, and they were bundled into Daniel's car and on their way to the airport. Andrea was bushed. She'd been up half the night packing. So that now, as Madison chattered on from the backseat, peppering Daniel with questions, she let her head sink back into the headrest and closed her eyes. Ahh... As they drove off the barrier island, the tension seemed to seep from her body, and she relaxed. Finally, she could take a breather. Andrea let her mind wander.

So much had happened in so short a time: first the housing bust, then the stolen escrows, followed by the mysterious man who'd stolen her heart and was about to steal away her familial estate, and—as if that weren't enough and most concerning of all—Madison's kidnapping. As usual, Daniel had been spot-on to suggest this trip. She and Maddy needed a getaway. A few days to do nothing but forget about their troubles and relax.

"Oh, just you wait," Daniel was saying. "I've booked us a fabulous suite overlooking the pool. You're going to love it. And yes, we can do Aquaventure first thing." He glanced over at Andrea and clasped her hand in his. "Isn't that right, Mama San?"

Andrea yawned and then opened her eyes wide. "Sure," she said, "so long as this tired mama can requisition a lounge chair and sit it out."

"Aw, Mom. You have to come with us," Madison pleaded. "Just wait and see. You're going to love it." At the parroting of his words, Daniel and Andrea burst out laughing.

"Daniel got it right," Andrea said. "You're a little mink!"

~

The drunkard at the reins struggled to control the spooked beast, but the startled mule was undeterred and pounded toward the church. Diana held the satchel tightly, and Floyd put his arms around her.

"Dios mío!" Father Ramos cried, as the cart bore down upon them.

At the sound of the old man's voice, Floyd's head snapped up, and he whirled around to face him. "Padre," he breathed, his eyes shining. Then he reached for Diana's bag. "This is for you, for the church." He wrested the satchel from Diana's hands and held it out to the priest. But before the transfer could take place, the donkey and cart were upon them.

Diana screamed, and with no thought to the consequences, Floyd —the tote still in his hands—put himself in front of her.

In a moment of quick thinking, the priest grabbed Diana and backtracked into the nave, dragging her along with him.

Just in time!

No sooner was Diana snatched from harm's way than the donkey charged Floyd. The next thing he knew, his feet flew out from under him, and the satchel went flying, releasing thousands of brightly colored COP.

Like confetti, the bills wafted on the gentle breeze.

The cart overturned, nearly crushing the three Bandidos and knocking them senseless. That finally stopped the terrified donkey's mad dash. Unable to pull the toppled conveyance, he stood rooted to the dusty street, his broad breast heaving as foam frothed at his mouth.

It all happened in a matter of seconds, but for Floyd, the scene played out in slow motion. The gray, wild-eyed beast had filled his field of vision until the four-legged wrecking ball slammed into him. At the force of the impact, Floyd's head snapped back. As he fell, he could see his money swirling about, the parishioners scrambling to retrieve the cash, all of them whooping and laughing at this unexpected windfall. Barely conscious, Floyd struggled to turn his head, and through half-closed eyes, he found Diana and the priest. The two were hurtling from the church doorway toward him. He tried to call out, to tell them to grab the cash, but no sound escaped his lips. By the time his head hit the ground, he was detaching from his body.

What a rush! He'd done it. Then he was looking down at himself. Dimly, he could see Diana kneeling beside him, weeping. With the last ounce of strength he possessed, Floyd forced his mouth to form the words he was determined to utter before leaving her—his parting bequest. Diana leaned in close to hear him.

"Money in freezer," he wheezed, and with that, the life force slipped from his body, and he expired.

~

Derrick had put in a long day in the fields. Somehow, he always forgot that, in the spring, everything insisted on popping out of the ground at the same time. So many vegetables to harvest! It was exhausting. But now, he was coming off a grueling work week, one that had seen his only child—the apple of his eye—kidnapped and traumatized. No wonder he, too, was feeling particularly fractured and fragile.

What he needed, Derrick decided, was a couple of ice-cold drafts and some female company. But where to find them? He sure as hell couldn't hang with Andrea and Maddy. They'd flown the coop, destination: the Bahamas. Derrick's brow lowered at the thought of their exodus in the care of that slick, snake oil salesman, Daniel Armstrong, and he fumed while wallowing in self-pity.

He climbed into his Jeep and tuned the radio to 92.7 the WAVW. Was it fate, he wondered, when the melodic strains of Jake Owen's newest release, *Made for You*, suddenly blared from the speaker? As he shifted to drive, the lyrics to that homegrown legend's hit record socked him in the gut.

> *The sky was made for the moon and stars.*
> *You were made to steal my heart.*
> *And I was made for you.*
> *Yeah, I was made for you.*

Before pressing a foot to the accelerator, Derrick paused and put his head in his hands. He still carried a torch for Andrea. She was *made* to steal his heart, and he'd nearly accepted the fact that she'd moved on, almost made his peace with that. But Maddy? She was made *from* him. She didn't have to steal his heart. It had been hers from the first moment she'd taken a breath. He remembered it distinctly, and a low growl of anguish escaped his lips. God, how he loved that girl!

His cellphone vibrated, and he tugged it out of his back pocket. "Hello," he barked while easing out of the field onto the highway.

"Hey, Mister Nelson, it's me, Garrett." The tech geek's familiar voice hoisted him from the depths of despair into a sort of limbo.

"Garrett, good to hear from you. What's on your mind?" Derrick headed south toward the East Orange exit. The sun was slipping below the horizon, and at this hour, there was hardly any traffic.

"Well, sir, I've been thinking…"

"Yes, son?"

"Gee, thanks for that, Mr. Nelson."

"Excuse me? What are you talking about?" Derrick navigated the feeder road leading to U.S. Highway 1.

"The son, sir. I appreciate that," Garrett said. "I never knew my father."

"Oh." Derrick considered. Perhaps this was TMI? But then Garrett was babbling, and he had to concentrate in order to keep up.

"Tyler and I have decided we need to be proactive. We can't just wait for that monster to strike again. And, sir, we think he *will* come for her. That he'll come for Maddy. And soon."

"I'm afraid I'm of the same mind," Derrick admitted. When he stopped at the traffic light at the highway crossroads, his hands were trembling. But he had to wrest hold of his emotions and deal with this. For all their sakes, he knew he had to act.

"You're absolutely right, Garrett. We can't just wait around for that pervert to strike again. So, here's what I propose…"

∾

Along a desolate stretch of the highway distinguished by a charmless cemetery to the east and an abandoned strip mall on the west, a cheery neon sign up ahead beckoned. The Dew Drop Inn, a mom-and-pop joint that served up good chow and stellar beer on tap. Derrick figured it was just what he needed, especially since his stomach was rumbling.

He sauntered in, only to find the entry empty. No one was manning the hostess station, but the dining room to the right was bustling with diners chattering away and filling their faces. He turned left, making his way to the bar, hadn't gotten but a few steps before a cute waitress, her dark hair pulled back in a ponytail, crossed his path. He pegged her at mid to late thirties. Bearing a tray laden with drinks, she paused to greet him.

"Hi, there. May I help you?"

"Yeah. Can I just seat myself?" Derrick nodded toward an empty booth by the window.

"Sure thing. I'll be with you in a minute." She breezed by him, heading for the dining room.

"Great, and bring me a draft," he called after her.

"You got it."

Derrick slid into the booth and immediately reached for the menu. Over the years, he'd stopped by the Dew Drop from time to time, but only for a quick beer. Now, however, he was ravenous, and the tantalizing aroma of char-grilled meats was more than he could resist. When the waitress came to his table asking, "What can I get you?" he ordered a burger, rare, with sides of fries and coleslaw. But before she could sidle away, he said, "What's your name?"

"Jasmine," she replied.

She was a foxy little thing, Derrick decided. Maybe, once fortified with food and drink, he'd muster the courage to ask for her number. Derrick took a long draught of his still-foamy beer. "Ahh…" He rested his head on the upholstered back of the banquette and sighed. What a week! Before he could dwell too extensively on the recent turn of events, his ears were suddenly attuned to a wheezy chortle coming to him from the other side of the banquette.

"Madison, ha! That's what she called herself. What kinda name is that? I ask you?" There was phlegmy coughing, followed by more laughter.

Then another lowered voice. "Sheeit! Madison. That's a street name. Am I right? Who the hell names their kid after a street?"

Derrick sat up straight, his ear pressed to the banquette back cushion. Just then, Jasmine sailed in bearing a pitcher of water and a small loaf of warm bread. Derrick gazed up at her and put his hands in the air, waving her away. She looked at him askance before rolling her eyes and vamoosing. Perhaps he'd live to regret it, Derrick thought fleetingly. Just now, the stakes were too high.

"What's that about the moon?" Phlegmy voice asked.

"There won't be one, Kurt," the other said. "And that's when the two of us are going to pay Ms. M. Street a visit and end this thing. Under cover of darkness."

"Gee, I don't know, brother. This mission might be above my paygrade."

"Don't give me that, Kurt. Remember. You owe me big time."

"Aw, hell... Calling in past favors, huh?"

"Damn straight." The two laughed.

Derrick failed to see the humor. He felt as though a pointy rock had dropped into the pit of his stomach, and his appetite vanished. What were the chances? Could this be possible? Had he really heard Madison's kidnapper outlining a plot to kill her? At the next words he strained to hear, cold hands seemed to grip his heart, leaving him breathless and shaken.

"I figured I'd go in by boat. Easy peasy. I'll make it look like an accident."

"Yeah. That should work."

"Uh-huh. And that will put an end to it."

The server swooped in again, this time with a look of caution on her face. Before she could unload her tray, Derrick climbed out of the booth. "Sorry for your trouble, miss," he said, pitching his voice loud enough to carry. "I just received a text. I'm afraid I have to go." He withdrew his wallet from his back pocket, pulled out a fifty-dollar bill, and tossed it on the table. "Keep the change."

"Oh, that's a darn shame," the waitress said, and the look that came over her face made him think she almost meant it.

"Yeah. Another time." As much as he wanted to, Derrick refused to glance at the men in the adjoining booth. Instead, he did his best to stay out of their field of vision while beating a speedy retreat. Once outside, enveloped in the warm night's exhalation, his knees wobbled. He put his hands to them and took a deep breath, willing his queasy stomach to settle down. A moment later, sufficiently recovered, he hiked to his truck and jumped inside. Peering out over the dashboard, he tried to get a look at the two men seated next to the now empty booth, but he was too far away to make out any details, let alone facial features. It didn't matter, he decided as he shifted to drive. He'd surely see them soon enough.

CHAPTER FIFTEEN

PROMISES PROMISES

Three hundred miles away from that desolate stretch of highway, Andrea was luxuriating in a bath of perfumed bubbles. She leaned back in the Carrera marble tub and gazed out at the panorama beyond her window. Daniel had not disappointed. The penthouse at the Cove in Atlantis was sinfully extravagant. The suite he'd chosen was ideally situated on the bridge between two towers, and the view from her vantage point was of a white, sandy beach fringed with graceful palms and the brilliant blue Atlantic beyond.

"Ahh…" Andrea closed her eyes and let her mind wander. The last twenty-four hours had been a mad whirlwind of packing and air travel, followed by a day of fun in the sun. She'd had no intention of taking this spur-of-the-moment holiday, but now she was glad Daniel had talked her into it. He'd been right. They all needed a little downtime. And the fact that the resort was far, far from Vero Beach made it all the more appealing.

"Hurry up, Mom." Madison's voice came to her from down the hall. Before Andrea had time to react, the teen wandered into the bath. "We have dinner reservations for seven," she cried petulantly.

"I know, honey." Andrea rolled her head on her shoulders.

"What are you doing, anyway?" Madison sat on the vanity stool before the dressing table and stared at her mother.

"Just getting the kinks out, darling. You must admit, it's been a bit of a hard charge. Especially keeping up with you and Daniel. I don't know where you get your energy."

"It was so much fun. I really like Daniel," Madison said.

"Me, too, sweet. And I know he likes you." Madison merely yawned by way of reply, and Andrea rose to her feet. "Oh, ho," she cried, carefully stepping out from the tub. "It looks like a certain someone's finally winding down."

Madison grabbed her mother's hairbrush from the dressing table and then drew it through her tangled locks. "Yeah, I'm getting tired," she admitted, "but I'm hungry." She gazed at her reflection in the mirror. "Do you think I'm pretty, Mom?"

"No." Andrea wrapped herself in an enormous bath towel.

Madison whirled to face her. "What?"

"Pretty doesn't define it. I think you're gorgeous, a real knockout, if you must know," Andrea said. "Now go put on your new dress. I'll join you in the living room in a few minutes."

Madison yawned again and padded out of the bath, leaving Andrea smiling at her daughter's retreating figure.

Night was falling over this enchanted setting as Andrea stepped through the sliding glass door out onto the balcony, an open bottle of champagne in hand. In the gloaming, her eyes were immediately drawn to the railing. Daniel, his broad back toward her, was standing there gazing out over a rapidly darkening sky where a few stars winked.

"Ah'm back." she called out gaily, crossing to him. "Madison is sleeping soundly. I swear, the moment her head hit the pillow, she was out like a light."

"And no wonder." Daniel turned away from the breathtaking view to gaze at her. "It's been quite the day. I, myself, am feeling bushed."

"No!" Andrea teased, as she poured champagne into the two flutes set on an end table between a pair of patio chairs. Glasses in each hand, she crossed to him. "Here you go." She handed him a flute and raised hers. "To paradise."

They touched glasses. "Are you glad you came?" Daniel asked, after taking a sip.

"Very much so," Andrea said, grinning. "In fact, I've a confession."

"Oh, dear. As serious as all that?"

"Yes. I want to tell you how sorry I am for being such a stick in the mud." Daniel made as if to protest, but Andrea touched a finger to his lips, silencing him. "You were absolutely right about this trip. It's been wonderful for Maddy, and certainly good for me. I only hope *you're* enjoying it. This," she tossed an arm about indicating the lavish surroundings, "must have cost you a fortune."

"You and Maddy are worth it." Daniel took Andrea's glass and set both it and his on a tile-topped, metal console table. Then, tucking a finger under her chin, he covered her lips with his.

Andrea lost herself in Daniel's sweet kiss, and as the kiss deepened, she felt her body respond. Wrapping her arms about his neck, she inhaled his masculine scent—bayberry and leather. Intoxicating! When she broke away from him, she chuckled. "And where is it you were off to, so mysteriously, this afternoon?"

Suddenly, Daniel's expression grew solemn. Taking her hand, he led her to a chair. "I have something to tell you." He waved toward the chair, implying that she should sit.

Andrea's mind raced as she imagined the worst, but she sat and presented a calm exterior. Daniel turned the other chair so that it faced Andrea's and seated himself. "I haven't been perfectly honest with you, Andrea, and I want to clean the slate."

Andrea's eyes grew wide. She had no idea where this was going, and it frightened her. "Goodness," she said. "This is unsettling."

Daniel gave her a rueful smile. "Now I hope you won't hate me for this…" Despite the warmth of the sultry night, Andrea felt a cold chill run down her spine, but she merely folded her hands in her lap and waited for him to continue.

"I'm not representing someone in the purchase of Casa Rio." He waited for a reaction, but Andrea merely tilted her head. "Did you hear me?"

"Yes."

"Well?"

Andrea exhaled as relief washed over her. So that was what this was all about. "Oh, Daniel, I'm afraid you're not a very good liar. Which, I guess if you think about it, isn't a bad thing…"

The creases in Daniel's brow deepened, and he peered at her. "I don't understand."

"I never really thought you were purchasing Casa for someone else. More than that, I hoped you weren't."

A look of consternation clouded Daniel's face. "Is that so?" Andrea could barely contain her laughter. "Well, what *did* you think?"

At that question, Andrea grew serious. "I thought… Don't get me wrong here. I thought that you were buying the place for yourself, that you didn't really know what you intended to do with it."

She sat back in her chair, ventured a look at the stars and confessed. "That you didn't want to make that information public and expose yourself to… I don't know… those who might not wish you well. And that, although you were well entrenched in Philadelphia, you were somehow drawn to Vero." She gazed into his eyes. "How am I doing so far?"

"I'll be damned." Daniel slapped his thigh. "You read me like a book. And here I thought I was being so clever."

"So secretive, you mean." Andrea's eyes locked on Daniel's, willing him to continue.

"That, too. You're right. I wasn't sure what I was doing. On the one hand, I was merely taking Nathan's advice—purchasing property that would increase in value—making a sound investment. Initially, I didn't have any intention of spending a lot of time in Vero. At least not for the foreseeable future. I figured it'd be a great place to retire." He paused and looked away, and then turned back and focused on Andrea. "But that all changed."

Andrea searched his eyes. "How so?"

Daniel reached out and took both her hands in his. "I think you know."

"I'd like to hear you tell me." She needed to hear the words, needed his reassurance.

"I fell in love with you," Daniel admitted. "Hell, I fell in love with Maddy. I want both of you in my life."

"Oh, Daniel," Andrea's eyes brimmed. "Maddy and I love you, too."

"So, you're not angry with me?"

"Ha!" Andrea exclaimed. "Are you kidding me? I'm thrilled."

"Good." Daniel came to his feet and reached for the sport coat he'd draped over the back of his chair. "And, as for what I was doing this afternoon... It was this." He withdrew a small box from the inside breast pocket and then took a knee.

Andrea gasped. Could this be happening? It was so unexpected she could hardly believe it.

Daniel placed the box in Andrea's hands. "Open it," he said, "and say you'll marry me."

With shaking fingers, Andrea lifted the lid from the jeweler's box. "Oh, my God, Daniel!" she exclaimed, for the ring he'd chosen was a huge, oval-cut sapphire, surrounded by a ring of fiery diamonds set in platinum. "It's splendid."

"It makes me think of oceans, which makes me think of you. Will you marry me, Andrea?" Daniel gained his legs and hovered over her.

"Yes, yes!" Andrea slid the ring onto her finger. "Nothing could make me happier."

Daniel clasped her hands in his and drew her to her feet. "I love you so much. You saved me." He explored her mouth, tasting her tongue, now sweet with champagne.

She returned his kiss, thinking that the opposite was true: Daniel had saved *her*. She'd never been more attracted to a man, and now, knowing that he truly cared for her, she wanted to give herself to him completely, to hold nothing back. She raked her fingers through his tawny mane, and then ran them down his beautiful arms, delighting in the firm muscles that held her fast in his embrace.

"Darling," Daniel whispered, drawing away, "as I'm about to rip the clothing from your body, might I persuade you to come to my room?"

Andrea laughed, glancing around at the adjoining balconies. "No persuading required. If we don't go inside soon, I may get arrested for indecent exposure."

~

They sat out on the balcony with mugs of freshly brewed coffee in hand. Andrea was wrapped in a Kimono-style silk robe, her glossy tresses piled atop her head in a clip, and Daniel thought she'd never looked lovelier. He smiled at the thought of their lovemaking. One wouldn't have imagined this lissome woman capable of the unbridled passion she'd unleashed a mere ten hours before. His X-rated musings were interrupted when Madison stepped out over the threshold.

"Morning, Mom." The teen slumped into a chaise lounge. "Hi, Daniel."

"Hey sweet-pea," Andrea swiveled around to face her daughter. "Sleep well?"

"Yeah."

"I'll just bet you did." Daniel grinned at her. "What's on the agenda for today?" Mountain climbing? Tiger wrestling?"

"Dolphin Cove?" Madison raised her eyebrows.

Daniel and Andrea exchanged bemused expressions. "Ugh," Andrea muttered.

"Come on, Mom," Madison protested. "It'll be fun. Don't you want to swim with Flipper?"

Daniel jumped to his feet. "Honestly? I think it'd be a blast, but Mom wants to sit this one out, so maybe we should cut her some slack. I know she'd like to hit some of the shops. Would you mind just hanging out with me for a few hours? Then we can all meet up for lunch and plan the next adventure."

"Sure." Madison peered at her mother, but Andrea merely shrugged, a small smile playing about her lips.

Then Madison's eyes were drawn to the enormous sapphire on her mother's finger. Glinting radiantly in the morning sunlight, it was hard to miss. "Jeez, Mom. Where did you get the rock?" Madison reached for her mother's hand.

Andrea's eyes cut to Daniel, and he nodded and then turned to Madison. "It's like this, kiddo." He sat down next to the teen and leaned in toward her. "I guess you've realized that I've fallen head-over-heels for your mother."

Madison bit her lip, mulling over his words. Moments passed before she met his eyes. "Yes," she finally said. "Mom loves you." She searched her mother's face, silently seeking her approval. Andrea smiled encouragingly, and she turned back to Daniel. "And I think you're great, Daniel."

"I care for you, too, Maddy," Daniel said. "So, I have something to ask of you."

"What?" Madison cocked her head.

Once again, Daniel took a knee. This time, Andrea couldn't

contain herself. She burst out laughing. "Daniel," she exclaimed. "What are you doing?"

"I'm proposing to your daughter," he said. "Now, be quiet."

As this was transpiring, Madison was wide-eyed and intent on Daniel.

"Madison," Daniel said, withdrawing a small box from his cargo pants pocket. "I've asked your mother to marry me, and she said yes. But now…" He opened the box and presented it to the girl. "Would you do me the great honor of being my stepdaughter? To have and to hold?"

Madison gasped when her eyes fell upon the tiny diamond ring nestled in the fold of a red satin cushion.

"Please, say something," Daniel pleaded. "The suspense is killing me."

"Yes!" Madison cried, throwing herself into his arms. "Oh, Daniel."

Daniel looked from her to Andrea and then back again. Elated, his heart expanded, and it was a feeling like nothing he'd ever experienced before. These two beautiful women were his family now, and life had never seemed so full of promise.

"Maddy," he said, "thank you, sweetheart. I promise to take care of you," He searched Andrea's face, and she gazed back at him with adoring eyes, "and your mom forever."

≈

That same morning found Garrett offloading a box of produce from the back of Derrick's truck. Too keyed up to sleep late, he'd wandered down to the park, knowing full well that Madison wouldn't be there and thinking that, perhaps, Derrick could use an extra set of hands. He hadn't been mistaken. Derrick had jumped at the offer.

It was a beautiful day, the height of season, and the market was enjoying a great turnout. A carnival atmosphere had settled over this stretch of beach. A solo guitarist performed Jimmy Buffett songs while eager customers circulated between the booths, eagerly snatching up grain-fed beef, freshly baked pastries, tropical plants, seafood plucked from the Indian River, and Derrick's organically grown vegetables.

"Heck, yes, I'd be much obliged for the help," Derrick had said. "You sure you don't mind?"

"Nah. What else do I have to do?" he'd answered. "It's Saturday; I've got nothing but time on my hands." Surprisingly, he found he liked the work, making small talk with the customers, tallying up purchases, running credit cards, or collecting cash. It wasn't like his nine-to-five tech gig—sitting in front of a screen with no real human contact. It was fun, and it gave him a chance to get to know Derrick better.

He'd hoped to talk about *the plan*, but they were so busy, with never a lull in the traffic. So that as the morning wore down, Garrett became more and more impatient to get at the heart of the matter that was driving him to distraction: namely, Madison. What were they going to do about the madman who was stalking her? He could see her in his mind's eye—so lovely. How were they going to thwart that creep? This was no video game. It was frighteningly real, and the girl of his dreams was hanging in the balance.

It wasn't until one o'clock in the afternoon—when the crowds had dispersed, and the market was winding down—that Garrett felt he could finally speak of their dilemma. "So, Mr. Nelson," he said, as the two worked in tandem, breaking down the booth, "What do you have in mind? How are we going to neutralize this Jack jerk?"

Derrick was unclipping the canvas awning from a metal strut, but at Garrett's words, he turned to face him. "I'm not sure, son." He glanced around at the few remaining stragglers. "But this isn't the place to discuss such things. What say I buy you lunch after we get this gear stowed? There's a new development. We can talk about it then."

By the time they were seated at a table at Bobby's Grill, it was after two. The lunch crowd had thinned, and Derrick felt as though he could speak freely, for there were no diners within earshot. "I'll get right to it."

Garrett propped his elbows on the table and leaned in, eager to hear the latest. "Shoot," he said.

"Believe me. That's what I'd like to do: shoot the bastard. But you're not going to believe what I'm about to tell you. On my way back into town last night, I stopped off at a little joint for a beer."

Derrick went on to explain how he'd overheard two men in an adjoining booth talking about taking care of a girl named Madison.

"Get out!" Garrett reeled. "You've got to be kidding me!"

"God's honest truth. I mean, what are the chances, huh?"

"What the hell did you do?"

"What could I do? I listened real hard. They were plotting to come in by boat on a moonless night, and—"

"Oh, jeez!" Garrett put his head in his hands and then peered up at Derrick. "When's the next moonless night?"

"Friday."

Garrett groaned. "This is worse than I thought." He met Derrick's eyes. "Shouldn't we call the police?"

"I was tempted. But think about it. What have they done so far— besides beefing up patrols? Don't get me wrong. I'm not bashing the cops, by any means. It's just that we've got nothing, no substantial evidence. Nada. And without that, we just can't expect too much from them."

"I hear you, but I'm tired of sitting on my hands, feeling helpless."

"Exactly, which is why I've decided to enlist some of my ex-marine buddies to help us lay the trap."

Garrett slapped the tabletop. "Now you're talking."

Andrea sat at a table at the open-air Lagoon Bar and Grill, peering up at a domed ceiling that had been painted to replicate the Atlantic Ocean. With brilliantly colored tropical fish darting in and out of coral reefs, life-like dolphins weaving through seaweed fans, it was so realistic. It reminded her of another domed ceiling, this one at Caesar's Palace. Newly single, she'd dragged Margaret along for the 2006 Realtor's Conference. One evening, when they'd set out for cocktails, they'd found themselves at another such magically manufactured place: the Forum Shops. Once seated, Mom had stared at the faux-painted sky twinkling with stars— pinpricks of halogen lights—and waxed on about how beautiful the evening was. Andrea smiled, remembering how they'd laughed when she'd pointed out that they were indoors in a purely manmade environment!

She drummed her freshly manicured fingernails on the tabletop.

What was taking Maddy and Daniel so long? But then she tamped down her impatience. They were probably having the time of their lives. She glanced down at the ridiculously large gem on her finger, thinking how lucky she was to have found Daniel. But then the horror of Madison's recent close call insinuated itself into her consciousness, and her ebullience dissipated. This was but a brief respite. Soon enough, she and Madison would be smack dab back in the horror.

"Say there, miss, mind if I join you?" Daniel swooped in for a kiss, and the upbeat lilt to his voice dragged her out of the depths.

Madison's giggly soprano calling out, "Hi, Mom," pitched her into the present. It was a good, safe place.

"I'm dying to hear about it." Andrea silently vowed to lay her troubles to rest for the duration of this little vacation. "Sit and tell me everything."

Madison plopped down on a chair next to Andrea's. "Honestly, Mom, you wouldn't have believed it."

Andrea grinned at Daniel as he seated himself across from her. "Really? Why not?"

"Because, woman, you had to be there to see it," Daniel said. Then his eyes fell on the shopping bags at Andrea's feet. "Had a good morning yourself, did you?"

"Oh, yeah. Picked up a few things for some of my homies.

A waitress swooped in. "Hi," she said, "I'll be your server. Do you have any questions about the menu?"

Before Daniel could answer, Andrea chimed in, "A pitcher of sweet tea, please, and when you bring that, we'll be ready to order our entrees." She looked to Daniel for affirmation, and he nodded.

"Coming right up," the waitress said before breezing away.

Madison's eyes fastened on the shopping bags. "What did you buy, Mommy?"

"Wouldn't you like to know?"

Madison's face took on a pained expression. "Yes."

Andrea rummaged through one of the shopping bags and came up with a small foil-embossed envelope. "Hmm…" she said, holding it before Madison and giving it a shake. "Wonder what this could be."

Daniel snaked out an arm and made as if to snag the thing, but it was pure theater, and Andrea snatched it back before he could grab hold of it.

"Mom!" Madison wailed.

Andrea relented and handed the envelope to Madison. "There you go, and don't ever say I'm sheltering you."

Madison tore open the package. "What's this?" She held two tickets aloft.

"It's your entry to the coolest teen nightclub on the planet. I figured you'd want to go."

Madison considered, screwing up her face. Then she shrugged. "It's nice, Mom, but... I don't want to walk into a place like that alone. Too scary."

"Yeah." Andrea shot her daughter a pointed look. "Which is why there are *two* passes. You see, I ran into the most darling couple and their daughter. We got to talking about activities for teens. Like you, this girl would never go to a place like Crush solo."

Madison thrust out her lower lip, and Andrea knew she had a selling job to do. "Look, Maddy. You'd be doing this girl a favor. She's here with her parents, and she'd like a bit of free time—to kick back with some kids her own age, listen to some good music, play a few video games. What do you have to lose?"

"Come on, Maddy," Daniel said. "If you don't go, I will. It sounds like an absolute blast."

At that, Madison narrowed her eyes and grinned slyly. "Daniel, that would not be right," she said. "Crush is for teens." She gazed at the passes. "No adults allowed."

"Humph!" Daniel muttered. He turned to Andrea. "So, who is Madison's date?"

"Oh, goodness!" Andrea exclaimed. "It's not a date; it's a girl's night out. Zoe Walker is as cute as a bug and smart as a whip. Also, painfully shy, which is why I thought my outgoing girl could help her have a fun evening while her parents had one of their own. But if you don't want to go, I'll see if I can return the tickets."

Before Madison could answer, their waitress arrived with a pitcher of iced tea and began filling their glasses. Then, after taking their orders, she darted off.

Madison squeezed a wedge of lemon into her tea. "I suppose that would be okay, but I'd like to meet her—this Zoe—first."

"And that's exactly what we're going to do. We're having dinner with the Walkers this evening." Andrea turned to Daniel. "You don't mind, do you?"

Daniel sat back and put his palms before him. "Fine by me," he said. "As usual, you've got it all figured out."

Shaking her head, Madison met Daniel's eyes. "She's very bossy, Daniel."

"Hmm…" he muttered. "I can see that. We'll just have to present a united front."

At those words, Andrea arched a brow. "Oh, no. Two against one isn't fair."

"We're not *against* you, dear." Daniel looked to Madison for confirmation.

"Right," the teen agreed. "We just have to keep you from steamrolling over us."

Andrea's eyes widened at Madison's succinct declaration, and for once, she was speechless.

～

It was late in the day. Sunlight slanted in through the veins of the white plantation shutters, casting strange bar-like patterns about the girl's bedroom. The phenomenon made Tyler think of a prison cell, which is where he hoped this enterprise would land Jack.

Derrick rummaged through Madison's closet while Garrett and Tyler hung back. Tyler didn't know about Garrett, but he felt uncomfortable invading Madison's inner sanctum. It just didn't seem proper.

"How about this?" Derrick withdrew a hanger on which was hung a floral-patterned halter dress.

Tyler's face took on a look of horror. He'd readily agreed to do his part to help neutralize Jack, but this gig was way more than he'd bargained for. "Excuse me! What the heck?" He reeled back, eyeing the garment Derrick held before him. "I'm not wearing *that*. Jeez!"

"You have to. It's for Madison." Derrick stepped toward Tyler. "Hell, would you rather we put her out there as bait for that psychopath?"

Tyler batted his hand away. "No! But I don't want to put *me* out there, either."

Derrick narrowed his eyes. "Yeah, we get it, Tyler, but you signed up for this tour, and you need to step up."

"Shit!"

"Yep, that about sums it up." Garrett said. "But you're the only one skinny enough to fit into Maddy's clothing. Got any better ideas?"

"I ain't wearing no dress, and that's final."

"Prima donna," Derrick mumbled, returning the gauzy confection to the closet.

Garrett felt a momentary pang of sympathy for Tyler. "I say we keep it simple, Mr. Nelson." He eyed the white cotton tee and navy shorts neatly folded on the bed and snatched them up. "Pure Madison, you ask me, and the next best thing to gender neutral.

Tyler shot Garrett a lopsided smile of gratitude. "If I die, at least I won't do it in a skirt."

~

In another bedroom, one affording panoramic views of the Atlantis resort and a shimmering ocean beyond, Madison lay propped up in bed. She was idly thumbing through a fashion magazine, her auburn tresses still damp from the shower splayed across the pillows. Then, suddenly, there was a rapping on her door, and she sat up. "What is it?"

Andrea opened the door a crack and peeked in. "Mind if I come in?"

"No." Madison tossed the magazine aside.

Andrea entered, crossed the distance between them, and perched on the edge of Madison's bed. "Tired?" she asked.

Madison had donned a white terrycloth robe provided by the resort, and her compact frame was nearly lost in it. "A little," she admitted.

Andrea's heart lurched. How defenseless this child was, and yet how resilient!

"We'll have drinks with the Walkers and then an early dinner and bed. How's that?"

Madison nodded. "Sounds good."

"Honey," Andrea took Madison's hand, the one with the petite diamond on its ring finger. "I want to talk to you about Daniel."

A guarded look came over Madison's face. "Okay."

"To say you've been through a lot is an understatement. I know you always hoped that your dad and I would get back together…"

"Yeah." Madison sighed. "But I know that's not going to happen."

"He will always be a big part of your life. No one can ever replace him."

"No kidding," Madison said, and they both laughed.

Andrea's tone became serious. "You've been through a very traumatic event. As if that weren't enough, Daniel's asked me to marry him, and I said yes."

Madison looked down at the ring on her finger. "He asked me to be his stepdaughter, and I said yes."

Andrea chuckled. "We're a fine pair, huh?"

A small smile tugged at Madison's lips. "It's okay, Mom. I love Daddy. I always will. But I really love Daniel, too. He wants to take care of us—"

"We don't need anyone to take care of us," Andrea interrupted, a troubled look on her face. "Tell me that's not why you agreed to this."

Madison shook her head emphatically. "Oh, no. Daniel's crazy about you, Mom, and you shouldn't be alone. You deserve a guy who'll always be there for you."

Suddenly, Andrea's eyes were bright with unshed tears. Sometimes, she forgot how sensitive and perceptive her daughter was. She thought about Derrick, how he'd constantly let her down, and she rubbed her thumb over Madison's ring. "I am so lucky to have all of you in my life."

"About tonight…" Madison's brow furrowed.

Andrea inclined her head. "What about it?"

"I'm nervous."

"Don't be," Andrea reassured. "Zoe's really sweet. I'm positive you're going to like her. Her parents, Mr. and Mrs. Walker are both professors at the University of Michigan—wonky, brainy, and kind of introspective, which is probably why Zoe is a bit of an introvert. A dose of Madison will definitely do that child good, and I'm certain that Zoe would enjoy spending time with some kids her own age.

You'll charm her. I'm confident of it, and you'll have fun in the bargain."

"If you say so."

"You can bet on it. Now, give me a hug, and then get dressed for dinner."

≈

Andrea's instincts proved spot-on. After an initial awkwardness, Madison and Zoe Walker hit it off splendidly. They sat next to one another at a dining table in the low-lit, atmospheric Bahamian Club, and while the adults exchanged pleasantries their two heads were more often together than not as they whispered confidences and giggled their way through the cocktail hour. At one point, Mr. Walker, a very trim, distinguished-looking Black fellow, raised an eyebrow saying, "My goodness, Zoe, I haven't heard you jabber this much since we got here," which set both girls off in gales of laughter.

Later that evening, Andrea and Daniel sat out on their balcony while overhead a scimitar moon cast its reflection on the slate black ocean. "I don't know how you did it." Daniel said.

"Did what?"

"How you managed to find Madison a partner in crime, and here, of all places."

"I know. It was serendipitous. I bumped into the Walker's in one of the boutiques, and we struck up a conversation. They were such attractive, interesting people—obviously brilliant—and Zoe was so adorable... I had a hunch she and Madison would click."

"Click they did! Click, click, click." Daniel snorted. "I bet they'll have a ball at the nightclub. They'll surely turn some heads—Madison with her porcelain complexion, looking like a Colleen from Derry Township, and Zoe, bronzed and beautiful, with those enormous green eyes."

"You're absolutely right." Andrea gestured toward the myriad glimmering lights of the resort far beneath them. "Thank you for this, Daniel. It's been a wonderful getaway. I can see the change in Madison. She's her happy, upbeat self again."

"It's been my pleasure," Daniel said. "Heck, without a kid in tow, how would I ever have managed to swim with dolphins and shake hands with octopi?"

Andrea chuckled and then grew serious. "Daniel... about Casa Rio, the closing—"

"I thought it was all set," Daniel interrupted. "We're on for a week from tomorrow. You're not having second thoughts, are you?"

"No! But I don't understand." Andrea's brow knit. "We're engaged to be married, and you're going to displace my mother? That seems a bit harsh."

Daniel reached out and brushed his fingers across her cheek. "I'm sorry, darling. With all that's happened, I'm afraid I haven't been a very good communicator."

"I'd say you did a damn fine job of communicating *some* things," Andrea quipped.

"Yeah. But as for future plans, not so much."

"Oh, dear. That sounds ominous. I hope I'm up for this."

"Me, too." Daniel dragged his palms down the slight stubble of his five o'clock shadow. "Here's what I've been thinking. Facts: You are thoroughly entrenched in Vero Beach. You're well-known, well-connected, and you've got a great career—star realtor with the town's premiere real estate firm."

Andrea arched a brow. "Assuming business will pick up one day."

Daniel shook his head, making light of her comment. "It most assuredly will. As for Madison, she loves her school, and according to you, she's made great strides in the last couple of years, both academically and developmentally."

"True on both accounts," Andrea agreed. "For the longest time I didn't think it would be possible, but now... I do believe she will not only be capable of living independently but of finding meaningful work and thriving."

"Exactly. Which is why I wouldn't dream of uprooting you two. Besides, Vero has seeped into my bones—the slower pace, sunshine, and sea breezes—I find I'm loath to leave." Daniel set his glass down and rubbed his palms together. "And if I'm going to be perfectly honest, you might as well know I can't wait to renovate Casa Rio. The architect's preliminary plans are really fabulous. Naturally, you'll want to weigh in."

"And about Mom?" Andrea turned a worried face to him.

Daniel huffed out a breath. "You said yourself the house was too big for her to manage."

"Yes, but—"

"There's more to my plan." Daniel rose from his chair. "I figured we could divide the project into two stages and renovate the guest house first."

"Okay?" Andrea shook her head, obviously not comprehending.

"State-of-the-art ADA-compliant, totally aging-in-place design." Andrea gaped at Daniel as his idea became clear. "When it's completed, Margaret could move in there."

Andrea clapped her hands in delight. "That is brilliant, Daniel."

"I thought so." He took Andrea's hand, and she allowed herself to be pulled to her feet. "We can stay at your place while the big house is being remodeled. The good news is, I happen to be personally acquainted with a top-notch relator who can list your Castaway Cove property, and I'll bet she'll get a pretty penny for it."

Andrea wrapped her arms around Daniel's neck and laughed. "And then?" she asked.

"When the main house is completed, we move in."

"Oh, Daniel, are you sure? What about Philadelphia?"

"There's a private jetport in Vero. I own a plane. As Disney says, *It's a Small World*. With a little juggling, we can make it work."

"This is too much." Andrea lightly ran her fingers down his prominent jawline, happy in the thought that she was free to touch him, hold him, make love to him whenever she chose to do so. He was her man, and soon it would be official.

"No. It's exactly right. Who says we don't deserve a happily-ever-after?" He buried his head in her lustrous tresses and then drew back and held her by her shoulders. "Remember that bit you fed me about Casa Rio needing new blood, someone to care for it, children running down to the beach, a family?" Daniel peered at her, and Andrea nodded.

"Well, I took those words to heart, and then it came to me. I realized that family was us. You and I will be purchasing Casa Rio, and your name will be on the deed—Mrs. Andrea Armstrong." He sighed. "Ahh, how I love the sound of that." Daniel bent to her, and all of Andrea's worries dissolved in the tenderness of his kiss.

When she drew away, her heart was so full she could barely contain her joy. "It couldn't be more perfect. Mom and Madison will be so thrilled. Could it be that fairytale endings are really possible?"

"I don't know," Daniel said, "but I promise you this: I'm going to do everything in my power to assure that this one is." No sooner were those words out than Daniel's cellphone vibrated. "Who could be calling at this hour?" He slid the phone from his back pocket, glanced at the display, and his smile vanished. "Uh-oh. It's Nathan."

"Take it," Andrea said. "I'll go pour us a nightcap."

When she returned with a brandy snifter in each hand, it was to find Daniel seated and scowling. "What's the matter?" she asked, handing him a glass and taking a seat beside him.

"Aw, hell! I'm afraid we're going to have to cut our stay short. I need to be back in Vero the day after tomorrow."

"Why?"

"Just some final details regarding the divorce." Daniel grimaced. "I hope you're not too disappointed, but I want to get that thing finalized and make a clean break from She-who-shall-not-be-named."

Andrea's mouth formed a perfect O. Then she said, "In that case, we shall return posthaste, for I couldn't agree with you more."

CHAPTER SIXTEEN

ANOTHER DAY IN PARADISE

As Daniel had predicted, Madison and Zoe caused quite a sensation at Crush. The two budding beauties had taken pains with their hair, makeup, and dress, and the results proved well worth their efforts. Clutching hands for support, they'd sashayed through the entrance, heads held high, and in no time, found themselves garnering the attention of several eager, would-be dance partners. Occasionally, the girls would grant some young man the privilege of accompanying them on the dancefloor, but they were so delighted to be in each other's company and exhilarated with the newfound freedom they'd been granted, that they spent more time playing video games and just and getting to know one another better.

It wasn't until nearly eleven that Andrea, Daniel, and the Walkers came to fetch them. By that time, Madison and Zoe were punchy but still ebullient.

"How was it?" Andrea asked.

"Oh, Mom," Madison looked at Zoe, and the two of them grinned. "It was so much fun."

"Really?" Mrs. Walker said. "You had a good time, Zoe?"

The girls hugged one another and giggled. "Mom, it was the bomb," Zoe said. "Best time ever."

Mr. Walker looked askance at his wife and then at Andrea, who merely shrugged. "Great," Mrs. Walker said. "Well, say goodnight to Madison."

~

The hours flew by, and before they knew it, they found themselves climbing the Gulfstream's airstairs. It was a sultry evening, the sky murky. "Bye-bye," Madison cried, waving a hand in the air before ducking inside.

"So long, Atlantis." Daniel followed Andrea up and couldn't resist patting her pert backside. Andrea turned to him and laughed. Once inside, the two plopped down in a pair of plush captain's chairs directly behind the cockpit and across from the small buffet console. Maddy had curled up on a seat in the back and was already nodding off.

"Looks like we wore the kid out," Daniel said, hitching his head in the teen's direction.

"I'll say." At the sound of the engines revving, Andrea sighed. "Back to reality."

Daniel reached over and took her hand. "This too shall pass. We'll get through it, and I'm not going anywhere, anytime soon." He brought her hand to his lips and kissed it. So!" He jumped to his feet and crossed to the buffet. It had been laid out with an open bottle of champagne chilling on ice and a mound of glistening, purple caviar with chopped hard-cooked egg, finely sliced red onion, and caper accompaniments. "I say we get the party started." He filled two flutes and handed one to Andrea. "Would you like something to eat?"

"Maybe later."

Daniel returned to his chair and then raised his glass. "To the new Mrs. Armstrong."

They clicked glasses, and Andrea said, "To Casa Rio."

"I'll drink to that," Daniel agreed. "I haven't been so excited about a project in a very long time."

Andrea nodded. "Yes. I can't tell you how happy I am to be fixing the old girl up. Honestly, it was starting to eat at me. I felt guilty watching the property slowly decline, but there was nothing for it." She looked away, lost in thought for a moment. Then she turned back to Daniel. "I have so many wonderful memories of my childhood there. Now, Maddy will not only continue that tradition, but be close to her Nana. That will surely be a joy for both of them."

"Humph! Daniel muttered. "Margaret's a piece of work, and I mean that in a nice way."

"You've got that right. She's feisty as all get out, but when it comes to looking out for her kids and grandkids, she's ferocious as a lioness."

"An apt analogy."

"Daniel?" Andrea's tone was suddenly pensive.

"Yes?"

"I have a big ask for you. Really big."

"Anything."

"You'd best hold off until you hear what it is."

Daniel frowned. "Alright."

"As you know, Madison adores Derrick." Daniel's face clouded, but he nodded. "I was wondering if it'd be alright for him to give me away at our wedding."

"What?" Daniel had all he could do to keep from spewing a mouthful of champagne all over himself. "That's a horrible idea. Next, you'll be wanting me to put She-who-shall-not-be-named on the guest list."

"No," Andrea snorted at the thought, "and it's not a deal-breaker. If you'd rather he not, that's fine. But hear me out. I think it's a wonderful idea for several reasons."

Daniel looked incredulous. "And they are?"

"First, it would make Madison very happy. Her dad could be part of the ceremony, and I believe that would provide Derrick an opportunity to save face. It would also signal to him and *everybody* that we're all keen on remaining on good terms. More importantly, he will finally have to deal with the fact that I have moved on. Having him give me away would not only be appropriate but send the right message."

Daniel put his head in his hands and groaned, but his fit of pique was a brief one. He met her eyes, saying, "You make good points. Let me think about it, okay?"

"Of course."

Daniel shook his head and narrowed his eyes. "You've got a lot of Margaret in you, woman. What am I getting myself in for? The Nelson females are all minks."

Andrea smirked. "Oh, yeah."

~

The Gulfstream was making its final descent into the Vero Beach Jetport, and as forecast, the night was moonless and black as sin. In the meantime, Derrick and company were setting their trap in Andrea's back yard. They'd erected floodlights and strategically plotted their positions on the lawn. Throughout it all, Garrett's dread only mounted. There were so many variables, so many ways this plan could backfire. Sure, Derrick was dead serious, and he'd assembled an impressive offense. Who could blame him? The dude had all the motive in the world. But that slimeball, Jack had plenty of motive, too, and that's what scared the hell out of him.

The sun had long since set by the time Tyler was tricked up—false eyelashes and auburn-tinted wig—transformed into a fair representation of Madison. Everyone seemed to agree that the disguise was good enough to fool someone expecting to encounter her under the cover of darkness. Tyler had made it known that he hated it, felt totally emasculated. But he figured Madison's wellbeing was worth the sacrifice.

"Tell me again how this works." He looked up, shielding his eyes from the powerful beam of the flashlight Garrett was pointing in his direction while Derrick positioned him on an outdoor chaise. "What makes you think this Jack guy will fall for such a ridiculous trap?"

"It's like this, kid," a burly fellow stepped away from a Startle security floodlight he'd been testing. Clothed in fatigues, there were black smudges under his eyes, all of which attested to the fact that he was taking this exercise seriously. "It's a mission. You never really know where a mission will land you, but preparation is key. As for us, we've done our homework: We've analyzed the area of operations and employed mission planning. All of that buys down risk. We've covered the situation, mission, and execution extensively. In the real world, we'd have air support, maybe maritime backup, but here? There is no backup. We have one option: mission success.

"As you can see..." Derrick gestured toward the back of the house, "the rest of the team is prepared to see this through. The elements of any successful ambush involve speed, surprise, and violence of action. Believe me, these guys can deliver all three." He rested a palm on Tyler's shoulder. "We'll do our part. Now it's up to you to do yours."

Tyler swallowed hard. "Aren't you terrified that something might go wrong?"

"Let me answer that," the husky ex-GI interrupted. "Fear is off the table, kid. It is a negative emotion—one that can doom a mission to failure. In spec ops, there's a line from the movie *Point Break* we use when training some of the younger guys to perform risky exercises like skydiving or swimming out of submarines. It goes like this: *Fear causes hesitation, and hesitation can cause your worst fears to come true.* In those high-speed, high-stakes maneuvers, fear or doubt can cause someone to pause. Sometimes that's all it takes to blow a mission. Just a split second can make the difference between life and death, success or failure."

"Well said, Keith." Derrick let his gaze rove over the property. Then he raised his voice so that it would carry. "And I want to thank all my comrades for volunteering for this assignment." Suddenly, the perimeter was alive with hunky beefcake. There were five of them in all—men who'd served with Derrick. Some had night vision goggles strapped around their necks, and all of them were heavily armed. "One more thing: Did everyone park their vehicles at the clubhouse? I don't want anything out of the ordinary to draw attention. Just in case."

The men nodded, said, "Yeah," or, "Sure thing," before retreating into the shadows.

Garrett took it all in, and the potential firepower was no comfort. All those trigger-happy ex-GI's, with their sophisticated weaponry, made him apprehensive. He agreed with Tyler. Were the two of them the only sane ones in the lot? Didn't the adults realize there was something so not right about this setup? It was too slick. Surely, Jack would never fall for it.

It wasn't until almost midnight when Jack gestured toward the spit of land jutting out into the river. "There it is, over there. That's the house."

Kurt steered the Boston Whaler toward Andrea's dock. "You've got the hammer?"

Jack merely nodded.

Derrick was the first to spot the light from the approaching boat, and he whistled an alarm.

Incoming.

Garrett's eyes had adjusted to the dark, and they sought out Tyler. They were both stiff from inactivity, not accustomed to waiting, hour on end, for a frightening unknown. The two exchanged anxious looks. Garrett breathed deeply and steeled himself. He nodded encouragingly at the boy, giving him the thumbs up. Tyler returned the gesture and managed a sickly grin.

It was going down!

≈

Daniel yawned as he pulled up into Andrea's driveway. His fiancée and Madison were dozing, and he was bleary-eyed and ready to hit the sack. "Come on, troops," he regaled. "We're home."

"Argh!" Andrea complained. "I don't think I can move. Can't we just sleep in the car?"

"Yeah," Madison grumbled, "I'm dead. Just bury me here."

"Girls," Daniel pleaded, "a little cooperation, huh?" He shook Andrea's shoulder. "You go get Maddy situated, and I'll see to the luggage."

"Ugh, okay." Andrea climbed out of the car and levered the backseat door open. She roused her lethargic daughter, and the two made their way to the front entrance while Daniel unloaded luggage from the trunk. "Come on, honey, let's go inside."

"Where's Beau," Madison mumbled.

"He's next door at the Mulholland's. I texted them, but it's much too late to try to retrieve him tonight."

"Aw," Madison wailed. "I want to see him. I miss Beau."

"Tomorrow." Andrea turned the key in the lock and opened the door.

≈

Jack tied off at the piling, and Kurt scrambled out of the boat and hoisted himself up to the dock. He was quickly followed by his brother, hammer in hand. The two paused on the riverbank, peering intently at the house. Jack put a finger to his lips and leaned into Kurt. "I can't believe it," he whispered, pointing toward the pool chaise where a figure reclined. "She's right there. This is going to be like taking candy from a baby."

The thugs crept toward the chaise, slowly advancing on Tyler. Suddenly, a high-pitched yapping cut the air. It was coming from the direction of the residence on the property next door. By then, Jack and Kurt were a mere twenty feet from Tyler, but the dog's insistent barking stopped them dead in their tracks.

In the next instant, the back door to Andrea's house flew open, and a slight figure dashed outside. "Beauregard! Beau, I'm home!" Madison cried. "I'm coming."

Then all hell broke loose.

Tyler bolted out of the chaise and struck a defensive pose. At the same time, four Startle floodlights popped on, illuminating Andrea's backyard in a dazzling glare. That was enough to momentarily blind Jack and his brother.

Having circumvented the pool, Madison froze, her eyes wild.

Derrick and his contingent of ex-Marines exploded from their cover and surged toward Jack and Kurt with weapons drawn.

At the same time, Andrea and Daniel burst out the back door, took in the eerily lit scene, and staggered to a halt. Wrapping their arms around one another, they struggled to make sense of what was beyond comprehension. "What the hell?" Daniel cried as Andrea whimpered, beyond words.

This was all turning into a nightmare, Jack thought as his brain went into overdrive. When, moments later, he was able to see again and process, he realized he needed to snatch Madison and make a run for it. He was blown big time, and the odds were against him. What else did he have to lose? He charged Tyler, adrenaline spiking through his veins, imbuing him with super-human power and speed.

"Don't even think about it," Tyler hollered, his voice spiraling to its upper register as he flailed his arms at the oncoming attacker. But Jack was upon him, raising the hammer above his head. Which is when the ex-GIs put an end to that madness. Keith pointed his gun in the air and discharged his weapon and the ex-GIs rocketed toward Tyler. Then, surrealistically, all the commotion came to a screeching stop while everyone tried to make sense of what was unfolding.

Not for long.

"Mom, Daniel!" Madison screamed. "Help!"

Kurt appeared out of nowhere, his eyes fastening on Madison, and Garrett was spurred to action. He shot out of the bushes and tackled the girl, bringing her to the ground, but that wasn't enough to thwart Kurt. The heavyset specimen loomed over them. Garrett went for the attacker only to be violently shoved away as though he were nothing more than a rag doll. Kurt locked the writhing girl in a vice-like grip and dragged her off.

"I've got her," he cried, holding the thrashing teen before him like a shield. "Let my brother go, and we'll be out of here."

"No!" Garrett cried. Scrambling to his feet, he ran, full tilt toward Kurt, and with no thought to his own well-being hurtled into the would-be kidnapper. It was a purely instinctive reaction and one which served him well. Kurt was completely taken off guard, and that was all the advantage the vets needed. They swung into action with the practiced efficiency borne of years of training. Working like a machine, they closed in on both Kurt and his brother. Within minutes, the situation was diffused. Jack and Kurt were handcuffed and subdued, and Madison and Tyler freed.

"Oh, my God," Andrea sobbed, her knees buckling.

"Sweetheart," Daniel cried, supporting her, "it's over. She's safe."

"Mom!" Madison slammed into Andrea's arms. "Are you okay?"

"Maddy!" Andrea cried through her tears. "Yes, sweetie. We're fine." She clutched her daughter to her breast. "We are always going to be okay."

Daniel wrapped them both in his arms. "Yes," he said. "Nothing will ever hurt you again, Maddy. I promise you that."

～

It was mid-morning, a brilliant sunshiny day, and Kara was sitting at her desk, gazing out over her verdant lawn, when her cellphone chimed. One look at the phone's display, and her face lit up. "Hey, Becca, you crazy woman. What's the news?"

"Rob and I have set the date."

Becca's whisky voice was like a tonic, her enthusiasm contagious. "Goody! When's the big day?"

"Two weeks from Saturday."

"What?" Kara reeled back in her chair. "I know you said as soon as possible, but isn't this rushing things a bit? I mean… can you even organize a wedding in so short a time?"

"Yes, to both questions. Rob's mother has taken it upon herself to arrange the entire event, which is fine by me." Becca laughed. "She's having the time of her life. I don't believe that woman has a lot on her plate, so this is simply consuming her. In a good way."

"Well, congratulations. I'll have to get busy and arrange to fly in. Have you told Lanie yet?"

"She's my next call. And listen, I'm emailing you a link to the three bridesmaids' dresses. Mom Barrow has given them her seal of approval, so, I imagine they'll be up to your standards. Will you and Lanie do me a favor; just decide between yourselves and order them?"

"Sure thing," Kara agreed. "My God, Becca! You're really marrying Rob Barrow. That is so great."

"Don't I know it? I am the luckiest girl. I got my Prince Charming. It's crazy, but he adores me."

"And he's filthy rich," Kara said.

"I love him, Kara. I really do. We have so much fun together. He's more than I ever imagined. I feel like I'm living a fantasy, that I'll wake up only to realize it's all been a dream."

"It's real, sweetie, and I couldn't be happier for you." As soon as Kara ended the call, she keyed in Michael's number.

"Well, this is an unexpected surprise."

The Brit's highbrow accent brought a smile to Kara's face. "Hello, Michael. I have a favor to ask."

"Anything."

Kara's smile broadened. "Becca is getting married in a little over two weeks. Please say you'll be my escort. It should be a grand affair."

"Sounds like fun. As you'll recall, I was going to pop over anyway. Count me in."

"Wonderful. And now for the big ask: Would it be possible for Laney and me to bunk at your place for the wedding?"

～

As she waited in that same airless, putrid-green room she'd hoped never to see again, Andrea fumed. It was a mere two days after the great debacle, as she'd grown accustomed to calling it. Nervously, she tapped the pointy toe of her pump on the terrazzo floor. Where was Officer Campbell? How she hated to be kept waiting! She hadn't done anything wrong. Nor had Madison. Still, their lives were, yet again, interrupted. And who was to blame? None other than the former love of her life and his half-baked plot to nab Madison's kidnapper. She had all she could do to keep from lunging across the table and strangling the man! Still, she had to admit that, despite his bungling, Derrick had accomplished that feat; he'd snagged the culprit when the police had failed to do so. But not without putting them all in grave danger.

It simply boggled her mind!

"Mr. Nelson," Campbell began, "what made you decide to... take the extreme measures that you did? You must realize criminal charges could be brought against you—an unauthorized military action, the discharging of a firearm? Need I go on?"

Andrea let her eyes rest on her former husband. He'd forgone his bib overalls for khakis and a classic polo shirt. More than that, he was clean-shaven, and his hair was cut short and stylishly. She had to give it to him; he looked quite respectable—handsome even.

The directness of Campbell's question seemed to catch Derrick off guard. He hesitated before responding, which lent him an air of gravitas. All eyes were on him when he finally said, "Officer..." But before Derrick could complete his sentence, he choked up, and it was plain to see it wasn't theatrics. He was speaking from the heart. "Sorry." He struggled to rein in his emotions. "Do you have kids?" he asked.

"That's neither here nor there," the policeman said, his face stony. "This isn't about me."

Derrick sighed. "You've got to understand. It was my daughter, my sweet, innocent girl those maniacs intended to..." He sniffed loudly, appeared to be on the verge of weeping. "When I learned that they were planning to come for her..." Derrick hunched over, putting a knuckle to his eye.

"Mr. Nelson?"

Derrick turned a tortured face to the cop. "I was desperate... a little crazy, I guess." He speared Andrea with a pointed look. "You can hate me for it, but I just wanted to save her." Then he broke down, sobbing openly.

As she watched her ex-husband fall apart, Andrea's emotions seesawed. The anger that had consumed her fled, and she struggled to keep her own tears from falling.

Derrick reached across the table for her hand, and for a brief moment, she allowed him to take it in his.

"Don't cry, Daddy," Madison implored. "You're my hero."

Campbell cupped his chin in hand as his gaze turned from Daniel to the girl. "I do have a daughter about your age, Madison," he said. "And I can't imagine what I would do if she had ever been put in the situation you were." His eyes returned to Daniel. "But we can't go running around like vigilantes taking the law into our own hands. Can we?"

"No, Officer."

"I'm going to dismiss this case, Mr. Nelson."

Derrick clapped a hand over his mouth.

"But I'm warning you…" Campbell looked hard at Derrick. "Never again attempt anything as hairbrained as this last exploit. You play by the rules from now on. Do I make myself clear?"

"Yes, sir," Derrick said, "absolutely. Thank you."

Campbell nodded and then turned to Madison. "Young lady," he said, and for the first time, a small smile played about his face. "You should be very proud of yourself."

"Me?" Madison's eyebrows rose, and she straightened in her chair. "Why?"

"I'll tell you why," the officer said. "I don't think many girls your age would have handled themselves the way you did throughout this ordeal. You, young lady, are one tough cookie, and don't you ever forget it."

Madison looked both dubious and pleased. "Okay."

Campbell turned his gaze to Andrea. "Mrs. Nelson, I understand that you've arranged for counseling for Madison. Is that correct?"

"Yes, that's right."

Campbell focused back on the girl. "Madison, I want you to continue with your therapy until the doctor says you no longer need it. Can I count on you to do that?"

Madison's eyes grew wide. "Yes, sir."

"Well, I guess that about wraps it up. I expect y'all will be called up as witnesses at the trial. So, unfortunately, you're not quite done with this nasty business." He looked at Madison, raised his eyebrows, and lowered his voice, saying, "The wheels of justice turn slowly." Then he offered up a smile to Andrea and came to his feet. "But they turn. And one day, you'll be able to put this all behind you."

"Thank you so much, Officer," Andrea said.

Derrick rose and thrust out his hand, and Campbell shook it. "I'm beholden to you, sir," he said.

"That you are," Campbell agreed. "So, do me a favor, huh? Don't ever let me see your homely face in here again."

Derrick snorted. "You have my word."

The policeman crossed to the door, but before stepping over the threshold, he swiveled back to face them. "This has been hard on all of you. Take my advice: don't dwell on it. Let it go." He turned on his heel and strode out the door, saying, "Or at least try."

It was the tenth of May, and the tropics had steamed under a scorching sun all day. Little wonder the encroaching night, with its attendant cooling sea breezes, came as a welcome relief. The Barrow estate was ablaze with light, every window glowing. Cut flowers and green garlands, gathered in white tulle ribbons, adorned the handsome molded railings, their perfume wafting on the gentle wind. Dressed in formal attire, guests surged up the wide stone steps toward the massive, mahogany double doors, which were open to the elements.

Once having gained admittance, Barbados's elite were greeted by a convivial liveried staff, for tonight's party was to be the social event of the season, and everyone–from maid to Prime Minister, Mia Mottley —was in high spirits.

Everyone, that is, except for the bride.

A disconsolate Becca was seated in front of a vanity table in a well-appointed guest suite—one which had been assigned to the females in the bridal party. "I look horrible," she wailed, ripping the veil from her head and tossing it aside. "These false eyelashes?" She batted her newly enhanced lashes. "It looks like I've got spiders in my eyes."

"You look gorgeous," Laney said, retrieving the veil and fluffing it.

"And if you start bawling, we're going to have a hell of a time dealing with puffy, red-rimmed peepers," Kara warned, her face stern. "So don't."

Laney set the veil aside and retrieved her impressively large makeup case. Placing it on the vanity table, she popped it open. "Now, listen to me. Those gals who did your makeup, they did a fine job."

"Yeah, perfect if you're a luscious, Latina beauty," Kara said, archly.

Becca made as if to bolt out of her chair, but Laney restrained her. "She's right," she soothed, "and who could blame them? That's their clientele. But yours, my dear gal pal, is a subtle, more refined, English countryside—"

"Jane Austen, less-is-more kind of beauty," Kara said.

Becca, her brow lowered, looked both rebellious and intrigued.

"So," Laney said, "shall we make a few adjustments and let the beautiful Becca we know and love shine through?"

Before Becca had a chance to reply, Laney was removing the ridiculously long, false eyelashes while Kara gingerly daubed at the heavy pancake.

Fifteen minutes later found a much-subdued Becca relaxing in the care of her friends. "Now," Laney said, "take a look, and what do you see?"

Becca swiveled around on the vanity stool, gazed at her reflection in the mirror, only to tear up again. "It's me! A very beautiful me," she cried.

"None of that now," Kara chided, sweeping in with a tissue. "No weeping allowed after your two best buds in the world created this masterpiece." She bent down and wrapped her arms around Becca.

"You really do look like a fairy princess," Laney said, once again securing the veil to Becca's head.

Becca sniffed but kept her tears at bay. "Oh, good gracious! I do believe this is actually going to happen." She rose from her chair and tossed her veiled head. "And, for the first time in my life, I feel beautiful."

"You *are* beautiful," Kara said.

"Freakin' drop dead gorgeous," Laney agreed.

Their girl talk was interrupted by a rapping on the door. "Who's there?" Becca whirled around. "Come in."

~

The door opened a crack, and a quivering, aging beauty peered in. "Becca?" A tremulous voice queried. "Are you ready? It's time."

"Yes, Mom B." Becca crossed the distance to the door and embraced her soon-to-be mother-in-law. "Thank you so much for this lovely party."

Celia Barrow's face was a well-tended garden preparing for a tsunami. Yet she allowed herself to be swallowed up in Becca's bear hug. She realized that times had changed—that the world order was evolving—and she knew she had to change with it.

Despite her initial resistance to this interloper, she had to admit there was a seductive quality about Rob's brash, in-your-face girl. And it was plain to see that Becca was madly in love with her son. More than that, she saw something of herself in this plucky American with little means and grand aspirations. She'd come to believe this hastily arranged marriage would be all for the good. New blood! Mix it up a bit.

God knows, she was eager for grandbabies!

CHAPTER SEVENTEEN

SALLY FORTH

"Are you coming, Mom?" Madison peered through the doorway, and her eyes came to rest on her mother. "It's almost time."

Seated at a dressing table, Andrea had her back to the door while putting the finishing touches on her makeup. At the sound of Madison's voice, she swiveled to face her daughter, and her breath caught in her throat. Had it really been only a year since their horrible time of trouble—a year which had seen such dramatic changes in all their lives?

One thing was for certain: Madison was coming into her own. This damaged child whom she'd been so protective of—the girl she'd thought defenseless—had, over the course of a year, grown a hard outer shell. Now Madison projected an aura of self-confidence, and there was a new lilt to her step. Although Andrea had never thought she'd live to see this day, she had to admit that Madison could, most likely, handle just about anything life threw her way.

Andrea's eyes roved over the young woman's svelte frame. The pale green sheath she wore did little to hide her budding figure, and it surely highlighted her green-gold eyes. "You look scrumptious, Maddy."

"Thanks." Madison tossed a head piled high with curls that were held in place by a pearl-studded clip. "I asked the hairdresser to copy a style I found in Glamour Magazine."

"It suits you." Andrea said, but in the next moment, she feigned a look of dismay. "Hey, I'm supposed to be the belle of the ball, and here you go stealing the show."

Madison hitched her shoulders and grinned. "I do like this dress."

"I'll bet Garrett does, too," Andrea muttered, extending her arms. "Come here and give your old Ma a parting kiss before she steps off the gangplank."

Giggling, Madison rushed into her mother's arms. "You're not Wendy, Mom."

"No, and you're not Tinkerbelle." Andrea held her daughter at arm's length, eying her critically. "You've grown up."

Madison drew away. "Not quite, Mom."

"Tell me, how are you handling Garrett and Tyler?"

Madison snorted. "Ugh! It's crazy. I like Garrett. He's the real deal... so mature." Andrea bit her lip to keep from laughing. "But Tyler is... so sweet. I don't want to hurt his feelings."

Andrea clasped her daughter's hand. "Honey, sometimes it's better to let a guy go, rather than to keep stringing him along." Madison's brow furrowed, and Andrea changed her tack. "For tonight," she said, "I suggest you three simply enjoy the evening and not worry about the future." She brought her daughter's hand to her mouth giving it a quick kiss before releasing it. "Oftentimes, the future simply takes care of itself."

Madison's face brightened, and she nodded. "Good idea."

"Hey, y'all!" Sally Bray swept into the room with her usual take-charge attitude. "My!" She looked the two up and down. "Don't you clean up nice!"

For the occasion, the voluptuous real estate broker had donned a pink, tea-length gown, which showed off her curves while playing up her peaches and cream complexion. "As do you, Sally." Andrea turned back to her reflection in the mirror and angled her head from side to side. "What do you think about this headpiece? Is it too much for an old broad?"

"Not at all!" Sally eyed the cream-colored, velvet headband studded with tiny seed pearls that crowned Andrea's head. "It coordinates perfectly with the lace on your dress. Honestly, I love it."

"Thanks." Andrea nodded toward the open door. "What's it like out there?"

"The clan has gathered and awaits your presence." Sally raised her brows, an impish grin on her face.

"Oh, dear," Andrea muttered, wringing her hands. "Suddenly, I'm wondering if I should go through with this."

"Mom!" Madison wailed.

"Oh, no you don't," Sally said. "You've simply got a case of the last-minute jitters. If you didn't have them, you wouldn't be human." She made a shooing motion. "I've been told we should take the back staircase. So come on! You don't want to keep that crowd waiting."

Ignoring her mother's troubled face, Madison grabbed Andrea's hand and pulled her to her feet. "To the gangplank," she cried merrily.

~

Casa's newly installed, commercial-grade kitchen was abustle with white-coated caterers busily preparing the wedding feast under Derrick's direction. A raven-haired woman darted in, toting a large box. She crossed to the sink, preparing to unload its contents. "Wait," Derrick cried, throwing his hands in the air. "Don't wet them!"

"Huh?" She held the box mid-air.

Derrick swooped in and snaked an arm about the attractive female's waist while, at the same time, relieving her of her burden.

A fellow with a jaunty toque atop his head looked up from a huge, steaming pot he was tending on the stove. "Are those the morels?"

"Yep." Derrick nodded and then turned back to the woman. "Jasmine, I'm afraid your stint at the Dew Drop Inn has not prepared you for the world of haute cuisine."

"What are you talking about?"

"All you need to do to these beauties is get out any of the sand that might have accumulated in their jowly little pockets. Then gently wipe them off with a slightly dampened paper towel." Derrick demonstrated, selecting a six-inch specimen. "You see how fragile they are?"

The comely brunette widened her eyes. "Got it," she said. "Didn't know. A-okay, boss."

"Sorry." Derrick pulled Jasmine close and nuzzled her neck before releasing her. "I get a bit crazy about morels."

"Why?" She reached for a paper towel.

Derrick turned back to her and shook his head, a rueful smile on his face. "I don't know. Maybe because they are not only delicious but rare." He returned to the enormous Norwegian salmon he was deboning. "Morels grow in the wild and are only available for a short window in the spring." He flung an arm out, indicating the mushrooms. These babies came all the way from Northern Michigan, shipped here by a friend of mine who owns a restaurant in the heart of the Sleeping Bear Dunes."

"Wow!"

"Jasmine, we are here to both nourish and entertain. It's a noble calling, one I bought into long ago. Perhaps you might consider what it is we're doing every time we feed someone."

Derrick's lecture was interrupted when Sally barged in. "Okay, people," the powerhouse realtor regaled, "time to get a wiggle on. A bride is waiting in the wings." She looked pointedly at Derrick. "She needs an escort. Do not let her down." Sally put hands to hips and glared at him. "Again."

At those words, Derrick came to attention. "No. I won't." He ducked in to plant a quick kiss on Jasmine's forehead. "Got to go, Jazz." He wiped his hands on his apron and then hitched it over his head and tossed it.

"Derrick!" Jasmine howled, "don't you dare leave me."

"I've got this, Mr. Nelson," the chef waved Derrick away, a sardonic grin on his face. "And you've got bigger fish to fry."

The caterers guffawed at Derrick's predicament, and he took the ribbing in good stride. "Really funny," he said, grabbing his tuxedo jacket from off the back of a chair. "Thanks guys. I'll be back soon." Then he clasped Jasmine's hand. "Come with me. It's about time you met the family."

～

Margaret glanced around at her new digs. She loved this newly renovated house. There were no stairs to climb, and everything was tidy—in its place and manageable. When all chicks had flown, and it was just her alone, Casa had become entirely too much of a burden. She'd found herself rambling about the place, unable to keep it clean, let alone maintained properly.

Now everything was perfect, and she felt as though a great weight had been lifted from her shoulders. Better yet, all she had to do was look out this window and see Casa resurrected in all its glory. Margaret put her face to the living room window. "Oh, John," she murmured, "how I wish you were here to witness this."

A rapping on the door brought her back to the present.

"Nana, we need you. It's time."

Margaret hurried to the door and threw it open. At the sight of her beautiful granddaughter, her eyes brimmed with tears. "Ah!"

"What's the matter?" One look at her grandmother's face, and Madison's eager smile faltered.

"Nothing, sweetheart. It's just…"

"You don't like my hair?"

"No! I love it. You look amazing." Margaret extended her arms. "You remind me… of me."

Madison allowed herself to be embraced before drawing away. "What do you mean?"

"Darling, until you have grandbabies of your own, you'll never really understand. Just know that you make me very proud."

"Why?"

"Because I see myself in you—your backbone and determination —to say nothing of the fact that you're a mermaid."

Madison giggled. "Yeah. We're swimmers."

"We know how to navigate, kid, you and I."

Madison grabbed her grandmother's hand. "That's right," she cried. "And we need to navigate over to the big house. Mom's getting married."

"Really?" Margaret allowed herself to be dragged out the door, laughing all the way.

Earlier in the week, Daniel had arranged for the pool to be drained and a temporary wood floor laid over it. The platform was now set with rows of white folding chairs facing a latticed bower festooned with orchids and cut roses. The guests milled about on the terrace and lawn, chatting with friends and neighbors. From her vantage point in the great room, Andrea peeked out from behind a linen drape at those who'd assembled to mark this occasion, and her anxieties fled. Here were the people she loved most in the world. Nathan McCourt, whose frame towered above the others, was the first of many friendly faces she picked out from the crowd. He glanced her way, and she caught his eye and waved at him. A silent communication passed between them, and when he responded with a thumb's up, she knew that this elegant man would always have her family's back.

Margaret and Madison bustled into the room, and Andrea spun around to face them.

"Andy," Margaret exclaimed, "how lovely you look!"

Andrea took in her mother's carefully made-up face, her form-fitting taffeta gown, and she marveled at the matriarch's ageless beauty. "Gosh. You, too, Mom," she said.

"Yeah," Margaret snorted, "just call me the *old* maid of honor," and they all chuckled.

"It's true, though," Sally quipped as she distributed bouquets—baby's breath and carnations for Madison and Margaret, calla lilies for Andrea. "The acorn doesn't fall far from the tree. Good genes at work in this family."

Derrick dashed in, shrugging into his formal jacket. "Well, darlin'," he said, eyeing his ex-wife. "Rather than meet you at the end of it, I'm ready to walk you down the aisle." He extended an arm. "Shall we?"

∼

Sally put two fingers to her lips and whistled loudly. "Alright, y'all, time to take your seats."

Eager for the party to get started, the guests quickly found chairs while the priest came to stand beneath the wedding bower. From an outdoor speaker, the first measured notes of Pachelbel's *Canon in D* sounded, and all in the assembly came to attention.

Flanked by a straight-faced Garrett on one side and a broadly grinning Tyler on the other, Madison was first down the aisle, and at the sight of the beautiful young people, there were titters of appreciation from the guests. Everyone in attendance knew of Madison's recent travails and seeing the girl looking so happy proved a balm to many a soul. Nathan followed the young threesome with an ebullient yet regal Margaret on his arm. The music segued to J. Clark's *Trumpet Voluntary*, and as one, the wedding guests rose to their feet.

Daniel appeared before the priest, and Nathan, Garrett, and Tyler fell in beside him. Madison and Margaret took their places to the right of them as Andrea and Derrick processed down the aisle. When the former couple arrived at the makeshift altar, Derrick shook hands with Daniel before bending to bestow a tiny kiss on Andrea's cheek. "Love you, babe," he said, a brief look of regret crossing his face. "Good luck."

The ceremony passed in a blur. Andrea tried to hold and capture every minute of it, but it simply wasn't possible to do so. It was as though she were dreaming.

Afterward, she looked out over the crowd and her eyes fell upon the usually dour Margo. Her former nemesis was looking surprisingly carefree and beaming at her so openly that Andrea couldn't help but think perhaps she'd judged her too harshly. The typically stoic realtor was surrounded by Stewart, Jeremy, and Craig and their attractive wives, and Andrea thought how fortunate she was to have such supportive colleagues. Together, they'd gotten through the worst of the housing bust, the stolen escrows debacle, the horror of Madison's kidnapping. They'd weathered the storm, and today, Andrea's heart was full to bursting.

≈

"Mrs. Armstrong, try one of these." Daniel forked a freshly shucked oyster from its pearly shell and brought it to her lips.

"Ulp!" Andrea put her hands before her and backed away. "My tummy says no." In the next moment, she bolted away. "Sorry," she called out as she charged up the stairs. Daniel followed her progress, a perplexed look on his face, but then Nathan's voice interrupted his reverie.

"Hello there," the tall man clapped Daniel on his back. "Congrats. You did it!"

"Yeah," Daniel grinned at his cohort, "sealed my fate."

"Well," Nathan looked out over the enormous tent, the manicured grounds, and then his eyes darted about the tastefully appointed interior. "It doesn't seem too onerous a task." He arched a brow and smiled. "With a smart, savvy, gorgeous wife factored into the mix."

"Ah, here she is." Daniel beamed at Andrea as she scurried toward him. "Is everything okay, sweetie?"

"Right as rain." Andrea turned to Nathan. "But I must admit whenever I begin to feel guilty for having waylaid this amazing man," She ducked in for a quick kiss with Daniel, "I am heartened to know that he is settling in near to his best friend in the world." She grinned at the financier. "That's you, Nathan."

"I couldn't be happier," the tall man admitted. "I've missed my brother. It'll be a great comfort having him close."

∾

The caterers had packed up, the wedding guests long since departed. Margaret had retreated to the little house—Madison dragged herself off to bed after having danced the night away. Now it was just Andrea and Daniel. They were sitting on the dock, perched over the ocean, staring out over a black expanse canopied by a gazillion stars.

"Are you still sure of this?" Andrea asked, lightly resting a palm on Daniel's thigh.

"Absolutely. Like it or not, I'm dug in."

Andrea tossed her head and laughed. "Good!"

"It was an amazing day, a wonderful party. I couldn't be happier."

"Me, too."

"But what came over you?" Daniel drew away, searching her face. "I was worried."

"There's something I need to tell you." Andrea ducked her head, suddenly unable to meet his eyes.

"Oh, my God," Daniel hooted, drawing away. "How could I have been so blind? Your loss of appetite, the nausea... Why didn't you tell me?"

Andrea gnawed at her lower lip. "I don't know what you mean," she dissembled, a small smile playing about her lips.

"You can't fool me." Daniel's eyes twinkled, and he reached for her. "You're pregnant!"

Playfully, Andrea made as if to pull away, but Daniel was

undeterred. He splayed the fingers of one hand over her abdomen. "Tell me it's true. You're carrying our baby, my child."

∽

Daniel had never experienced a birth, and this was much more than he'd bargained for. To see the love of his life convulsed in agony had never been on his agenda. But Madison and Garrett were offering their support from the waiting room, and he knew he had to step up. "Breathe," he insisted, clasping Andrea's clammy hand in his. "Come on, sweetie. Almost there."

"Oh, my God!" Andrea cried, convulsed by another contraction. "You do it."

The female OBYGN doc laughed. "Maybe in the next life, huh? Your husband's right, though. The baby's head is crowning. Almost there, Mrs. Armstrong. One last push."

∽

"Nana, he's too little to swim," Madison cried as she clambered into the pool.

Margaret stood waist-deep in the water, feet firmly planted, the baby held snuggly in her arms. "Nonsense," she said. "This little guy's a swimmer. Just look at these sturdy limbs."

"Mom," Andrea entreated, "are you sure about this?"

Margaret turned to her daughter and lowered her brow. "I taught each of my three children to swim—you included," she said, in an aggrieved voice, "and you are all terrific swimmers. Isn't that so?"

Daniel drew his wife close. "Let her be. She knows what she's doing."

"Ugh," Andrea grumbled. "I hate this."

Margaret raised her arms, hesitated for a moment, and then tossed the nine-month-old before her into the water. Almost immediately, the little tyke flipped onto his back, flailed his arms, and somehow managed to keep afloat.

Madison couldn't contain herself a moment longer. She dove under, only to come up beside her baby brother. Positioning her hands beneath him, she supported his tiny back. "That's right,

Haydon, you got this," she said, all the while assuring his head was elevated.

"He does, indeed," Margaret cried. "Bring him to me, Maddy. We have a very rare creature on our hands!"

"What's that?" Madison asked as she slogged through the water, her baby brother in arms.

"A merman," Margaret hooted. "A real live merman, Madison!"

~

Andrea was standing at her bedroom window, gazing out over a slate black sky dusted with a smattering of twinkling stars when Daniel came up behind her. "What are you thinking?" he asked, nuzzling her neck.

Andrea allowed herself to melt into Daniel's broad chest. "Just that I'm so grateful you came into my life." She turned to him, throwing her arms around him. "Never in a million years would I have imagined I'd be back here—living in Casa—with my..." She stood on tiptoes, kissed him lightly on the lips, and then drew away, her eyes shining, "my wonderful, handsome husband."

"Mom!" At the sound of Madison's strident voice, the two jolted apart, panicked expressions on their faces.

"Coming," Andrea cried as she and Daniel charged out of the bedroom and down the hall to the nursery.

"Maddy, what is it?" Daniel was the first to burst through the doorway. No sooner had he gained entrance than Andrea plowed into him.

"You scared me half to death, Madison." Andrea pushed past her husband. But before she could take two steps into the room, Daniel's arms had encircled her waist, and he was whispering in her ear, "Shh... don't frighten him."

Andrea took in the sweet tableau that greeted her eyes: Madison, amid an assortment of toys and stuffed animals, sitting cross-legged on a braided rug and tottering before her on unsteady feet, a rosy-faced Hayden. The babe's wee fingers were tightly clasped around his sister's thumbs, and he seemed determined to keep them there.

"You see," Madison chortled, "he is *so* strong." Gently, she pried her thumbs from her brother's hands, at the same time scooting backward, her arms outstretched. "Come on, Hayden, show Mommy and Daddy how you walk to Maddy."

Andrea gasped as the toothless, grinning child took first one, then another uncertain step toward his sister.

"I can't believe it," Daniel breathed. Madison moved out of the way at the same time, motioning to Daniel, and he scrambled to take her place. Crouching down and extending his arms, he said, "Come to Daddy, Hayden."

The boy took three more staggering steps and then fell, giggling, into his adoring father's arms. Andrea dropped to her knees beside Daniel, and Madison snuggled up next to her. The three let their arms fall around one another.

"Madison, how long have you been... practicing?" Andrea asked.

The teen shrugged. "I don't know. A week maybe. Ever since he took his first swim."

"Ah," Daniel said. "I guess you figured if he could stay afloat—"

"Yeah." Madison snorted. "I thought if he could swim, he sure as heck could walk."

"Oh, honey!" Andrea kissed Madison's forehead. "You were absolutely right. What an amazing sister you are."

"Your mother's spot on." Daniel squeezed Madison's shoulder. "That kid is lucky to have you looking after him, Madison." He swooped in for a quick kiss. "And I'm really lucky to have the sweetest, kindest step-daughter on the planet. So very proud of you, honey."

Andrea awoke to an orange glow shining directly into her eyes. It was winking at her from between the narrow slats of a plantation shutter. Perhaps it had been a bad dream that roused her from sleep, but now she was wide awake, and she couldn't ignore the inexorable pull the moon exerted. Daniel lay somnolent beside her, and as tempting as it was to snuggle up next to him and go back to sleep, she felt compelled to creep from bed and pay homage to the moon.

Once outside, Andrea surrendered to the warm night's embrace. With ears full of the whirring of insects and the shrilling of tree frogs, she darted down the lawn and out to the dock.

"Hey, Andy!" Her mother's distinctive voice came to her from out of the darkness. Andrea's eyes soon adjusted, and she could make out a form perched at the end of the pier.

"Mom, what are you doing?" Andrea hunkered down next to her mother.

"Same thing you are, silly!"

Andrea chuckled. "Sally was right about us."

"What do you mean?"

"The acorn doesn't fall far from the tree."

"Ah! I guess it's true." Margaret leaned back, propping her hands on the dock and gazing at the night sky. "But look at that moon, would you?"

"It's glorious."

"I'd say!" Daniel's voice startled the two women, and they swiveled to face him. "What are you two sorcerers doing out here?"

"Daniel!" Andrea cried, "I thought you were asleep."

"And I thought you were sleeping beside me. I missed you."

"Your timing's perfect," Margaret said, extending an arm in his direction. "Daniel, help this creaky old lady up, won't you? It's time I toddled on."

"Don't let me scare you off," Daniel said, but he reached for Margaret.

"Not at all. I'll leave you in good company."

"Shall I walk you?"

"Good heavens, no! I know this property like the back of my liver-spotted hand. But thanks, Danny." Margaret gave him a quick hug, patted Andrea on the shoulder, and headed back up the dock. "Night, you two."

Andrea scrambled to her feet. "Nighty night, Mom," she called after the retreating figure. In the next moment, she was in Daniel's arms. "Do you remember the last time we saw a moon like this?" she asked.

"I do," Daniel bent to kiss her. "And this is what I wanted to do then—"

"But I rebuffed you. Foolish me."

"Yes," Daniel said. "I got my feathers ruffled. But look at us. It's what I have the privilege to do now."

There was such a tug and pull with Daniel, Andrea thought, before all reason fled, and she surrendered to his kiss.

When she drew away, breathless, she smiled at him. "Yes. It was a little over a year and a half ago when that swollen moon beamed strange emanations down upon us."

"Bewitching me, for sure." His laugh was rich and warm as he gazed about, feigning confusion. "How is it I came to be in this place, anyway?"

"Just damned good luck, mister!"

Daniel turned back to Andrea and drew her close. "I guess that's so," he said. "I got lucky, alright. I never imagined I'd end up here, in Vero Beach." He ran his fingers through her hair, letting them gently come to rest against the nape of her neck.

"When I think of that first night... how confused I was..." Andrea shook her head.

"What?" Daniel lightly rubbed a thumb against Andrea's ear.

"It seems like a lifetime ago," Andrea admitted. "I was attracted to you, and you, my dear husband, were so mysterious."

"Didn't do a good job of *that*," Daniel said, a self-deprecating tone to his voice.

"Then there was the horrible abduction business."

"Yes, we've been through a lot. But, hey! Casa's been restored. I have a stunning wife. We're parents to a beautiful daughter and a darling baby boy." He shook his head, marveling at his good fortune. "The future's looking rosy, my dear."

Daniel drew her close, and Andrea clung to him with an urgency that could not be ignored. "Let's go to bed," he whispered. "We'll open the shutters and make love under this beguiling moon."

"Best offer I've had in a long time." Andrea clasped his hand, and the two ventured another look at that distended, gleaming orb. "Goodnight, moon," Andrea cried gaily. She dropped his hand and capered up the dock and across the lawn, and Daniel raced after her, laughing.

Andrea tore through the doorway, but Daniel paused on the threshold for one more glance skyward. "You, old devil moon," he breathed, "work your magic again."

THE END

～

Don't miss out on your next favorite book!
Join the Melange Books mailing list at
www.melange-books.com/mail.html

THANK YOU FOR READING

∼

Did you enjoy this book?

We invite you to leave a review at your favorite book site, such as Goodreads, Amazon, Barnes & Noble, etc.

DID YOU KNOW THAT LEAVING A REVIEW...

- Helps other readers find books they may enjoy.
- Gives you a chance to let your voice be heard.
- Gives authors recognition for their hard work.
- Doesn't have to be long. A sentence or two about why you liked the book will do.

ABOUT THE AUTHOR

Award winning author of the
gripping memoir, *Dancing with the
Devil*, and the children's book, *Dune
Dragons*. Gretchen Rose spent most
of her adult life operating a high-end
interior design firm in Vero Beach,
FL. A classically trained soprano, she
has performed in countless
professional musical and theatrical
venues and penned four musical comedies. Gretchen's love of music
and theater colors all her writing. She is currently at work on an
historical fantasy novel set in San Antonio's Japanese Tea Garden.

www.gretchenroseauthor.com
www.gretchenroseauthor.com/blog

facebook.com/Gretchen-Rose-Author-2163047320474640

instagram.com/rose_gretchen

ALSO BY GRETCHEN ROSE

Very Vero

Veni Vidi Vero

A Little Vice in Vero

CPSIA information can be obtained
at www.ICGtesting.com
Printed in the USA
LVHW040707260422
717220LV00001B/151

9 781955 784597